I Am Hürrem

A novel by Julia Wood

Copyright

I Am Hürrem
© 2025 Rubicon49 Inc.

This is a work of fiction. While inspired by real people and events, many elements have been adapted or reimagined for the purposes of storytelling.

ISBN: 978-1-0697212-1-1
Published by Rubicon49 Inc.
First Edition – 2025

Cover design by Russell Wood

Printed by Amazon KDP

Map of Istanbul

Drawn from memory by Katherine Elizabeth Dubois

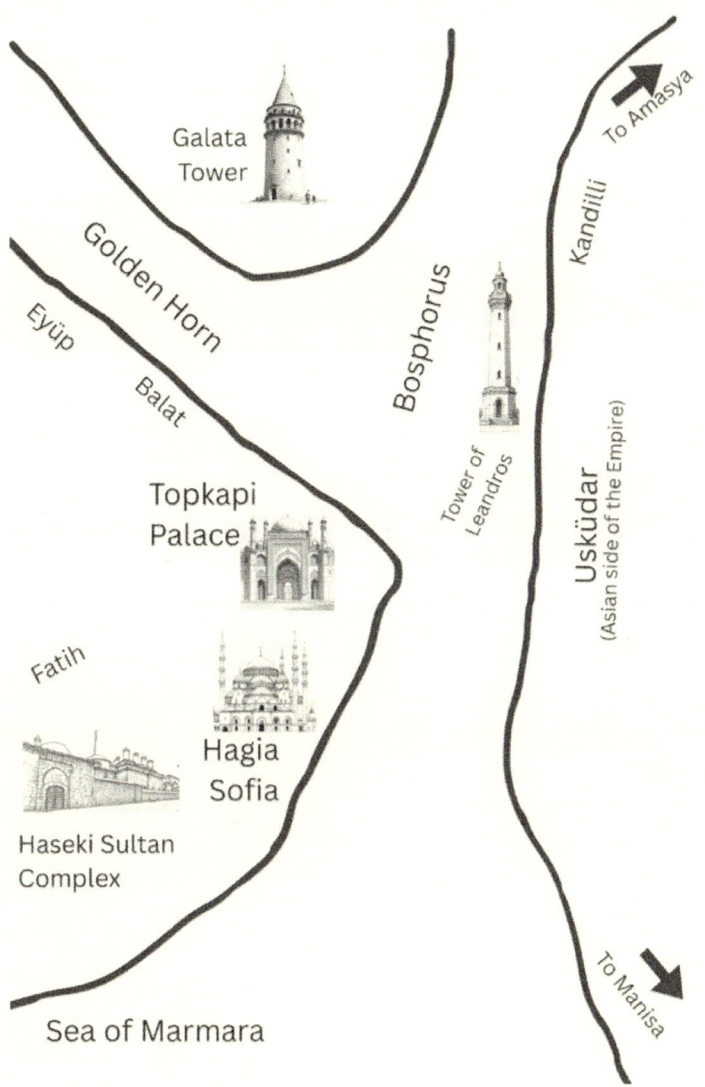

Lexicon of Turkish and Ottoman Terms
In alphabetical order

This lexicon is provided for reference. Readers are invited to consult it if they wish to better understand Turkish terms throughout the novel.

Agha – A title of respect, often for high-ranking officials, guards, or heads of households. Can also be used to refer to a butler, military officers, or prominent eunuchs.

Anne – Mother

Arabesque – An ornamental design consisting of intertwined flowing lines in the patterns of flower, foliage, fruit, animal or figural outlines to produce intricate patterns, originally found in Arabic or Moorish decoration.

Aşk – Love

Baba – Father

Bebek – Baby

Benim güneşim – My sun

Bey – Governor of a district or province in the Ottoman Empire.

Çok iyiyim, teşekkür ederim – I'm very well, thank you

Dervish – A member of a Muslim (specifically Sufi) religious order who has taken vows of poverty and austerity. Dervishes first appeared in the 12th century; they were noted for their wild or ecstatic rituals including dancing, whirling, or howling.

Divan – The imperial council or court where state matters are discussed.

Eunuch – A castrated man, often serving in palace administration, especially within the harem.

Galatasaray – A professional football club located on the European side of Istanbul.

Golden Road – The central corridor of the imperial harem in Topkapi Palace connecting the private quarters of the Sultan and the women of the palace. Access to the Golden Road was strictly controlled and only select women and officials could traverse its length, reflecting the rigid structure and protocols of the harem.

Güzelim – My beauty

Hafez – A 14th-century Persian poet celebrated for his lyrical ghazals (a type of poem) that are considered a pinnacle of Persian literature. His work, particularly his Divan-e Hafez, is widely revered in the Persian-speaking world, with many Iranians knowing his poems by heart and using them as proverbs.

Hafiz – A person, male or female, who has memorized the entire Qur'an.

Hammam – A traditional bathhouse that is characterized by its emphasis on steam, heat, and cleansing rituals. It's a place for physical purification and social interaction.

Haram – Any act that is forbidden by Islamic law.

Harem – The harem refers to the private, inner quarters reserved for the women of the household. This included the wives, concubines, female relatives, servants, and eunuchs. It can also refer to the women who inhabit this space (e.g. the Sultan's harem).

Haseki Sultan – A title in the Ottoman Empire designating the chief consort or favorite of the Ottoman Sultan. It was a powerful position, and the first holder of the title was Hürrem Sultan.

Hatun – Ottoman Turkish word primarily meaning "lady" or "noblewoman".

Hatim – The practice of reciting the entire Qur'an, either in one sitting or over a period of time, often by individuals or groups. It is a form of worship and spiritual practice within Islam, where the complete text of the Qur'an is recited, either from memory or from a copy of the text.

Helva – Helva (also spelled halva, halwa, or halvah) is a confection found throughout the Middle East, North Africa, Eastern Europe, and parts of Asia. The term covers a wide range of recipes, generally involving a paste or thick mixture sweetened with sugar and often featuring ingredients like tahini (sesame paste), semolina, flour, butter, and nuts.

House of Osman – The Ottoman dynasty, named after Osman I, which ruled the Ottoman Empire from c. 1299 to 1922.

Imam – An Islamic leadership position. For Sunni Muslims, Imam is most commonly used as the title of a prayer leader of a mosque.

Inshallah – If Allah wills it.

Iznik – Named after the town of İznik in Anatolia, a decorated ceramic that was produced from the last quarter of the 15th century until the end of the 17th century.

Janissary – A member of the elite infantry unit that formed the Sultan's household troops and bodyguards. They were the first modern standing army.

Juz – Literally meaning "part", refers to each of the thirty volumes of the Qur'an.

Kadi – A judge responsible for enforcing Islamic law in the provinces.

Kaftan – A variant of the robe or tunic that originated in Asia and worn by a number of cultures around the world for thousands of years by both men and women. It may be made of wool, cashmere, silk, or cotton. In cooler climates, it is often worn as an overdress, usually having long sleeves and reaching to the ankles. In warmer climates, it is worn as a lightweight, loose-fitting garment.

Kalfa – A senior female attendant or supervisor within the Ottoman harem, often responsible for training concubines and overseeing daily operations.

Khan – A traditional Turkic-Mongol title meaning "chief" or "leader." Among the Ottomans, it was used alongside "Sultan" to assert ancestral legitimacy rooted in Central Asian and steppe traditions. This duality linked them to both the caliphal tradition of the Muslim world and the khanates of their nomadic forebears, signaling power, lineage, and legitimacy across cultures.

Kohl – A dark powder used as eye makeup. Kohl has been used for centuries as eye makeup, believed to have cooling and cleansing properties and sometimes associated with warding off the "evil eye".

Mangala – A traditional Ottoman version of the modern game of mancala.

Mashallah – An Arabic phrase expressing appreciation, joy, or praise for something that has happened, often implying that it is a blessing from God. It can be translated as "what God has willed" or "God has blessed" and is used to acknowledge divine intervention in positive events.

Muhibbi – Muhibbi was the pen name used by Sultan Süleyman I.

Orhan Gazi – Second sultan of the Ottoman Empire from 1323/4 to 1362.

Osmanlıca – Refers to Ottoman Turkish, the standardized form of the Turkish language used in the Ottoman Empire. It is characterized by its heavy borrowing from Arabic and Persian languages and its use of the Arabic script. While not a spoken language today, Ottoman Turkish is still studied to access historical documents and literature from the Ottoman era.

Oud – The oud is a short-necked, pear-shaped, fretless lute-type stringed instrument, primarily used in Middle Eastern, North African, and Central Asian music.

Padishah – Padishah is a title of nobility roughly meaning 'emperor' in Persian languages, primarily used for the Sultan of the Ottoman Empire.

Pasha – A high-ranking title in the Ottoman political and military system, typically granted to governors, generals, dignitaries, and administrative leaders.

Qur'an – The holy book of Islam, believed by Muslims to be the literal word of Allah, as revealed to the Prophet Muhammad over a period of 23 years. Written in Arabic, the Qur'an is composed of 114 chapters (*suras*) and addresses spiritual, moral, legal, and social matters. It is recited and memorized by Muslims worldwide and serves as the foundation of Islamic faith and law.

Rumi – A 13th century Persian poet, Islamic scholar, theologian, and Sufi mystic. He is renowned for his lyrical poetry, particularly his epic Masnavi-yi Ma'navi (Spiritual Couplets), which has significantly influenced mystical thought and literature. Rumi's philosophy centers on the idea of achieving union with the divine through love and self-abandonment.

Safavid – The Guarded Domains of Iran, commonly called Safavid Iran, Safavid Persia or the Safavid Empire, was one of the largest and longest-lasting Iranian empires. It was ruled from 1501 to 1736 by the Safavid dynasty. It is often considered the beginning of modern Iranian history, as well as one of the gunpowder empires.

Sanjak – An Ottoman administrative division, similar to a province or district, ruled by a bey.

Şehzade – Refers to the male descendants of an Ottoman sovereign in the male line and equivalent to "prince of the blood imperial" in English.

Selam, nasılsın – Hello, how are you ?

Şeyhülislam – In the Ottoman Empire, the şeyhülislam was the highest-ranking religious authority, serving as the Grand Mufti of

Istanbul and the head of the Ottoman religious-legal hierarchy. This position played a crucial role in both religious and political spheres, advising the Sultan, issuing legal opinions, and influencing appointments to judicial and educational positions.

Sharbat – Sharbat is a refreshing, sweet beverage originating from Persia, often made from fruit or flower extracts, and typically served chilled. It's a cordial, meaning it can be consumed as a concentrated syrup or diluted with water to create a drink. Sharbat is the ancestor of various chilled desserts and beverages like sorbet, sherbet, and syrup.

Sultan – A sovereign ruler, especially of a Muslim state. In the Ottoman context, the Sultan was both the political and, later, spiritual head of the Empire. The title emphasized the ruler's Islamic legitimacy. Also used for royal women (e.g., Hürrem Sultan).

Tekke – A dervish or Sufi lodge, a place of worship and gathering for Sufi brotherhoods, e.g. the Mevlevi Tekke.

Teşekkür ederim – Thank you

Topkapi Palace – The name of the primary Ottoman palace in Istanbul, where the Sultan and his court resided.

Tughra – A calligraphic monogram, seal, or signature of an Ottoman sultan that was affixed to all official documents and correspondence. It served as a symbol of the sultan's authority and validation of documents. The tughra typically included the sultan's name, his father's name, his title, and the phrase "the eternally victorious".

Valide Sultan – The mother of the reigning Sultan, often wielding great political influence. The Ottoman equivalent to the Queen Mother.

Vizier – A high-ranking political advisor or minister in the Ottoman Empire and other Islamic states. Viziers served directly under the Sultan and held considerable administrative, military, and diplomatic power. The highest of them, the **Grand Vizier**, acted as the Sultan's chief minister and head of the imperial divan (council), often wielding authority second only to the ruler himself. Viziers were instrumental in managing the empire's vast bureaucracy and were often selected for their intelligence, loyalty, and strategic insight.

Waqf – Refers to an endowment made by a Muslim for charitable or religious purposes, such as building mosques, schools, hospitals, or other public institutions.

Yasak – Forbidden

A note on Istanbul

Though the city known today as Istanbul was officially called *Constantinople* during the years of Hürrem Sultan's life, the name *Istanbul* was already in common spoken use by the Ottoman population throughout the 16th century. In this novel, I have chosen to use *Istanbul* consistently for clarity and continuity, as it reflects the city's identity within the Ottoman context and aligns with modern understanding. This choice is intended to enhance the reader's immersion in Hürrem's world, not to impose an anachronism.

Author's Note on Cultural Sensitivity
and Historical Adaptation

This novel is a work of historical fiction inspired by real individuals and events from the Ottoman Empire. While many characters—such as Hürrem Sultan, Sultan Süleyman, and members of the imperial court—are based on historical figures, the story is a highly adapted interpretation. Events have been dramatized, timelines adjusted, and private conversations imagined to convey the emotional truth of the narrative.

Every effort has been made to portray Islamic culture and history with care and respect. I hold deep admiration for the legacy of the Islamic world and the richness of its traditions. Though I do not come from this background, I have endeavored to write with thoughtfulness and humility.

Any errors or unintentional misrepresentations are entirely my own and are not meant to offend, but reflect the challenges of writing across time, language, and culture.

This book is offered as a tribute to the spirit and strength of those whose lives shaped a great empire—and especially to the resilience of the women who lived within its walls.

To Emily and Russell, who have always shown me that creativity is a gift to be shared.

I Am Hürrem

Chapter 1
The Awakening

The birds wake me—shrill cries slice through the stillness of my room, a fierce defense against some unknown intruder.

Kah-kah, kah-kah.

The air trembles with the flapping of wings. For a moment, I lie motionless, trying to place the noise in the context of where I am. The wings flap again, followed by a sharp squawk—too close to be outside my bedroom window. I bolt upright.

My mind rushes to make sense of the world before me. There is no ceiling, no walls, no floor. The sun hangs low over the horizon. Long shadows stretch across a vast beach. A wave rolls in, slow and deliberate, hissing as it licks at my toes. The sting of saltwater makes me gasp. The sand is warm, almost feverish in contrast. My thin nightshirt clings to my skin, damp with sea mist as more waves crash against the shore, loud and constant.

The air smells different, not the usual hot, humid air of Boston in the summer, but something heavier and more organic. A shiver crawls up my spine, despite the warmth of the day. The air tastes like fish and earth, sun-warmed wood and something faintly spiced.

I blink, disoriented, pulling my knees up to my chest, wrapping my arms tightly around them. I listen—no distant wail of sirens, no background noise of a modern city, only an uneasy calmness. Fear creeps in, a growing sense of wrongness, a foreboding feeling that I should run. I force myself to breathe slowly, methodically, trying to center myself.

Scanning the beach, only an empty shoreline stretches out before me. Just water and birds and wind and… nothing. No buildings. No piers. No sign of the world I know. My chest tightens, my heart pounds like a beating drum. The waves keep coming, steady and dispassionate. Time feels broken, like I've stumbled into a dream.

Voices cut through the silence. Five or six men, their outlines blurred by the mist, chat in the distance. Their wide trousers flap like sails in the wind. Headscarves cling to their brows, ends fluttering above sun-browned faces. They move toward the surf, nets and poles in hand, their attention on the sea.

They see me and stop; the sound of their footsteps dies away. They gesture. Their eyes hold mine—wary, assessing. One starts forward. Another follows. Their pace quickens.

I scramble to my feet, nearly slipping in the wet sand. "Stop!" I say, my voice fierce. "Where am I?"

They ignore my words, their faces hard, eyes narrowing as one grabs my arm—rough and uncaring. I jerk away, but another hand catches me from behind. My breath hitches as I twist. Fingers dig into my shoulder. Panic explodes in my chest.

"Let go!" I scream, my voice breaking. "Please, stop!"

Their voices harsh, tones I don't understand, foreign words shouted over me. A slap, sharp and blinding, breaks across my cheek. The world turns white. Time slows down to a moment of suffocating stillness.

I scream—wordless and primal. I kick and thrash, but it's useless. My limbs feel uncoordinated, heavy with fear. They drag me through the sand, their grip like iron. The beach blurs past in a haze of foam and shells and sunlit chaos.

Another slap. My head reels. My fight dissolves.

Someone throws rough cloth around me, thick with the scent of smoke and brine. I stop struggling. My breath comes fast and shallow, my stomach twisting in a knot.

I glance over my shoulder as they haul me away. The sea watches in silent witness.

Chapter 2
The City of Strangers

I'm moving too fast, stumbling forward, half-dragged, half-walking, my breath coming in sharp gasps. The rough fabric draped over me is coarse and foreign against my skin. My bare feet slip in the soft sand.

The shore falls behind us, sand giving way to a rocky path. The air thickens, warm and oppressive, carrying the scent of wood smoke, charred meat, and something more pungent, the lingering stench of animals, and of human waste. My nose recoils at the invasion. The sounds of the sea fade, replaced by the murmur of voices—distant at first, then swelling as we crest a low hill.

A town sprawls below, its stone buildings low and squat, weathered and gray from years of salt and wind. The roofs are flat, with large wooden beams jutting out at odd angles, creating the impression that the entire city is stacked on top of itself. There are no neat rows of houses like in Boston, no paved roads or modern structures, no cars or streetlights.

Narrow, twisting alleyways crisscross like veins, their dark mouths hidden in shadow. The path turns to cracked stones, uneven and rough, their jagged edges biting my feet. The stones give way to cobbles baking in the sun, making me wince as the heat seeps through the soles of my feet.

This can't be real, but the dream seems too palpable to ignore. I ache for my bed, for the drone of traffic, the bark of my neighbor's dog.

Instead, I see a sky washed in pale blue, the sun glaring down mercilessly, casting long, sharp shadows. The buildings seem to lean in, suffocating me. Black flecks dance at the edges of my vision. I bite my cheek—the pain, sharp and immediate, keeps me on my feet.

The streets pulse with life—a dance of human figures weaving in and out of the shadows. Women in flowing dresses move with the soft chime of brass jewelry. Men in loose robes, scarves shielding their heads, barter loudly.

I lunge toward a passing woman, her veil fluttering as she balances a basket on her head, and shout, "Help me! Please!" My voice, hoarse from fear, strains to reach her as she turns away, her eyes averted as if I'm a ghost. I twist against the fishermen's grip, calling to a man nearby, "Please, I don't belong here!" He mutters something in that unfamiliar tongue, waving me off like a stray dog. My pleas echo against the stone walls, swallowed by the clamor of the market, ignored against the relentless pull of my captors dragging me deeper into this feverish hallucination.

In a dusty square, market stalls overflow with color—crimson and saffron fabrics, piles of spices, baskets of dates and pomegranates. The air hums with cinnamon and cloves, undercut by the raw stench of fish. Vendors haggle; their voices raised over the clink of coins and the distant clang of a hammer on an anvil. Old women in tattered shawls whisper at the edges, their eyes flickering over me. A boy stands behind a wooden cart, his dark eyes wide with curiosity.

I must look like something dragged from the sea—barefoot, hair wild, soaked nightshirt clinging to my skin beneath the makeshift wrap. Children chase each other through the dust; their skin darkened from the sun. They pause for a moment when they see me. Their laughter falters. I force a smile, but it collapses into a tremble. Around me, words tumble in a language I don't recognize, thick and fast. I strain to catch even a single word that makes sense. Nothing. It's as if I've been dropped onto an alien planet.

The road narrows, winding between buildings. The scent of what I hope is animal waste clings to the walls of some of the houses. In a small courtyard, I catch a glimpse of a donkey tethered to a post, its eyes drowsy from the heat.

We round a corner, and a building rises before us, its towering wooden doors stand like sentinels. Soldiers in long robes linger nearby, hands resting on the hilts of their swords. One of the fishermen calls out, gesturing toward me. My stomach lurches. This is bad. This is really, really bad.

I turn to the soldiers, my voice strained but steady. "Please, tell me where I am." I search their eyes for any sign of understanding.

Blank stares. More words in their foreign tongue. I take a step back, only to be yanked forward again. My panic flares.

"Let me go! I haven't done anything!" I shout, twisting against their grip, my shoulder burning under their hold.

The soldier's frown deepens. Without warning, he grabs my chin, tilting my face up. I gasp, his rough fingers scraping my skin. He inspects me like livestock in a market, muttering to the fishermen.

The decision is made. I can feel it—a shift, a verdict, a fate being sealed.

My heart hammers in my chest as they pull me forward, a frantic beating of a drum. I don't know where they're taking me, but one thing is clear: this isn't Boston. And I have no idea how to get home.

Chapter 3
The Cage

Two guards flank me, each gripping an arm like I might try to bolt. They are rough, impatient, like men used to dragging prisoners from one place to another. I see it in the way they grip me—not cruel for cruelty's sake, but utterly devoid of concern, as if I were a runaway goat.

The guards bark at me to move along. I struggle to keep up with their hurried pace. My feet, already bleeding from multiple small cuts, scrape painfully on the uneven cobbles. We pass more low buildings, domed roofs, and narrow alleyways. The city feels like a maze, ancient and unknowable, as though it has risen from the earth just to swallow me whole.

We pass through a narrow gate in the city wall before arriving at a grim-looking compound, windowless, with iron bars and heavy doors. A guard pounds on the door and exchanges a few words with the man who opens it—a broad-shouldered brute who barely looks at me before waving them in.

Inside, the thick smell of unwashed bodies and old straw clings to the walls. Caged pens are located on opposite sides of the building, housing dozens of men. They look dejected, beaten, half-dead. Most sit or lie on straw strewn across the floors of the pens; some stand huddled in little groups, hanging onto the bars, engaged in quiet conversation. They pay little attention to me.

At the far end, a lean-to shields more guards from the summer sun. In this recessed alcove, several men lounge behind a large wooden table. One leans back on a stool, legs stretched out and crossed at

8

the ankles, a curved dagger peeking out from his belt. Another pours dark, steaming liquid from a copper pot into a small ceramic cup. They are drinking tea, though it smells stronger than what I am used to—perhaps bitter and spiced, brewed strong to keep them awake for their guard duty.

A small fire glows in the corner, a dented pot suspended above it—from the smell, a stew is simmering over the heat. A guard sips slowly, eyes half-lidded with boredom, while another scratches his beard and laughs at something muttered in their strange language. The whole area has a cluttered, lived-in feel, stinking of sweat, tobacco, and dust. The guards look up briefly as we pass, their eyes sliding over me with disinterest. Just another prisoner. Just another day.

Down a corridor to the left of the lean-to, the guards push me into a small room with a barred door and stone floor. I collapse onto the cold ground, my body shaking with fear. The interior of my prison is dark and damp and hot, airless—the only light a faint glow from the shaded corridor beyond. The atmosphere is dense, an invisible wall of heat—the walls close around me thick with silence and judgment, the weight of confinement clinging to my skin, oppressive and unrelenting.

"Mother! Save me!" I plead to the emptiness.

I stay there alone for what feels like hours, my arms wrapped tightly around my knees, thinking of home. Late for work, again— my boss won't be happy. He'll roll his eyes, mutter something about responsibility, not knowing I've vanished. My thoughts drift to my mother, grieving alone in a house far away, probably pacing the floor, waiting for my call. Does she already know I'm missing?

The thought of her breaking down, thinking I've been hurt or worse, is heart-wrenching. Tears land hot on my cheeks as I curl in on myself, willing the nightmare to end.

Eventually, the door creaks open, and a matronly woman enters— older, her shoulders stooped, with kind eyes set deep in a lined face. I begin to scream and scream until my throat is raw. I was too stunned before by the strangeness of my surroundings to fight, but now I must and once I begin, I cannot stop.

"Let me out of this prison!" I yell like a wild thing, crazy with fear.

I throw myself at the old woman, all semblance of rationality gone. She yells and backs out of the cell as guards enter. One shouts something, sneering at me. Another gives me a shove between the shoulder blades that drives me to the floor.

I howl until my voice cracks, tears running down my cheeks. "Please, I don't belong here!"

No one understands me. Or if they do, they don't care. My arms are bound in front of me with coarse rope, the fibers bite into my wrists. The guards shout at me, and one slaps me twice, hard. My words dissolve into broken sobs, meaningless to the people surrounding me.

Locked in that small, dark room that smells of damp straw and sweat, I pound against the wooden door, ignoring the sting in my fists and the bindings that chafe into my skin. I feel adrift, cut loose from my life, lost in someone else's dream. Broken, exhausted, afraid, a hollow shell of my former self, I huddle in a corner and wait for salvation.

Night comes and the darkness is complete. I whisper to myself to keep from being utterly overwhelmed by the fear that is now a constant companion. I think of my apartment, of running fingers over the spines of books from my favorite authors. *Dickens, Shakespear, Austen, Tolstoy.* My body remembers running in Boston Common just yesterday. Over and over, I repeat phrases and words, the familiarity soothing me. Breakfast at my favorite café, discussing modern sculpture with my mother, analyzing ancient battles with my father.

My heart skips a beat. We buried my father just two months ago—his illness swift, his death a wound still raw. Grief is still a fresh shadow. And now I am missing—vanished without a trace, somehow stolen from my life and thrust into this foreign world. I am a ghost to the people I love, lost to them. A stranger in a strange land. The weight of it is too much to bear.

Days pass. I try to keep count, though the haze of captivity and the lack of sunshine make it difficult to remain certain. Still, I scratch little lines in the dirt to mark the passing of each day. And every night, I think of my mother. She must be frantic by now. "Please," I whisper to no one, "let her not despair."

My stomach is hollow, aching with hunger, and my body throbs from sleeping on the cold floor. I am still only dressed in my nightshirt; the rough cloth draped over me by the fishermen serving as a blanket against the dampness. My feet are caked with dried blood. I am filthy and my own smell is insufferable.

The matron enters every so often, bringing water and a bowl of thin soup. She is always accompanied by a guard. At first, I repeat my pleas to them, though without the histrionics of our first encounter. Even saying my name brings another slap. I learn to stay quiet.

One day she comes in alone. She eyes me hesitantly. I don't move from the corner. I don't speak. Her shoulders loosen; she gives me a caring smile. She speaks to me for the first time, gently, though I don't understand a word. She doesn't seem cruel like the men.

"My name is Katherine!" I say to her quietly, hoping she doesn't summon the guards.

To my surprise, she tries to repeat it, but stumbles over the foreign syllables—she frowns. "Katerina," she finally says, nodding as if settling the matter.

Katerina. I want to correct her, but the fight has drained out of me. Maybe it doesn't matter. Maybe I don't matter.

Later that day, she returns with a bundle of clothes. The guards bring in a bucket of water. I flinch seeing them, fearing another beating. They untie my wrists, ignoring my tears and sounds of pain from the days of having the rough cord bite into my flesh, then they just turn and leave. She hands me a cloth and some soap that smells of olive oil and motions for me to undress and bathe. I hesitate but strip off the nightdress—the desire to be clean outweighing all else.

The water is cold. I start to shiver from it but still wash myself as best as I can. The clothes are simple, rough-spun fabric that smells of soap and something herbal. A long tunic and loose pants, nothing like the clothes I am used to. But at least they're clean.

She points to my tangled hair, mimicking a brushing motion. I nod weakly. She takes a comb and begins working through the knots with surprising patience. Standing close to me, she smells faintly of rosemary. Her hands are rough, but her touch is careful as she applies a thick salve to my feet and wrists, gently to avoid causing me more pain. For the first time since waking on that beach, I don't feel entirely alone.

By my count, I have been here fourteen days when she leads me outside into a courtyard. There are others—women and girls, all huddled together in a large, caged pen, where straw covers the floor, and the stink of too many bodies pressed together fills the air. Some are crying, others silent with blank, empty eyes. Guards stand near the door. They push me in among them. I want to protest, to cling to the matron who treated me with kindness, but she only gives me a sad look before turning away.

I spend many nights here, sleeping on the hard ground among the others. There is no escape, nowhere to go. Other women are brought in—girls, mostly, dirty and thin. They avoid me at first. I must look strange to them—I have fair skin, amber-red hair, and speak in a foreign language. I laugh bitterly at the realization that I have begun to think of English as foreign. I cannot explain where I am or why I am here. I am always afraid. But when one of the girls begins to cry in the night, I crawl closer and hold her hand. After that, we huddle together, sharing body heat, fear, and silence.

On the fifth morning, they come for us. The guards rouse us roughly from sleep, and hand us worn shoes and long veils that cover our heads and shoulders. There are about two dozen of us, eyes downcast, too tired or too scared to resist. They maneuver us into a single line. Ropes are tied around our waists and then each rope tied to the person in front and behind, creating a human chain. The chain is then tied to the back of a horse-drawn cart. Two guards sit up front. Two more accompany us on horseback.

We are herded out of the building and down a dirt road that winds its way out of the city walls. I look up once, just once, to see the city behind us and the distant shimmer of the sea. I arrived in this world on a beach. Now I am being marched into its unknown interior—away from the water, away from prison, into something even more unfathomable.

My feet hurt and my legs ache. The sun is already high and hot. No one speaks. No one cries anymore. We just walk. We pass by travelers on their own journeys. Some avert their eyes, pretending not to see, others watch with open curiosity, their gazes crawl over us as if we are nothing more than objects.

We walk through the countryside, through dust and heat and exhaustion. With every step, returning home seems less possible. This world, which my mind reels to understand, is unravelling the very fabric of who I am. I wish I could explain it. But in the absence of a tangible explanation, only hellish imagination remains.

Chapter 4
Domes and Minarets

For days, our procession continues. A line of women, chained together at the waist. When one falls, the guards yank her back to her feet; sometimes she is just set upright, other times beaten. When one of us slows too much, we are struck with sticks or the butts of their knives—not so much with cruelty, but indifference, as if we are just beasts that need correction.

We are not permitted to speak—talking leads to another beating. We march in silence, broken only by the occasional sharp cry of a guard barking orders. We are gaunt, dirty, and silent, our eyes blank. We are cattle now, bound and voiceless.

The days bleed together, indistinguishable in the blur of heat, pain and confusion, without beginning or end. My feet are raw with blisters, the grit of dirt and tiny stones stabbing through the soles of my shoes with every step. I bleed. I limp. Still, we walk on— the guards don't care about our misery.

We move during the daylight hours, under the sun that bears down on us mercilessly. The air shimmers above the road, reflecting off stone and dust. Our heads are covered, the veils making the heat underneath stifling. My legs ache, my shoulders throb from multiple beatings, and my stomach is twisted in knots with hunger. Some among us are no older than children and their footsteps drag, for which I am thankful as it keeps the pace slow and steady. Most have long since given up crying.

We are given bowls of watery gruel—thin, tasteless, barely enough to sustain. The guards ladle out warm, metallic-tasting water from a single barrel. I eat because I must, not because it brings any relief. My stomach is still clenched, as much from fear as from continued unsatisfied hunger. I drink greedily, taking in large gulps of stale water, knowing I won't get more until the next meal. No one speaks. We are too afraid, too weary, too broken.

At night, we are herded to the side of the road and made to lie down in a ditch, beneath the sparse trees lining the countryside or where the tall grasses give way to patches of packed earth. The guards don't bother with tents or even blankets. We sleep on the cold, hard ground, huddling together for warmth as the nights are starting to get noticeably cooler, a cruel tangle of our roped chains and bruised limbs.

Despite the aching weariness I feel, I can't immediately fall asleep. I lie curled on my side, hugging my knees to my chest, listening to the groans of the others and the muttering of the guards. Above me, the heavens unfold in their full glory without the light of big cities, a vast, unbroken dome of deep indigo, scattered with stars that pulse like living embers. The Milky Way arches overhead in a luminous sweep that inspires worship, but I have no awe left in me—only lingering pain and bone-weary fatigue.

I stare at the stars, wondering if anyone back in Boston is looking at them too. It has been perhaps three, maybe four weeks since I disappeared. Mother must be hounding the police, anxious to receive news. The next session at Harvard started without me. I wish it were as easy as finding me.

But a hard truth has inched its way into my mind, despite its impossibility. A truth I dare not say aloud, one I barely venture to whisper inside my own thoughts, for its implication means my world will have to move on without me. The tears come without warning, silent and hot. I cry until the chill of the night air dries them on my cheeks and I fall into a dreamless sleep.

On the fourth morning, the road widens, and I notice more travelers—carts, donkeys, men on horseback, women balancing baskets on their heads. The dust of the countryside gives way to the heavy scent of people, animals, sweat, and smoke. On either side of the road, the landscape is a patchwork of parched grass, thorny shrubs, and the occasional grove of olive trees, their silvery-green leaves fluttering in the breeze. The soil is dry and chalky, dotted with wildflowers. Small farms appear here and there, mud-brick homes with low stone walls enclosing fields and patches of vegetable gardens.

Men herd goats and sheep along the roadside, prodding them forward with long sticks, the animals bleating and clattering their hooves over the stones. Donkeys trudge past us, carrying bundles of firewood or great baskets of produce. One man leads a camel draped with rugs, its expression bored and slightly disdainful, its large, hooded eyes give off an air of indifference, as if it has made this journey a hundred times.

Stalls and makeshift markets begin to spring up along the road. Simple canvas awnings are stretched over wooden frames, their fabric faded and flapping in the wind. Vendors call out to passing travelers in singsong voices, hawking fresh dates, figs, bundles of herbs, and roasted chestnuts. The smell of cooked meat drifts in the air—something spicy and charred, making my stomach churn from its emptiness. It is chaotic and noisy, yet vibrant and alive. The road itself feels like an artery pulsing with life.

Their wares are not for us. We are ignored, sneered at, or worse. An old man spits in the dirt as we pass and barks a word that makes the other merchants laugh. A woman behind a fig stall clucks her tongue and shakes her head, muttering something under her breath, giving us a look of contempt. Boys point and laugh, jostling each other as they whisper and mimic our slow, shuffling walk. But not all look at us with cruelty. A girl, no older than ten, clutching her mother's skirts, stares at us with wide, solemn eyes. Her mother pulls her away gently, whispering something to hush her questions.

Suddenly, just as the sun is cresting over the hills, the scene changes. At first, it is only the sounds that I notice: the din of voices, distant bells, the occasional clang of metal on metal, a low, steady hum that vibrates in my bones. And then, I see it. It takes me a moment to understand what is before me. It is only a shimmer on the horizon—stone walls rising out of the earth like a mirage. But as we draw nearer, it becomes undeniable. A city lies before us, and the skyline strikes me dumb.

Rising above the chaos of buildings are the spires and domes of a place unlike anything I have ever seen. Grand mosques loom in the distance, their towering minarets reaching toward the sky, graceful and strange. The largest among them seems to float above the city, its great dome is flanked by half-domes and sweeping arches.

The architecture is both alien and majestic, and I stare at it with wide, uncomprehending eyes. The call to prayer rings out across the land, haunting and beautiful. It echoes through the air in long, undulating tones, as though the very earth is singing in exaltation.

We pass under a stone archway and enter a narrow street; buildings rise on either side, some crumbling and faded, others freshly whitewashed. People crowd the streets—men in turbans and flowing robes, women in veils, barefoot children darting between carts pulled by donkeys. The air buzzes with their voices. No one stops to look at us. No one seems surprised by the procession of chained women moving through their streets. We are invisible, a common sight.

The city is enormous, not the vast sprawling metropolis of modern steel and glass, but a city alive with activity, and magnificent in its grandeur. A haze of dust and smoke hangs in the air, lit golden by the afternoon sun. The scent of it hits me—a mix of spices, smoke, sweat, and sea, so different from the briny sharpness of the beach or the sour reek of prison. Here, it is layered: cardamom and cloves, roasted meat, burnt wood, animal dung, and human labor. There is something vibrant about the smell, something intoxicating.

We turn off the main road and into a narrower alley that winds through what must be the market district. There are fabrics hanging from balconies, bright like spilled paint—crimson, indigo, saffron. A man passes carrying a cage of squawking birds, and boys chase after him, laughing. Somewhere nearby, a woman is singing, her voice rising above the din.

The city pulses with life, overwhelming in its color and noise. Every turn brings more sounds, more smells, a sensory overload that seems to keep pushing me further from any semblance of something familiar.

Around a bend and down a sloping road, we arrive at gates, tall and black and menacing. There is a charge in the air, like a thunderstorm waiting to break, something raw and tense that makes the hair on the back of my neck stand up. My heart races faster. I can feel the weight of the moment pressing down on me, the sensation that I've crossed some invisible boundary.

Once inside, the iron creaks shut behind us with an echoing clank. My eyes refuse to accept the view. My stomach sinks. I blink, trying to assimilate the sight before me, but the reality of it all is too much to process. Whatever misery awaits me, it lies ahead— a slow descent into something I cannot escape.

Chapter 5
The Market of Souls

Beyond the gates lies a sprawling yard, hemmed in by tall wooden fences. Inside, it's a madhouse—crowded, noisy, chaotic. Guards mill about, whips attached to their belts. Men stand on platforms, hands bound, faces stoic or desperate. The scent of sorrow and resignation makes the air feel thick with suffering. We've reached what can only be a slave market.

I don't know why, but I can't look away. My eyes flick from one figure to the next—boys, young men, older men—all herded together like livestock, their bodies on display for the buyers to assess. It feels like I'm seeing the very essence of humanity reduced to nothing more than property.

My stomach churns with disgust and fear. A hundred voices shout over each other, eyes cold and calculating, bargaining, discussing the worth of each captive, reducing them down to a value in coin.

The guards drive us deeper into the complex, past an alcove where soldiers lounge in the shade, here perhaps to keep the peace in case any prisoner gets ideas of escape. Simple awnings are strung above stone pens. Onlookers drift past, inspecting men of all ages, some pale-skinned, some dark. They look like they haven't eaten in weeks. Most bow their heads, their eyes glassy from hopelessness. A few shout out, trying to catch the attention of passersby. Others simply cry.

They unchain us and begin sorting—those too sick or old are pulled away and disappear through a side gate. I don't want to know where they are being sent. The rest of us huddle together, awaiting further instruction. I feel my panic start to rise again. My throat tightens. I look up once more at the distant domes gleaming in the sun. Whatever solace they offer their patrons, none filters into this hell.

A detachment of female guards approaches in silent formation. They push us forward through a narrow arch into a smaller, more enclosed area, this one buzzing with the sounds of women's voices and soft cries. My breath catches in my chest as I take in the scene before me.

This part of the market is cramped, almost suffocating. Women and girls of every age are packed tightly together in cages, their eyes empty, hollow with the devastating understanding of their fate. Some hold each other, their thin bodies curled together, looking for comfort in each other's presence. The scene is a chaotic mixture of shame, grief, and utter surrender. There's no fight here—only the quiet, dull acceptance of a life that has already been decided for them.

I try not to let the horror sink in too deeply, but it's impossible. A woman nearby sobs harshly, and a girl, no more than sixteen, presses her face into the shoulder of an older woman who strokes her hair gently. I can hear whispers. I may not understand the language, but the tone is unmistakable—words of comfort, of sadness. One young woman meets my gaze for a moment, her expression hollow, before turning away, ashamed of her own helplessness.

They lead us past the front portion of the women's market to a dark corner. Secluded behind thick curtains, a woman waits. Her face is etched with deep lines from a life lived in misery. She indicates for us to line up, and then to undress. After a few awkward glances at each other, we begin to remove the filthy travel clothes.

She approaches each in turn, examining us. I'm exposed to her gaze, shame burning within me. She hands me a simple unadorned dress, made of thick, scratchy fabric. It fits me, neither too tight nor too loose, but it makes me feel more like an object than I care to admit. I'm glad, however, for the simple shoes she hands me to replace the worn-out ones from the journey; I put them on quickly over my filthy damaged feet, pain stabbing me with each movement. When I look up again, she has already turned her back on me, moving to inspect another.

When she is done, we are guided back into the main section of the women's slave market. A round stout woman jerks me aside with rough, uncaring hands, away from the other women, who are already being corralled into cages. She walks me briskly down a side corridor to a wooden cage with steel bars, thick and heavy, the kind that might hold wild animals. With a hard command, she ushers me inside. When I hesitate, she growls, her voice gruff and dismissive, like I'm little more than an inconvenience.

The cage is small and dark, with barely enough room for me to stretch my legs. The air is thick with the mingling scents of sweat, dirt, and something acrid that makes my stomach turn. My mind screams at me to escape, though I know that I am trapped. My legs tremble beneath me, but I force myself to stay calm. I close my eyes for a moment, letting the sounds of the market wash over me—the distant chatter of the crowd, the occasional rattle of metal doors opening and closing.

I feel unanchored, curling inward, retreating into a fog of pity and self-preservation. And then I hear it—soft, anguished wails that echo through the air, rising and falling like the rhythm of some cruel lullaby. The sound makes me shiver, as if the very air in this place is pregnant with sorrow.

It's only when I hear the clatter of a wooden bowl being dropped in front of me that I snap back to reality. A woman in a drab dress, her face weathered from years of hardship, stands outside the bars. She says nothing, just watches me for a moment, before she turns and walks away.

I look down at the bowl, my stomach twisting. It smells faintly of stale bread and something sour. I eat, not out of hunger, but out of fear, not knowing when my next meal will come. Scooping up a handful of the slop, its texture is thick and gooey and sticks to my tongue. I force myself to swallow despite the taste, feeling the heat rising in my chest as I try to choke it down.

I drift in and out of consciousness, the cage like a tomb, the sounds of the market lingering in the distance, taunting me. I want to believe that when I wake, the hard metal bars will be gone, and I will be home in my own bed.

Lost in reverie, I'm pulled back by the distant echo of pops and crackles as flashes of red and green dance across the heavens. It takes me a moment to realize—fireworks. The people in the city are rejoicing. It astounds me to see something so familiar in the middle of this otherwise alien world.

In a hazy blur of exhaustion, both physical and mental, I finally close my eyes, as sleep drags me down like a stone into the depths of the abyss.

I wake to the cries of women, the wailing of children. The low murmur of men haggling over prices hums beneath it all. It all bleeds together, a backdrop to the oppressive silence in my mind. The metal bars are still there. I want to scream. I want to run, to break free of this nightmare.

Footsteps approach my cage. A lone guard beckons me out. He takes a firm, bruising hold of my arm, and drags me into the open courtyard. He pulls me roughly to a raised platform and forces me onto it. No matter how bad things have been so far, this is worse.

There are other women and girls already standing, motionless, eyes downcast. Their faces are blank masks of indifference, as though the very spirit has been drained from them. Most appear to be like me, somewhere in their late teens, but some of the girls are as young as ten and a few women appear older, perhaps in their thirties.

I look out at the sea of men, my stomach knotting—the buyers, watching, waiting. They examine the women on display like one would look at vases, inspecting both functionality and beauty. A man approaches the platform. He peers at me with small, twitchy eyes—birdlike, watchful, and far too interested. I avert my eyes, shrinking inward, willing myself invisible.

He steps closer, scrutinizing me from head to toe, lingering on my face, studying me as if I'm something new, something strange, and I suddenly feel naked, exposed in a way I never have before. The feeling is like a rush of cold water. I swallow hard. I want to say something, anything, to get out of this, but the words catch in my throat.

Bidding begins. The seller is a man with a thick black beard and a scar across his cheek. One by one, a woman is pulled forward to the front of the stage, various men shout and then the woman is carted off. Some go silently, some wail and cry, some try to reach out to a loved one still in line. It is heartbreaking.

Then, it's my turn. Before bidding begins, the man who inspected me earlier steps up and hands the seller a leather pouch that he pulls from his belt, the faint sound of coins shifting inside. And just like that, I'm bought. I am someone's property. I am a slave.

The man takes me by the arm, pulling me off the platform. The slave market disappears behind me in a blur of noise and stone. I'm half-dragged through narrow streets, too dazed to resist, my thoughts a mire of fear and confusion. Piece by piece, I vanish— every breath a slow suffocation. I'm trapped in this strange brutal world that sees me as nothing more than a possession.

We stop in front of a large stone archway with a massive iron gate, different from the others I've seen. The walls are high, and the gate is decorated with vines and flowers. There are guards standing at attention just outside the entrance, their eyes cold as they watch us pass them. The gate closes behind me with a loud clang that makes my heart race. My fate is sealed.

The man walks briskly, saying nothing, and I have no choice but to follow. We pass under archways and through open sun-dappled courtyards. In sharp contrast to the acrid smells of the market, the

26

air smells faintly of roses, the first beautiful scent I've breathed in days. It feels wrong—beauty in the wake of such horror.

We finally stop in front of a large, ornate door. The man knocks, and the door creaks open, revealing a woman dressed in rich, flowing robes. She is perhaps in her thirties, strong and well-fed— she studies me for a moment, her gaze sharp and calculating. She nods to the man, who leaves without looking back.

Her hand is warm, her grip tight. I draw in a shaky breath. The door shuts with the finality of a tomb, and I step into whatever nightmare waits on the other side.

Chapter 6
The Initiation

Right, then left, then left, or was it right? I try to remember which way we are taking—an opportunity may come to escape. But there are more corridors, more twists and turns, each hallway looking the same as the last. The maze seems endless. I ponder the thought of trying for a surprise attack, but the route has completely turned me around and the thought of ending up back at the slave market makes me shudder.

The air smells thick and perfumed, filled with hints of roses and sandalwood. I look for patterns on the brightly colored walls that can help me backtrack, but they are too alike to stand out. The hallways are dimly lit by hanging oil lamps, casting a flickering golden glow. There are candles shining in small alcoves. I hear no voices; just silence, thick and watchful, that feels oppressive and heavy with secrets. I shiver—not from cold, but from the weight of the unknown.

At last, we stop before a large, ornate door. She knocks once. It creaks open on ancient hinges, and I'm ushered inside. The door shuts behind me with a soft, deliberate thud—quiet, but absolute.

The room is not large, yet it commands attention. Authority clings to the air like smoke. A single window, its wooden lattice carved in intricate patterns, filters the sunlight into slanted beams that catch the haze of burning incense. The scent—jasmine and roses—floats heavy in the heat. Though fragrant, it does nothing to calm my nerves.

Floral tiles in rich blues, deep reds, and golds climb the walls in elegant symmetry. A wide wooden desk dominates the space, crowded with parchment stacks, ink pots, and thick, spine-worn books that look like accounting ledgers. A silk-covered divan runs the length of one wall, its cushions plump and pristine, untouched. It is a room designed to impress—and to intimidate. I feel smaller with every breath.

There are four women in the room other than myself and my guard. At the center of the room stands a woman dressed in deep crimson. She holds a long, slender cane in one hand and a narrow writing tablet in the other, its dark surface gleaming faintly with a wax-like substance. She moves to stand in front of me, eyeing me critically from head to toe. Her sharp gaze runs over my body, making me feel exposed and vulnerable. She is older, perhaps in her late forties, her face stern as she takes in my appearance. The look in her eyes makes me hesitate. Caution seems prudent. I don't dare speak; her authority is clear.

But it is the woman who is seated in the corner that grabs my attention. Her rich velvet gown in hues of dark green and threaded with intricate golden embroidery declares her a queen, and she commands the room with her very presence. She does not speak, but I know without a doubt that she is the one who will decide my fate.

My guard releases me, and I barely have time to steady myself before hands grab my arms. The two other women who have been standing silent near the door begin examining me with practiced efficiency. They lift my chin, tilting my face toward the light. One of them inspects my teeth, pulling at my lips before nodding slightly. Another lifts my arm, pinching the skin as if testing for

29

softness. I stand stiffly, swallowing back my discomfort. My hair is examined for lice. My nails are checked. My arms, my shoulders—every inch of me is scrutinized. I want to pull away, to tell them to stop, but I bite my tongue. Resistance feels futile.

Finally, one of the women steps back and murmurs something to the official with the tablet. The woman records something quickly before glancing toward the silent figure in the corner—the woman in velvet.

There is a pause as Velvet Woman looks at me. Seconds tick by. The tension in my chest tightens. Then, she nods, only once, and the other women react instantly.

Tablet Woman speaks, but not to me, her voice as cold as the stone floors beneath my feet, and I catch one word that she repeats more than once, addressing the guard who remains standing by the door. *Kalfa*, that must be this one's name.

The order given, Kalfa escorts me out of the room and down more corridors, ever deeper inside this massive building. The hallway stretches on, twisting and turning, until we arrive at a set of heavy wooden doors. They open to reveal a steam-filled room, warm and humid.

Inside, the heat hits me immediately, thick and steamy, like a comforting blanket. The walls are smooth, pale marble. The floors are warm beneath my feet. Water echoes everywhere—dripping, splashing, flowing into great basins where the steam rises in soft tendrils. The bathhouse is something between a temple and a dream—an ancient ritual in stone.

There are other women in the bathhouse. They lounge on stone platforms, their bodies wrapped in thin cloth, their hair slick and faces flushed. Attendants, strong and quiet, move through the fog with practiced grace, scrubbing, massaging, rinsing. There is a rhythm to the place—a slow pulse of cleansing and release.

We move to a recessed area in back and away from the others. Kalfa steps closer to me, her hands reaching for the rough fabric dress, pulling it up and over my head without hesitation. I freeze, my skin prickling with the suddenness of it. I want to fight, to scream, but I don't know what to say or how to make her stop. I'm now standing there naked, exposed, vulnerable—an object to be scrutinized.

Another woman steps forward and wraps me in a cotton towel. She touches my skin, examining me, pulling the fabric this way and that. Her fingers are impersonal, clinical, as she inspects my body from head to toe with even greater scrutiny than was done in the small room moments ago. I protest but am ignored. I don't know why she's doing this or what it means. All I can do is stand there, shaking, the silence in the room deafening.

She gestures for me to sit and doesn't hesitate to spread my knees apart. Her fingers touch me, examining. Every movement of her fingers feels like an eternity. Her touch is harsh, unfeeling, as she checks me over, scrutinizing me too intimately. The humiliation is defeating. My heart stops in my chest. I don't need to know their words to understand what she is searching for. I'm not a virgin, but not very experienced either. I can only hold my breath.

Finally done, she nods at Kalfa who signals to even more women—silent, faceless guards, who guide me to a stone basin filled with warm water. I'm forced to kneel, and as the warm water pours over me, I catch sight of my reflection—my hair is a mess, my skin pale and streaked with dirt. I can feel the water washing away the dirt, the grime of the journey. But it doesn't feel like relief. It feels like a reminder that I no longer control anything, not even my own body.

One of the women begins to scrub, her hands firm and purposeful as she works the soap into my skin. She is gentle but insistent, as though there is nothing more natural than washing the filth off a woman like me. I want to scream, but I dare not. As unbearable as this is, the thought of being sent away, into something worse, is more than I can risk. The tears that have been threatening to spill for so long burn in my eyes, but I won't let them fall, I won't let them see me cry.

My skin is scrubbed raw, my hair—damp and combed through— falls in loose waves down my back. I feel lighter, cleaner, but also stripped bare in more ways than one. The women who bathed me have not spoken to me much, not that I could have understood them anyway, but their hands have been firm and practiced, leaving no doubt that they have done this countless times before.

They lead me to a stone bench where clothes—a silk robe and cotton tunic—lie in waiting along with odd wooden platform shoes. They dress me quickly, pulling the robe over my head, fastening the silk at my waist and adding the cotton tunic over top. Though soft and finely woven, it feels strange against my skin, foreign and unfamiliar. They fit me well enough, but it feels as though I am disappearing. These clothes are not for comfort, nor for beauty. They are for concealment, for subjugation. The robe is too loose, too soft, like a shroud.

32

I barely have time to adjust to the sensation before Kalfa pulls me back out of the bathhouse. My heart beats erratically as we walk through more halls, my head spinning with the unfamiliarity of it all. Finally, we stop before a large door, gilded and imposing, as if to protect something precious within.

Kalfa pushes it open, and I'm ushered through. The courtyard is lush with gardens, fountains trickling softly in the distance. It is unmistakably beautiful. I don't know what I expected, but it certainly wasn't this—nothing in my life has prepared me for the reality of this place. The air smells of flowers and herbs, and I can hear the soft hum of voices from women inside. The grandness of it all weighs on me.

This may be a palace, draped in luxury and gleaming with gold, but to me it feels more like a prison. Every step echoes with the truth—I am no longer a person, but a possession, something to be controlled, displayed, and dispensed at will.

There is no freedom here. Only a gilded cage, woven of silk and shadow, beautiful and inescapable.

Chapter 7
Whispers in Marble Halls

Past the first courtyard, I enter a world unto itself—grand, enclosed, and utterly separate from the rest of the palace. It is quieter here, though not silent. Soft murmurs, the rustling of silk, and the occasional laughter of women echo through the halls, bouncing off the high, domed ceilings.

The corridors are long and winding, some narrow and dimly lit, others opening into bright courtyards where sunlight spills across polished marble floors. The walls are covered in elaborate tilework—brilliant blues, deep reds, and lush greens forming intricate floral and geometric patterns. Tulips, carnations, and twisting vines stretch in delicate arabesques, their vibrancy almost dizzying, a subtle language of curves and symmetry. The designs seem to pulse under the flickering light of oil lamps mounted in bronze sconces.

Carved wooden doors with latticed panels line the halls, some slightly ajar, revealing glimpses of rooms beyond—private chambers where women sit on low divans, reclining against embroidered cushions. The scent of burning incense lingers in the air, mingling with the faint perfume of rosewater and the distant, mouthwatering aroma of freshly baked bread.

The main courtyard is breathtaking, an open-air space surrounded by colonnades. Here, women gather in small groups, their laughter and hushed whispers filling the space. A central fountain gurgles, its water shimmering in the midday light. The floor is a mosaic of marble, cool underfoot, the patterns flowing seamlessly with the decorative arches overhead. Potted plants—jasmine, orange trees, and small roses—line the edges, their fragrance drifting on the warm breeze that flows through the open archways.

It is seeing the women lounging on cushions that finally strikes me—I know what this place is. In a college seminar in my first term, we studied *The Arabian Nights*—the story of Scheherazade, the clever girl who saved herself by spinning tales to a sultan. I remember the animated discussion about power and storytelling, and how none of us—sitting safe in our chairs in Harvard—believed that women would so meekly accept being part of a harem.

In the absence of any other possible explanation, I must accept something unbelievable. My journey has lasted too long to be a dream, the pain has been too real to be a hallucination and the differences from everything known, no matter how culturally distinct, too extreme to be a kidnapping. Sherlock Holmes had it right: When you have eliminated the impossible, whatever remains, however improbable, must be the truth.

And the truth is that I am in a harem, in a foreign world, in a different time. Until the fates bring me home, this is where I must stay. The cold reality provides clarity. I will survive this ordeal, drawing on all my strengths and every ounce of knowledge. I will pay attention, learn, thrive, because there is no alternative.

As I move deeper inside, I notice the layout is not straightforward. The harem is a labyrinth of interconnected rooms and hidden passages, courtyards, gilded halls, and gardens, a breathtaking array of vaulted ceilings, golden domes, fountains whispering in stone basins, and fireplaces carved with royal emblems. Some hallways are grand, adorned with gold-leaf calligraphy and

35

detailed carvings, while others are stark, functional, almost forgotten.

This place is beautiful, but beneath its beauty, there is something else—a feeling of containment. The high walls and latticed windows ensure that no one looks in, and no one looks out. It is a golden cage, designed for comfort but still, unmistakably, a prison.

Kalfa leads the way. She strides ahead with the confidence of someone who belongs here, while I feel like an intruder in a world that is not my own. The occasional servant passes us, their eyes flicking to me briefly before they move on. Some glance at me with interest, others with indifference. Head held high; I will no longer cower in fear.

At last, we reach an arched doorway that leads into a vast, enclosed two-story room. Sunlight floods the space from windows set high in the walls, warming the stone beneath my feet. Around me, women are gathered in clusters—some lounging on cushions, others standing and talking in hushed voices. Their clothing is rich with color, soft silks and embroidered fabrics draped elegantly over their figures. Jewelry glints at their ears and wrists. They are beautiful.

When they notice me, their conversations falter. Heads turn. The weight of their stares presses down on me, heavy with curiosity, amusement, and something else—concern. A few whisper behind their hands, others simply watch.

I am ushered into a side chamber, where another woman is waiting. She is perhaps in her thirties, strong and clearly in charge;

she gives me a long, assessing look before speaking. Her tone is measured, clipped—she is telling me something that I strain to understand. After a pause, she sighs and gestures toward a small sleeping space along the wall. A simple mattress lies on the floor, covered in crisp white linens. A folded blanket rests at its foot. This, it seems, is where I will sleep.

I flop onto the mattress, weary from the day's events. My stomach twists—not just from nerves but from hunger. I realize that I haven't eaten today. As if sensing this, the woman calls for something, and within moments, a young servant girl appears carrying a tray. She places it in front of me on a small low table that was pushed against the nearby wall, offering a hesitant smile before retreating.

The food is simple but warm—fresh bread, a small bowl of lentil soup, dates, and a cup of water. I eat slowly, my hands trembling slightly. The soup is thick and comforting, the bread soft and slightly sweet.

The woman in charge stays with me while I eat. She waits until I finish my meal before speaking again. "Melek Kalfa" she says, pointing at her chest. I look confused for a moment. I thought Kalfa was the name of the woman who led me to the bathhouse. "Melek Kalfa" she repeats. She summons another woman. "Cennet Kalfa" she says, pointing at the woman. Unless they are all sisters, Kalfa must be a title. Melek Kalfa points at me, asking for my name. I hesitate.

My name is Katherine Elizabeth Dubois; I settle on telling her Katerina. Melek Kalfa smiles and repeats my name. "Katerina" adding other words after it that elude me. She nods to the bed, inviting me to sleep. It is probably only midafternoon, but I admit that I am bone tired. I lie on the soft bed; within seconds, sleep is pulling me under.

I wake to the sound of voices—soft murmurs, hushed giggles, and the occasional sharp whisper cutting through the dim room. My body aches from exhaustion. The scent of flowers and incense cling to the air, unfamiliar yet soothing.

I push myself up from the thin mattress, my fingers pressing into the soft fabric of the bedding. The room is filled with rows of sleeping spaces, each separated only by the bodies of the women occupying them. Some are still asleep, curled beneath fine woven blankets, while others sit up, combing their hair or whispering to one another.

In the calmness of my new surroundings, I reflect. It feels like an eternity since I woke up on that beach, though it has only been a month, give or take. My realization that I am in a different time is stomach churning. How to piece together what time it is? The architecture points to somewhere in the Middle East: Persia, perhaps, or maybe the Ottoman Empire.

My mother would love the intricate designs. I reflect on the language, but don't know enough to declare whether it sounds more Turkish or Arabic. The people, the clothes, the scenes I saw on my journey; they indicate premodern, but that could still mean any time before the 17th century.

Humans can adapt to anything, and I am no different. Even if I can make it back to that beach, I have no idea what great cosmic force I would need to employ to bring me back to my own time. I cannot wail against the unknown.

Though resolved to adapt, sadness clings to me, mostly for my mother's sake. I miss her deeply and mourn that she has lost me so soon after my father. They have been my pillars, saving me from a life in foster care, adopting me, loving me, nurturing me. I will draw on every ounce of that love to survive, every lesson to help me thrive.

A kalfa approaches and pulls me from my reverie. She hands me a new dress, simple but fine—long, flowing, made of a soft fabric that drapes over my body. My hair hangs loosely down my back. I feel exposed without my usual layers, without a bra or underwear.

A girl beside me stirs, blinking up at me with large, dark eyes. She looks younger than me, maybe fifteen, with delicate features and an expression that is equal parts curiosity and fear. She speaks, her voice gentle, but I can only shake my head.

"I don't understand," I murmur, knowing it is useless.

"Aleksandra" she says, tapping herself on the chest. I offer her my name in return. Aleksandra gestures toward the door, where the sound of footsteps signals movement. The other women have already risen, adjusting their clothing, braiding their hair. I hesitate before following her out of the room.

We go down a corridor into a larger chamber, where low round tables are set with food. The sight of it makes my stomach clench with hunger—I have only eaten the bowl of gruel at the slave market and lentil soup yesterday afternoon. The women sit cross-legged on the floor, forming small groups. I hesitate, not knowing where to go, until Aleksandra tugs me down beside her. We might not be friends yet, but I feel better having a companion by my side.

The meal is delicious and comforting—soft bread, fresh cheese, olives, honey, clotted cream, a variety of fresh fruit and a soothing herbal tea. I eat slowly, listening to the conversations around me, trying to catch any words that might make sense. The women glance at me now and then, some with curiosity, others with disinterest, but many others still with a look of disdain or jealousy.

I realize, with a sinking feeling, that this is not a place of sisterhood. This is a place of survival, filled with rules and customs I will have to learn, and master.

I survived the first night. And I will survive the days to come.

Chapter 8
The Quiet Becoming

At first, I expect the days to blur together in shapeless monotony—but instead, they press in with strange clarity. Each morning arrives with the soft shuffle of slippers and the distant ring of a servant's bell. There is no clock, yet time is kept with eerie precision: prayers echo through the walls, trays clink in unison, water splashes in fountains at regular hours. I begin to mark the passage of days not by dates, but by the slow unfolding of ritual—baths, meals, silences, glances. The rhythm is not comforting, only inescapable.

The kalfas move efficiently, tending to daily tasks. Children weave through this world as well. The younger girls, no older than ten or eleven, sit in their own lessons, giggling when they think no one is watching. They practice curtsies and learn the art of graceful movement, their small hands delicate as they trace embroidery patterns.

Once, I catch a glimpse of a different kind of child. A little boy, dressed in rich silk, dashes past the corridor, pursued by a servant who calls after him in exasperation. A prince, no doubt. His laughter is high and bright, vanishing down the hall before I can see his face.

This world is strange, beautiful, and terrifying all at once. I do not know what my future holds here, but for now, I survive. I learn. I wait.

Each morning, we rise with the sun and set to work. The harem must be kept spotless—sweeping, polishing, and tidying the countless rooms and corridors. The higher-ranking women do none of this; the newest or lowest among us bear the burden.

I rise when the others do, following their lead as we fold our bedding and tidy our sleeping area. No one tells me what to do, but I have learned quickly that standing idly invites scorn. The older girls, those who had been in the harem longer, take their duties seriously and expect the same from everyone else. So, I work—sweeping the floors, dusting the carved wooden furniture, and polishing the delicate inlaid surfaces.

Breakfast is simple—bread, cheese, fruit, honey and clotted cream—and though the food is plain, it fills my stomach and gives me the energy I need for the long day ahead. The other women eat in silence or whisper in a language I barely understand. Their voices are hushed, careful. I listen, trying to catch words, but I am still lost in a sea of unfamiliar sounds.

Aleksandra is my frequent companion. Though younger than me, she gives me the impression she has been here for years. She chats to me constantly, helping me to pick up bits and pieces of words. The formal lessons help even more.

The first is language, *Osmanlica*, Ottoman Turkish. I sit cross-legged on the floor with a group of other new girls, our teacher—a stern, older woman called Halime Kalfa—paces before us as she drills new words and phrases into our slowly-developing vocabulary. I struggle at first to understand the unfamiliar sounds twisting in my mouth, but I am a quick learner. I listen closely, memorizing words by their rhythm, attaching meaning to gestures and expressions.

Halime Kalfa places a small pillow under her dress and points. "*Bebek,*" she says. I understand clearly the meaning of baby.

"*Anne,*" Halime Kalfa says next, pointing to herself while gently stroking her imaginary baby. And then more slowly "*An-ne.*"

"*Anne,*" I repeat, along with the others, perhaps the word for mother.

Halime summons a man into the room and interlaces their arms. "*Baba,*" she says, pointing to the man. I now know mother, father, baby. From Aleksandra, I have picked up words for various foods; word by word, I build a means of exchange with the world.

The music lessons are easier. The harem girls are expected to know how to entertain, how to sing sweetly or play delicate melodies on the *oud*, a short-neck, pear-shaped lute. I was never musically gifted, but rhythm is universal. I pluck at the strings of an oud feeling the vibrations hum beneath my fingertips. The melodies are unfamiliar but enchanting. I imagine how these songs must sound when played in grand halls, drifting through candlelit chambers.

We are taught more than language and music. There are lessons in embroidery and dance—skills meant to refine us, to prepare us for the life we are expected to lead. Sewing is a skill that requires patience I do not have. We sit in a circle, embroidering fine silks with golden thread, our stitches meant to be perfect and even. My first attempt is a disaster. My stitches pull too tight, puckering the fabric, and when the girl beside me looks over, she smirks and whispers something. I understand enough—my failure is amusing to her. My face burns, but I force myself to keep going. Gradually, with time, I might become proficient though I doubt I will ever be an accomplished seamstress.

Next comes the lessons in curtseying. Halime Kalfa stands at the front of the room, her hands clasped in front of her. She watches as we line up along the tiled floor. I can feel the sweat forming at the back of my neck from the heat of the room, but I keep my back straight, my eyes focused.

She speaks in slow, deliberate Turkish, demonstrating as she moves. I don't understand all the words yet, but the motion itself is clear.

"One foot behind the other," she says, tapping her slippered foot against the floor. She adjusts her long, flowing robe and gracefully steps back, her right foot sliding behind her left. Her knees bend slightly, and her upper body tilts forward—not too much, just enough to signal deference without lowering herself completely.

I try to mimic the movement. My foot slides back, my knees bend, but something feels off. My balance wobbles, and I quickly step forward again before I make a complete fool of myself.

The instructor sighs, moving toward me. She grips my arm lightly, repositioning my stance. "Slowly," she instructs, demonstrating again. "Graceful. Controlled."

I exhale, focusing on the placement of my feet. Right foot behind, bend, tilt forward slightly, keep the spine straight. My muscles protest at the awkwardness of the movement, but I push through it.

Across the room, a few of the other girls perform the motion effortlessly. Some are clearly experienced, their movements smooth and elegant. Others, like me, struggle with coordination. A girl beside me stumbles, nearly losing her balance, and a quiet chuckle ripples through the group.

The instructor claps her hands sharply. "Again."

I inhale and try once more, this time keeping my weight centered. Right foot behind, a gentle bend, a soft tilt forward. It's not perfect, but it's better.

The instructor nods approvingly. "Good. Now, the hands."

She lifts her arms slightly, fingers resting gently on her thighs as she dips into the curtsey. It's a delicate motion, meant to appear effortless. I copy her, trying to keep my movements fluid, but my arms feel stiff, unnatural.

The instructor frowns. "Relax," she says, tapping my shoulder lightly. "Like water."

I close my eyes for a second, taking a slow breath before I try again. This time, I let my arms move naturally with the curtsey, letting them follow the motion instead of holding them rigid.

When I straighten, the instructor gives a small nod.

"Better," she says.

I exhale in relief, only to hear her next command.

"Again. All of you."

The lesson continues, each repetition etching the motion into my muscles until my body begins to understand what my mind struggles to grasp. By the end of the session, my legs ache, my back feels tight, but I no longer feel like I'm about to trip over my own feet.

I still don't understand all the words spoken in the room, but one thing is clear. This lesson is not just about movement, it's about learning to carry myself like I belong.

By far the most important lesson is *yasak*—learning what is forbidden in the strict routine of our lives.

"No looking directly at the Sultan," she says.
"No speaking unless spoken to."
"No loud laughter."
"No wandering the corridors without permission."
"No whispering. No secrets. No gossiping."
"No quarrels."
"No men."

This last one confuses me as I have seen men about.

"They are eunuchs," explains Halime Kalfa. "Men who are not men, so they may serve within the harem, so they may guard us without dishonor. No desire. No threat. That is their purpose."

By the time the midday meal arrives, I am exhausted. Lunch is more substantial than breakfast—steaming lentil soup, fragrant rice, stewed vegetables. I eat in silence, watching the other girls as they chat and laugh. I am still an outsider. I cannot yet joke in their language, cannot share in their gossip or their stories. I have no friends here, except Aleksandra in whom I have come to appreciate her quiet reserve and patient lessons.

After lunch, we are given time to rest. Some nap in the shade of the courtyard, others lounge on cushions, fanning themselves slowly. I sit either alone or with Aleksandra, observing, listening, piecing together the fragments of my new world.

The afternoon brings more work—sweeping, dusting, fetching water from great marble fountains. I grip the handle of a broom, pushing it across the cool tiles. My arms throb from days of unfamiliar labor, my back sore from hours spent bent over scrubbing floors. I have never cleaned so much in my life. There are no mops, only cloth and buckets of water scented with lavender. The head kalfa, Melek, watches over us with keen eyes, her voice snapping like a whip when someone moves too slowly.

As the sun dips lower in the sky, the harem grows quieter. The evening meal is richer than the others, with meat and sweet *sharbat*—a refreshing drink made with various fruit, flowers, or herbs. I learn that there are favored girls who dine separately, their laughter carrying through the halls. I wonder if I will ever be among them.

Evening comes and the oil lamps flicker, casting shadows on the tiled walls. At night, I lie on my mattress, my body sore, my mind heavy with new words and unfamiliar customs. I don't know what I am becoming—but I am becoming, nonetheless. I close my eyes, thinking of the sounds of my former life, the feel of my own bed, the familiar streets of Boston.

And every night I send love through the cosmos to my mother, willing her to feel my arms wrapped around her, to hear my whispers on the wind.

Chapter 9
The Art of Survival

My tongue still stumbles over unfamiliar sounds, but the words come easier now. I no longer feel like a child learning to speak for the first time. Each day, I listen carefully, memorizing phrases, mimicking the way the other women speak. The more I understand, the more dangerous this world becomes.

At first, I only hear the name spoken in reverence—Süleyman. His name alone commands respect. Even though the women whisper about him constantly, they are always careful. In the harem, one wrong statement can lead to punishment—or worse.

Sultan Süleyman Khan—young, recently ascended to the throne. I remember his name from a lesson in European history class, and from bits of information my father once shared. He used to talk about world-changing battles: the Battle of Mohács, the siege of Vienna. I wish I could remember the exact years those events happened. Dates used to seem like trivia. Now, they might be the only compass I have.

16th century Ottoman Empire—at least I now know exactly where, and when, I am. The knowledge fills me with dread. This is not a time and place in history when women have rights. Every thought fills me with fear, each one more terrifying than the last. I am a slave in the court of Süleyman the Magnificent. I have no rights, no freedom, no say in what happens to me. I am at the whim of people with a very different set of moral and cultural values than modern America.

What happens if I break the rules or displease someone in power? I have already seen girls with bloody feet, beaten for some misstep. And some girls have disappeared altogether—one day there, the next gone. My modern mindset encourages me to stand up for myself, to declare that I am a strong woman with rights. But this is not the time nor the place for such thoughts. Here, I am disposable. I know that I had better learn the rules fast or risk being drowned in a time that I don't understand.

The harem is a place of beauty, but beneath the gilded walls and silken cushions lies something sharper. A hierarchy, an invisible chain of power that dictates who rises and who is forgotten. I see it now in the way the women move around each other—the way some lower their heads in deference, while others walk with a quiet, assured grace.

As I listen carefully to the conversations around me, I begin to piece together the fragments of knowledge from the concubines in the harem, to learn about the people who hold the most power in my new world.

The harem is filled with eager women vying for the attention of the Sultan. Some of the younger concubines are utterly mesmerized by the idea of Süleyman. They talk about him as if he were larger than life.

"He is the shadow of Allah on earth. They say he is the most powerful ruler in the world. To be chosen by him is the highest honor," Aleksandra tells me one day.

Aleksandra explains to me that many of the concubines dream of being noticed by him, though most will never even see him up close.

"He only has eyes for Mahidevran Hatun, his most favored, the mother of his only son. The rest of us are nothing," says Aleksandra.

Legend says that if a concubine bears the Sultan a son, her feet will never again touch the ground—she'd be carried in a litter, served by others for the rest of her life.

"Why have so many concubines if he only favors Mahidevran?" I ask, confused.

"Because hope keeps the harem alive," Aleksandra says, stars in her eyes. "A glance, a night, a son—that's enough to change a life."

She explains that those who share Süleyman's bed become his favorites, those who live in the semi-private rooms—private rooms are reserved for the royal family. The Sultan's favorites do not work as we do. They do not scrub floors or polish brass. They wear fine silks, they are served the best food, and their days are spent in leisure. Their monthly stipend is increased compared to the rest of the concubines. But for the other girls in the harem, they live to serve the royal family, to care for the children and to attend to the sisters of the Sultan.

"But only Valide Sultan chooses who goes to him. Most of us never will," she adds.

Aleksandra's words echo in my head. I think about their meaning. Some women never get summoned, spending decades in the shadows, aging behind silk screens, until one day they're quietly sent to the Old Palace to live out the rest of their days in obscurity, useless and forgotten. If I want a chance to be anything but a lowly slave, I must win the Sultan's mother's favor first.

I really understand her true power here when I first set eyes on her—Valide Sultan.

She enters the chamber like a storm dressed in silk, her presence commanding absolute attention. The women around me instantly curtsey. I follow, putting to use those hours of lessons. When I lift my head, I catch a glimpse of her face. She is the velvet woman I met on my first day, regal and severe, her eyes sharp with intelligence. She is the mother of the Sultan. The most powerful woman in this palace. Probably the most powerful woman in the Empire.

She sits proudly, confidently. Her gaze lingers on the women around her, and briefly on me.

A beautiful woman is moving up the dais to sit on a cushion near Valide. She carries herself like a woman who knows her place— and her place is above the rest of us. She is striking, with dark, almond-shaped eyes that seem to see through anyone who dares to look at her too long. Her features are severe yet undeniably beautiful, her high cheekbones accentuated by the flickering light of the oil lamps. Her hair, thick and dark as ink, is meticulously braided and adorned with delicate golden threads that shimmer with each movement.

Her robes are richer than those of the other concubines. While many women in the harem wear silks and soft linens in muted colors, this one's garments are deep jewel tones—crimson, sapphire, emerald. The fabrics cling and flow in a way that speaks of status. She does not wear the plain slippers that the rest of us do; instead, her shoes are embroidered, stitched with pearls and fine thread.

But it is not just her beauty or clothing that sets her apart. It is the way she moves—graceful and deliberate, like a panther that knows it is the queen of its territory. The other girls whisper about her as she passes, their voices hushed but urgent. I catch one word—Mahidevran.

I know who she is. She is the Sultan's most favored. The harem girls always speak of her with a mixture of admiration and fear. She holds a power none of the other women have.

And I know, suddenly, what I must do. There is no future in this palace as a servant. I will never be free. I will never go home. But I can rise. If I am to live, truly live, I must become one of his favorites. I must make the Sultan see me—not just as another veiled girl, but as something unforgettable.

The harem isn't just a bunch of pretty women—it's a battlefield. Women whisper in corners, they measure each other like opponents before a duel. This place is just as cutthroat as the halls of power in modern-day America. If I want to do more than survive, if I want to thrive in this place, I will need to play the game better than anyone else.

I look at her again. Mahidevran, mother of Prince Mustafa, the only son of Sultan Süleyman—that alone secures her place in the harem's hierarchy, but there is a sharpness in her eyes, a wariness that tells me she is not as secure as she once was.

She walks with confidence, but I notice the way her gaze lingers on those around her, always assessing, always aware. She is alert, which tells me that there have been rivals. She is the favorite, and favorites do not share their thrones willingly. She may be the favorite now but now is not forever.

Getting his attention is only the first move. Keeping it—on my terms—that's the real challenge. I have a few advantages over the other harem girls. I am confident, independent, and educated. I know that I can shape my own destiny.

I may not yet master their customs, but I understand power—the subtle game of influence, the art of survival. I will use every shard of knowledge, every scrap of will, to carve my place. I refuse to be a passive player in my own destiny. I am no ornament—I am a force to be reckoned with.

Chapter 10
The Day the World Changed

I have spent the past few months learning the rules of the harem. Women whisper about ambition, about beauty, about fate. But I am not here to simply exist—I choose to rise.

Süleyman.

That name has settled deep into my mind, the man who rules this Empire, the one who holds power over every life in this palace, including mine. I spend my nights piecing together scraps of knowledge, trying to remember anything useful. The Magnificent. That means he must be famous for something—but what? Military conquests? Being a fair ruler? My limited knowledge offers but scraps, breadcrumbs to follow.

But I do know one thing: if I want a future, I must make him look at me.

I watch the other women in the harem. Women who have never seen him worship him like an untouchable god. The favorites live comfortably, with silks and perfumes, their lives a delicate game of keeping his favor.

If I am going to matter here, I have to matter to him.

The problem is that the Sultan doesn't simply wander into the harem and pick a woman at random. He is busy ruling an empire. If I want him to see me, I have to find a way into his path. And that way is with Valide—as she can support a concubine or bury her. Valide rules the harem and the lives of every female of the royal family, every concubine, every servant, kalfa or eunuch depend on her favor.

I brainstorm at night, fictional conversations with my mother. We have spoken before about men; I can hear her words of wisdom. "Be warm, be kind, be real," she might say. "Be unexpected; don't play games. Be the girl who isn't afraid to look him in the eye, and the woman who doesn't need him to survive, but might just choose him anyway."

Valuable lessons, but only once I get to Süleyman. It is Valide that I must win over first. What sage advice will my imagined conversations conjure? It is in the early hours one morning that it comes to me. "Find the one thing she values most—be it devotion, loyalty, cleverness, or piety—and reflect it back to her like a mirror. If she sees herself in you, she will guard you like a jewel. And once she favors you... the Sultan will follow."

That is my course, my path to success. Now, I must ensure that the Valide Sultan notices me and then discover what she values above all else. And so, I hatch a plan to stand out by virtue of my excellence.

Over the coming weeks, during music lessons, I begin to lose myself in the strings of the oud. My fingers learn their way across the instrument with increasing confidence, plucking each note with growing precision. I no longer simply follow the melodies—I breathe them. Music becomes my refuge, a place where I can shape beauty with my own hands, even in captivity. Sometimes, I close my eyes and let the sounds transport me back to the forests of my childhood, or to imaginary gardens filled with cypress trees and the scent of jasmine. The oud, I discover, speaks a language older than sorrow.

In language lessons, I redouble my efforts, my pride stung each time I stumble over a phrase. I repeat the same sentences over and over until the syllables no longer catch in my throat. I whisper them to myself while walking in the courtyards or falling asleep at night. Turkish begins to form on my tongue like a second skin, no longer foreign, no longer feared. Though still an amateur, with each word I master, I feel a sliver of power return to me—to understand and to be understood, to shape my place and become master of my destiny.

And I walk—not with the uncertain steps of the frightened girl who arrived here, but with deliberate grace. I watch the Valide Sultan closely, her every gesture measured and majestic. She moves like the moon in water—serene, untouchable. I study her posture, the tilt of her chin, the way she folds her hands in her lap with silent authority. Her elegance becomes my guide, her composure my armor. In the mirrors of the harem, I practice her expression: calm, composed, distant. And slowly, I feel myself transforming. Not vanishing—no, never that—but emerging. Like steel drawn from fire.

And then, one morning, fate decides to smile down on me. Some days arrive like storms—you know they'll change the shape of your life before they even touch you.

A kalfa appears in the dormitory, her expression unreadable. "You will come." She says simply, "Valide Sultan wishes to see you."

I rise and follow her, my heart hammering. We walk from the concubines' quarters to Valide's suite, passing through dimly lit corridors lined with intricately tiled walls and arched doorways. Servants and eunuchs move through these halls in near silence, carrying messages and fulfilling the daily needs of the harem.

Before reaching Valide Sultan's private domain, we pass by several restricted sections that I have never seen before. These are the private quarters of the Sultan's sisters and the senior concubines, the ones most favored by the Sultan—of which there is currently only one—Mahidevran. The final stretch before entering her suite is marked by a set of grand double doors, guarded by the highest-ranking eunuchs of the harem.

Valide Sultan's suite is in the privileged inner sanctum of the harem, separate from the general quarters where the concubines live—separate even from the restricted section. While still within the harem complex, her chamber is positioned in a way that symbolize her authority—closer to the Sultan's private apartments yet still accessible to the women she governs.

This placement ensures that Valide is physically separate from the concubines, reinforcing her status as our ruler while maintaining proximity to the Sultan's chambers—always near enough to wield her influence over both the harem and the Empire.

Valide Sultan's suite is unlike any other space I have seen in the palace. It is not simply a room—it is a world apart, a realm gilded in authority and refinement.

The ceilings are high, decorated with intricate geometric patterns and delicate gold filigree, catching the soft glow of the oil lamps that line the walls. Carved wooden panels, inlaid with mother-of-pearl, gleam in the dim light, their delicate floral patterns casting shadows that dance as the lanterns flicker.

The walls are covered in silk brocade, deep hues of sapphire and crimson woven with golden threads. Large cushions, embroidered with intricate floral motifs, are arranged on the low divans that line the room, forming a space for receiving guests and holding court over the harem.

In the center, a marble fountain trickles with gently flowing water, filling the chamber with the softest murmur of movement. The air smells of lavender and amber, the faintest trace of burning incense lingering in the background.

Along one side of the chamber stands a grand screen of latticed wood, separating the private sleeping quarters from the reception area. Beyond it, I catch glimpses of luxurious bedding, a plush mattress piled high with silken sheets and fur-lined blankets. Even in rest, Valide Sultan is surrounded by opulence.

At the far end of the room, an ornate chair sits on a raised platform, more throne than seat. Every detail of the suite is a testament to her status as the gatekeeper of the fates of the entire harem.

Valide Sultan sits on a cushioned settee, dressed in embroidered silks. Her presence fills the room. I stand before her, lower my head and curtsey. I take my time with it, demonstrating her proper respect. I stay in the curtsey, waiting for Valide to speak. She takes her time, perhaps to test my resolve—my legs begin to shake.

"You have adjusted well," she says, her voice measured; it was not a question.

I finally rise and meet her eyes.

"I am learning, Valide Sultan."

She studies me for a long moment.

"I purchased you myself," she says finally. "You are meant to be a gift," she continues, "for my son. A woman unlike the others, a rare offering on the occasion of his ascension."

I stop breathing for a moment, stunned. Her revelation explains much about my time in the slave market, my segregation from the other women, the man who bought me without bidding. She purchased me for the Sultan. I am not meant to be a simple concubine. She intended for me to stand out, to be special.

"I am honored, my Valide," I reply, taking a risk by ascribing kinship.

"You should be." Her expression is unreadable. "But honor alone is not enough. You must prove worthy of the gift."

Her meaning is clear. If I want to survive, I must succeed, I must please the Sultan.

"I will," I answer softly. "My only purpose is to please the Sultan and serve the Empire."

Silence for minutes as she examines me. My heart skips a beat as I wonder if I read her wrongly.

Finally, she nods. "Tonight, you will be presented to him."

The words feel both like a victory and a challenge. I thank her, curtsey again, and shuffle out of her presence without ever showing her my back, another sign of the respect I owe her.

I glide back to the harem. I am his gift. I know that I should be upset by this—after all, I am a person, and it should not be possible to gift me to someone—but I do not feel slighted; I feel elated. In this strange situation in which I find myself, in a different time and place than where I am meant to be, I know already that my circumstances could be far worse than they are. I am fortunate to live in this oasis of luxury, and I am determined to make the most of the opportunity.

Since arriving in the harem, no concubine has been prepared for the Sultan. I will be the first. The harem girls are already aware of the news by the time I arrive in our courtyard and the harem is atwitter at the prospect that one of us will be so fortunate. I can hear their chatter—if she was chosen, we can be chosen too. But I have no intention of sharing—I will catch the Sultan, and I will keep him.

The process of preparing a concubine to be presented to the Sultan is a ritualized, luxurious affair, with every detail carefully managed by the kalfas and eunuchs of the harem. First, I am brought to the *hammam*, the bathhouse. The large pool has been prepared and the warm water infused with rose petals and orange blossoms. The scent is intoxicating. Platters of fruit are prepared. I laze in the water, eating grapes, pomegranates and dried apricots.

The kalfas use a raw silk mitt to exfoliate my skin, infused with olive oil and musk-scented soap. They rub me down until my skin is soft and glowing. It feels good to be pampered and I relax into the ritual.

To my surprise, after the bath, the kalfas use a special paste to remove all hair from my body, save the eyebrows and scalp. I find it a little embarrassing to have the kalfas work on every nook and cranny of my body, applying the paste and then using a bronze scraper to remove any trace of hair. Our lessons taught us that cleanliness is of great value in Ottoman culture, and I can understand that the Sultan's bed is no place for anything less than perfection.

Smooth and hairless, I return to the bath for my hair to be washed. The scented soap smells of lavender. Each scent builds on the last, creating a unique blend that is a heady, exotic perfume. After the bath, I am anointed with a specially prepared mix of resin scented with musk, jasmine, and rose. This perfumed mixture is applied to my wrists, neck, between my breasts, and even to my ankles. It is a seductive fragrance that further complements the lingering smells from the bath.

My hands and feet are massaged with scented cream. My pubic area is decorated with henna in swirling patterns reminiscent of a flower—exactly four fingers breadth above the vulva, as is custom. The kalfas then begin the laborious process of drying my long hair. Finally, stage one is complete—I am bathed, shaved, and perfumed.

Escorted out of the hammam, I am brought to a private chamber for dressing. As the kalfas begin to brush and style my hair, I am permitted to graze on fruits, nuts, and figs. I am told to eat lightly to avoid "any necessity for bodily functions" during the night, so says the kalfa working on my hair. I sit still as they apply *kohl* to the waterline of my eyes, creating a smoky effect. They sent my skin with various powders—the kalfas explain that sandalwood is the Sultan's favorite.

The kalfas talk to me throughout the afternoon, their hands careful as they prepare me for the night ahead. Don't forget to kneel when you enter the room. Don't forget to kiss the hem of his robe. Wait until he invites you to stand. Be demure. Don't talk too much. Don't move too much. On and on with instructions. They explain that taking the Golden Road—a gilded corridor leading to the Sultan's private chamber— is a privilege that can change my life forever.

"Remember, the Sultan is not obligated to receive every concubine sent to him. But please him and your life will be filled with joy."

Those words roll through me like a bulldozer. If he doesn't like me, I am unlikely to get another chance. I will forever be stuck in the harem as a servant. I must please him.

It is hard to sit still after that, but there is still much to do. With my white skin and autumn amber hair, the kalfas choose a ruby-red sheer gown of the finest silk to accentuate my features. The only thing stopping it from being transparent is its multiple layers, creating a dreamy ethereal effect. It is held together by thin straps that tie together above my shoulders, making it both easy to slip off and tantalizingly seductive. I wear no undergarments. A bejeweled sash is tied around my waist to emphasize my figure. My hair is adorned with ruby and pearl hair clips on my right side—a design that exposes my neck on that side while leaving my long hair free to drape over my left side down to my breasts.

"You are ready," one of them declares, smiling at their accomplishment.

I stare at my reflection in the polished brass mirror. My skin glows like a lantern, my lips are stained a deep red and my eyes are dark and mysterious. I barely recognize myself.

A kalfa steps forward and fits delicate slippers on my feet. A small glass of sharbat is offered—it is both refreshing and leaves a nice scent on my breath. A red veil is carefully placed on my head to avoid messing my hair. I look like a sultry candy—exotic and delicious.

The corridor stretches ahead, dimly lit by flickering torches. My heart drums in my ears as I take my first step down the Golden Road. Tonight, everything will change.

Chapter 11
Between Fear and Flame

The massive double doors stand as a silent proclamation—imposing, beautiful, and unmistakably regal. Their polished walnut is carved with intricate geometric shapes and crowned by a golden emblem shaped like a stylized lute, surrounded by tiny blue and red flowers. Delicate ivy tilework creeps along the doorframe; the bronze handles, curved into tulips, gleam with a soft, worn sheen.

Two guards flank the entrance, their eyes never meeting mine. The eunuch who escorted me knocks once, then pulls the door open from the center without waiting for a reply. Everything here is predetermined—I am expected.

For a moment, I stand there, stunned into stillness. A fire burns brightly in the grand hearth—the air is warm and fragrant with scents of sandalwood, a hint of cinnamon, and something deeper, more ancient. This isn't just a room; it is a world, vast yet intimate, bathed in warm light from dozens of hanging lanterns. Their glass is stained in hues of amber and crimson that dance across the walls, painting the room in flickering pools of firelight. Each light whispers a different mood as if the room itself is alive with emotion.

The walls are covered in intricate tilework of cerulean blues, deep teals, and white floral patterns that spiral in delicate flowing lines, evoking shapes of flowers, fruits, and animals. Verses of the Qur'an and poetic blessings curve around the room in graceful gold leaf. The shallow-dome ceiling is painted with celestial patterns of stars, suns, and moons, winding together in harmony.

Beneath my feet, the floor is layered with thick carpets, a tapestry of reds, ochres and forest greens. In one corner stands multiple low tables of inlaid wood and mother-of-pearl holding brass ewers, delicate crystal glasses, and shallow dishes of dried fruits, sugared apricots, and roasted almonds. Everything is arranged with such care, intentional and precise.

The bed sits atop a dais, rising from the floor like an island. Wide and low, it is framed by sheer drapes that hang from the ceiling in cascades. The bedding, a brocade of plum and ivory, shimmer like water under moonlight. Velvet cushions are piled high, inviting, nearly imposing. This is not a bed for rest—this is power, a throne by any other name.

A small screen alcove lies beyond—a low divan, stacks of scrolls and books, perhaps it is his study. The scent of ink and beeswax drifts faintly from that corner. To my right, the chamber leads to a private garden balcony, the doors shut tight against the cold winter air. This private sanctuary is a place for solitude, a quiet pause between the responsibilities of the Empire and the intimacy of private life.

Sultan Süleyman stands near the doors to the balcony, his back to me, looking out at the dark sky. I have never even seen him before and yet here I am, painted, perfumed and polished—an offering for the most powerful man in this world.

I drop to the ground, head touching the floor as a supplicant, and wait, my heart racing. In my many months here, I have often thought of how I should react in this moment—timid and shy, or strong and self-confident. I am running out of time to decide.

I sense more than see that he has moved to stand in front of me. Without raising my body more than a fraction, I reach delicately for the hem of his robe, kiss it and press it momentarily to my forehead—a symbol of respect and reverence. After a moment, his hand scoops my chin, and he gently raises me to my feet. I keep my eyes lowered until finally he tilts my chin up with one finger, and I meet his gaze for the first time.

His eyes are dark, thoughtful. There is an intelligence in them—this is a man who rules armies and changes the fates of nations. I hold his gaze, trying to pierce the veil and see into his very soul. It is deeply intimate. For a brief moment, I see confusion, or perhaps curiosity, and then a softening, a flicker of a smile as though he can see not only who I am, but who I might become—perhaps who he needs me to become. There is a sadness to his eyes and in that moment, I want nothing more than to chase it away and bring him joy.

"Come," he says in a voice low and calm, neither offering a command nor a request, as he takes my hand in his.

We walk hand in hand toward the dais. We sit side by side on the massive bed. He doesn't ask me my name or where I come from. It doesn't matter to him. Not yet. I am still only another woman in his harem.

Leaning into me, scenting my skin, his lips brush along the curve of my neck. I close my eyes, trying hard to relax into the touch of a stranger. Our eyes lock again as he gently urges me to lie back on the bed. Instinctively, I reach up to touch his cheek and guide him into a kiss, tentative at first then more passionate. He touches me here and there with kindness. I was expecting force, but there is nothing harsh to his touch. He seems to study me, curious.

The next few hours take us both by surprise. Maybe it is because I engage with him, coax him, urge him gently with kisses, allow my hands to roam his body, moan slightly at his touch. At some point, I forget that he is a stranger, forget that I am his slave stuck in a foreign land and time from my own, forget everything but the feel of him. It is simultaneously hesitant and passionate—a delicate blend of the unknown and the newly discovered.

Süleyman rolls over, sated. He laughs, a full deep belly rumble that is contagious. I laugh with him as he scoops me up in his embrace. We are both too tired for more, but it is not from lack of desire. We lie on our sides, facing each other, him stroking my hair, me his shoulder. Gradually, he eases toward sleep, his eyes closing. Just when I think he has dosed off, he opens his eyes. Staring deeply into mine, almost whispering "where have you come from?"—he holds my gaze a moment longer, kisses me one last time on the forehead and turns over to sleep.

I lie beside him, watching the flicker of lantern light dance across the ceiling. My mind is spinning, thinking over everything that has happened to me in the last few months, from waking up on that beach to the slave market to here in this room tonight.

I may never understand why or how this journey was possible, or see my mother again to tell her all that has happened to me. But looking at Süleyman, I feel—for the first time—that this is exactly where I am meant to be.

Chapter 12
Becoming Hürrem

The quiet rustle of linen and the low murmur of voices just outside the chamber wake me. I prop myself up on velvet cushions, pulling the silk coverlet around me. The room seems even more overwhelming than last night. There are many intricate details to catch the eye and an endless stream of colors to explore.

As I turn my head, I see him. Süleyman.

He is sitting by the window, the heavy winter drapes slightly pulled aside, his head turned toward the horizon where the sky is slowly bleeding from a morning rose to the golden rays of the day.

I remain still, unsure whether to speak, to rise or to wait. The gravity of last night settles on me: I have just spent the night with the most powerful man in the Empire, and he hasn't sent me away—the usual fate of concubines is that of a quick dismissal after the pleasures of the night. I am lost in thought when I realize that Süleyman is looking at me. His expression is soft, almost bemused—like he can't quite believe what he's seeing.

"You are awake," he says, the words slow and deliberate. "Good."

He crosses the room, slowly and purposefully, as if afraid of frightening his prey. Watching him move toward me brings back memories of last night, unreal and yet utterly vivid, and I find myself blushing at some of the more intimate moments. He sits on the far side. I watch him closely, reading every shift in his expression. He reaches forward to brush a wayward curl behind my ear.

"You are not frightened of me," he says, not so much a question as an observation. After a pause, "many women are," he adds.

"No, I am not afraid."

Leaning forward, he lays the briefest kiss on my lips before rising to pull closed the bed-curtains, encasing me in a cocoon of sheer drapes and plays of light. He claps his hands once, sharply.

"*Aghas*!" He summons the two attendants at the door, who enter immediately and bow before their Sultan. "Breakfast," he commands. They withdraw without a word to fulfil their mission.

In a surprising display of playfulness, Süleyman sticks only his head through a crack in the drapes.

"Past the alcove, you will find a place to dress and refresh yourself. Hurry or I'll start eating without you." He winks as he says the last part and withdraws to the terrace.

Chuckling quietly, I wrap myself in silk sheets to walk to the alcove. The antechamber beyond boasts a large dressing room, washbasin and private facilities. The dressing room is long and spacious, with sunlight streaming through intricate stain-glass windows, painting the floor in a rainbow of color, highlighting the elaborate floral motifs. The walls are lined with carved wooden wardrobes inlaid with mother-of-pearl and tortoiseshell. A full-length mirror of polished glass stands near the corner; its surface slightly warped with the imperfections of the era. A low divan rests beneath another window; beside it, a carved ebony table holds an array of small glass jars.

Beyond the dressing room, separated by a latticed arch, is a private lavatory. A small fountain trickles in the corner, its soft bubbling casting a hush over the tiled floor. The toilet itself is made of smooth white marble with a round basin and a pitcher of water is provided for drainage. A copper ewer stands on a marble pedestal beside a carved wooden towel rack, draped with finely woven linen cloths embroidered at the edges. The space smells faintly of the lavender oil used for purification and fragrance. Though simple, the lavatory is impeccably clean, and no detail is overlooked in its upkeep.

My dress from last night is draped over the edge of the divan. I freshen up and dress. Looking in the mirror, I am not as polished as upon my arrival yesterday evening. I look more like myself than a doll to be admired.

Returning to the main chamber just as the aghas are bringing in breakfast, the smell of fresh bread fills the room, and I am reminded that I have barely eaten in the past day. Butter, honey, fig jam, several types of cheeses, bowls of olives, fresh fruit lightly dusted with sugar, a tahini and molasses spread, and a dish of fried eggs served with tomatoes, onions and spicy sausage. This breakfast is far grander than that served in the harem.

"Come," he says, extending a hand to me. "Eat with me."

The aroma is warm and comforting. He pours me some water from a tall jug and gestures to the food.

"Eat," he says again, gently. "You must be hungry."

I am ravenous. I reach for some cheese and a piece of bread, forcing myself to eat slowly. He watches me with amused curiosity. We eat in silence for a few minutes until he is satisfied that I finally have some food in me.

"What is your name?" he asks.

"Katerina," I say automatically.

"From where do you come?"

I hesitate, then say the only word I can think of that might make sense, the homeland that my friend Aleksandra has described to me: "Ruthenia."

He nods, satisfied with that answer. I watch him tear a piece of bread and dip it into honey. His hands are strong, calloused—these are hands that hold both swords and pens.

And then something shifts. He asks me about music, stories, and verse. It becomes almost a game—a clumsy dance of amateur Turkish, hand gestures, facial expressions, and occasional laughter. To his clear delight, I recite, in my best efforts of a translation, some lines from Plato—who knew that my studies in literature would actually come in useful—and he surprises me by reciting poetry in Persian. I don't understand the words, but I hear the rhythm.

Time slips away. Morning turns into afternoon as the sunlight moves across the floors, catching the gleam of golden inlay in the walls. And still, he does not send me away.

All afternoon, we talk, and he shows me things—beautiful manuscripts, scrolls, miniature paintings, a globe he keeps near the fireplace. He tells me of battles and cities I've only ever read about. He describes his ancestors and their achievements— Mehmed II who conquered Constantinople, his own father Selim I who conquered the Mamluks of Egypt. He talks about his friend and brother-in-arms, Pargali Ibrahim Pasha. I ask questions, encouraging him, delighting him.

He takes his time with his explanations, ensuring that I understand before moving on, displaying patience and a resolve to communicate with me. I do my best to entertain him with stories from the harem, mimicking eunuchs and kalfas as they try to instill discipline in us, and we frustrate them with pillow fights that send feathers into every nook and require days to remove. He laughs at my stories and broken Turkish, not mocking me, but enjoying my attempts to explain the frustration of feathers. And I watch him—not as a sultan, but as a man, a lover of knowledge, history, poetry.

By evening, another meal is brought to us, richer than the last, served on silver trays covered with embroidered cloths to keep them warm. Stewed lamb with apricots, saffron rice, warm flatbread, savory pastries filled with spinach and cheese, stuffed eggplant in olive oil, an array of pickled vegetables, and sweet baklava for dessert. We eat slowly, beside the fire, our shoulders nearly touching, speaking in soft tones, trading stories, laughing until tears run down our cheeks.

And then, as the sky turns black and the stars bloom above Istanbul, he reaches for my hand. No words are needed. This night is already different from the last. No hesitation, no nervousness. It

73

is more bold, more urgent, steamy yet gentle, a curious exploration of each other's bodies. Exhausted and well loved, I rest my head against his chest, listening to the beat of his heart; I fall asleep wrapped in silk, the warmth of our burgeoning closeness a soothing balm to the pain of my lost life.

I wake to the golden light of morning and Süleyman looking at me. His eyes hold a depth I cannot yet read, a mixture of curiosity and need with hints of weariness and concern. He might never have been alone, but his eyes tell me he has always been lonely. He smiles down at me. He reaches for my hand; his thumb tracing circles along the inside of my wrist.

"Where have you come from?" His voice is like velvet, the question caressing me with its implications.

"I come to you from far away and was lost until you found me. I am yours, heart and soul."

He kisses me, passionately, desperately. "You are fire and joy," he says. "From this day, you are *Hürrem*—my joyful one, the one who brings me happiness."

I repeat the name, over and again, until I have the pronunciation right. It feels strange in my mouth, but it blooms inside me like a seed awakening to sunlight. Katherine was the girl who wept for her mother—lost, powerless. Hürrem is the woman who made a sultan smile, and perhaps, someday, the one who will make the world bend.

"Now Hürrem, I must work. Even a sultan cannot spend his days in pleasurable pursuits."

"Is that what I am, a pleasurable pursuit?" I raise my eyebrows provocatively as I say it, to make sure he understands the jest.

He laughs, full bodied. "Oh! That you are. That and more." A light kiss on my nose.

Before I can respond, he claps his hands once and the aghas open the door. A kalfa enters quietly and bows low, waiting to escort me back to the harem. I stand, smoothing the delicate silk of the robe handed to me by the kalfa.

He turns to me once more, brushing his fingers lightly against mine. "Go now. Rest. But I will summon you again, my Hürrem."

I look back, smiling at the man who had, in a single night, changed the course of my entire life. His eyes find mine again, and something passes between us—something wordless, something real.

I follow the kalfa out into the corridor and back down the Golden Road, my new name echoing through my chest like a newly lit flame. I have spent the night—no, night and day and night again—with the Sultan. And I am not the same woman who entered that chamber.

Chapter 13
The Favorite

In the strict rhythm of the harem, where every woman knows her place and what a night with the Sultan usually means—brief, fleeting, transactional—my extended stay breaks all precedent.

Every eye turns to me the moment I step through the carved wooden door. A hush falls over the women like a veil; they watch me as though I had sprouted wings. And then multiple conversations all begin simultaneously, twittering like a thousand small birds sensing a cat nearby. I catch bits and pieces of their conversations.

"She stayed for two nights?"

"A full day?"

"No one's ever done that—not even Mahidevran."

Few of the comments are directed at me; they are talking around me as if I was not standing right there listening to them. More than I expected, the gazes are hostile, sneering, the comments meant to belittle and minimize me. I know already that this place is no sisterhood, and my triumphant return only reinforces the malice and fear that permeates our lives. I have disrupted the balance.

But despite their initial reactions, curiosity is a powerful mistress and gradually a small group forms around me.

"Katerina, what happened to you? Have you spent this whole time with the Sultan?"

"Did you dance for him?"

"Will he see you again?"

"Hürrem," I say simply, and loudly enough for the entire harem to hear me. "My name is Hürrem, given to me by Sultan Süleyman Khan himself."

That is all I offer in response to their many inquiries.

The twittering begins again. Though they resume other activities, their attention remains fixed on me. I see the jealousy gleaming in their eyes. For a flicker of a second, my jubilation falters. If even the concubines, most of whom have never met the Sultan, treat me with scorn, I dread what Mahidevran Hatun will do. She hasn't barged into the harem—yet—but her shadow stretches long.

Soon, the kalfas bark for chores to begin, and the women scatter. Scrubbing floors. Polishing brass. Preparing embroideries for the Valide's suite. No one tells me what to do, so I wait, standing immovable in the center of the harem.

A young girl, maybe twelve, an apprentice kalfa, approaches hesitantly. "You don't have to work anymore," she whispers before scurrying off.

I sit alone for the rest of the morning and afternoon, my day interrupted only by the return of the harem girls for lunch where Aleksandra, as always, sits by my side, talking pleasantly of the latest embroidery stitch she has mastered—I am more grateful

77

than she knows for both the company and the simple exchange she is content to have.

I stare at the gold thread of the pillow's embroidery, tracing it absently. My mind wanders. I retrace every detail of my time in Süleyman's chamber. Süleyman the Magnificent is unlike any other man—not merely because of his status, but because of the aura that surrounds him. It isn't just power. It is his very presence.

Tall and broad shouldered, his posture is impeccable, upright with the kind of effortless elegance that comes from being born into authority and honed by years of command. He moves with purpose, like a man who has never once questioned whether the world will bend to his will.

His face is striking, eyes sharp and dark as ink, with a thoughtful intensity that seems to weigh and measure everything they see. His skin is lightly tanned, weathered only slightly by travel, suggesting a man who has spent time in the sun, leading rather than hiding behind his title.

But it is his voice that I recall the most, low and calm, threaded with warmth and command in equal measure—the voice of a man who does not need to shout to be obeyed. His laughter is soft and surprised, as if he doesn't expect to laugh. And when he kisses me, I melt into him—there is something terrifying in how natural it is and how safe he makes me feel.

I share my happiness with my mother, a conversation across space and time. She smiles at me, eager to meet my new beau. We laugh at his stiffness when meeting father and at my dad's attempts to seem tough and protective of his daughter. And tears well in my eyes that none of this will ever happen.

"Mom," I whisper, "you would love him." I miss her so much.

In the evening, the concubines gather for the evening meal. I can still make out snippets of conversations about me, but other topics are also being discussed. Small groups of women gather on cushions in the corners, drinking sharbat or sweetened rose water, and talking in low voices, sharing often embellished stories—tales about home and family, love stories, or palace gossip.

Some women play board games, usually Mangala, some sing or play their instruments; others work on their embroidery, tiny needles moving back and forth under the low light of oil lamps. Occasionally, informal dance performances might happen, where girls show off their talents. Lessons are not uncommon, learning Turkish, Arabic, and Persian, reciting verses, or exploring the finer details of court etiquette.

But tonight, the parade of kalfas and eunuchs that enter the main courtyard attracts everyone's attention, especially since they are carrying wooden chests bound with iron latches. The room falls silent.

Emine Hatun, the harem treasurer and advisor to Valide Sultan, leads the procession. I still think of her as Tablet Woman. Melek Kalfa stands beside her, and the eunuchs flank them all, setting the chests down.

"For Hürrem," says Emine Hatun in a loud clear voice, "gifts from Sultan Süleyman Khan for his favorite."

The largest chest is opened, revealing folded silks—deep crimson, sapphire blue, and shimmering gold that gleams like sunlight on water. The second chest is overflowing with a mountain of coins. The third and smallest chest contains golden bracelets, necklaces heavy with pearls, and brooches set with emeralds.

My heart skips a beat. The word *favorite* lands like a stone in the water of my mind, sending out silent ripples I can't yet name. I rise to examine the chests, running my hands over the silks and eyeing the beautiful jewels. Concubines inch closer, eyes wide. Gasps and murmurs ripple across the courtyard. This isn't just a reward. It is a message. And every woman in the harem has heard it.

Emine Hatun commands me to follow her. She starts walking without a backward glance, her cane tapping on the tiles as she moves. Concubines start to trail behind but are stopped by Melek Kalfa. I reach out to Aleksandra, who takes my hand with the brightest smile. The eunuchs trail behind.

We walk past the main courtyard with its inner gardens and bubbling fountains. I expect to keep walking toward the common bedchamber, whose second floor contains the semi-private quarters of the favorites. I am surprised when she leads us down a quiet hallway off the garden courtyard. The doors here are taller, inlaid with mother-of-pearl. One opens into a private chamber with windows facing the inner gardens.

"This is your new room," Emine Hatun declares.

The room is not grand by palace standards, but it is mine, a private oasis only for me. The walls are painted with little blue and gold flowers. The carved wooden bed is piled high with silk cushions. A lacquered cabinet stands in the corner, many new dresses waiting to be worn. Several small low tables, set against the walls, are host to a myriad of small glass bottles of fragrances and oils. A latticed window provides a view of the central courtyard. A polished copper mirror reflects the stunned look on my face.

For the first time since waking up in this strange foreign world, I have a place where I can close the door, take a breath, and feel something like me again. The room is modest compared to the grand chambers of the royal family—but for a concubine, even a favored one, it is a rare gift. It sets me above every other favorite who looks down from the second floor. This is a room for privacy, comfort, and status. And it is mine.

I am no longer one of them. I am a favorite. I made the Sultan laugh, and now, I have been chosen.

As night falls, I etch my initials—my own initials from my first life—into the base of one of the columns, as a silent farewell.

I am no longer Katherine. I am Hürrem.

Chapter 14
The Rival

Word of the festivities spreads through the harem—a first experience for many of the newer concubines. Lessons are cut short to allow time to appropriately prepare. I spend much of the day in the hammam, the soothing steam curling around me, luxurious and invigorating.

This is a first for me too, and my new status as favorite adds a level of complexity. I have little doubt that many eyes will be watching me. As with all things in the harem, these festivities are not just for pleasure—they are part of the game of competition, strategy, and silent maneuvering. I choose a gown the color of crushed violet, my hair is braided and laced with pink silk ribbons and seed pearls. The combination is striking against my fair skin and auburn hair without being ostentatious. I must be clever tonight.

The scent of orange blossoms and jasmine clings to the night air as the harem's grand salon glows with the light of a hundred oil lamps. Shadows dance on the walls, flickering across tiles with intricate designs of flowers and cypress trees, while delicate silks sway from the domed ceiling like banners in a gentle breeze.

The festivities begin at dusk. The atmosphere is charged with unspoken hopes—that the Sultan might make an appearance, that a glance could change one's life, that a dance might draw favor.

Eunuchs sit cross-legged along the edge of the room, plucking at ouds, tapping handheld drums, and coaxing sorrowful, winding notes from flutes. The melody curls around the gathered women like smoke—fluid, hypnotic, ancient.

Cushions, velvet and satin, in hues of deep wine, indigo, and emerald sit arranged in wide half-moons around low tables. The concubines, dressed in their finest silks and adorned with silver jewelry and bright sashes, recline in clusters, sipping sharbat from crystal cups and nibbling candied almonds, figs, and sugared chestnuts placed on bronze trays.

Everyone falls silent when the doors open and aghas announce the entrance of Valide Sultan. A beautiful young woman enters just behind her, then Mahidevran. All concubines bend into deep curtseys as they pass.

Valide Sultan moves to sit on an elevated dais, her posture regal, her face unreadable. She is quickly flanked by her chosen concubines, waiting to respond to her every whim, and by her trusted head kalfa, Emine Hatun. Valide is dressed in a robe that shimmers with gold, rubies and pearls. Her royal headdress is wrapped in layers of the finest white silk, adorned at the front with a plume of delicate feathers held in place by a brooch of gold filigree and emeralds the size of olives. A pearl-studded veil trails behind her ears, falling to her shoulders. Her entire ensemble shimmers softly; this is not a woman trying to dazzle—this is a woman who has already conquered.

The beautiful young woman moves to sit beside Valide with the serene assurance of someone born to power. She is dressed in a silk robe of forest green embroidered with silver pomegranates. She is slender, with delicate features and eyes the same rich shade as Turkish coffee. She nods to the musicians while the others are still seating themselves. Music immediately fills the grand salon, conversations resume, and several concubines rise to dance, their bodies undulating with the rhythm, a sensuous display of grace.

"Who is she?" I ask a cluster of girls sitting nearby.

"That is Hatice Sultan," a concubine named Mariia answers me. "She is Sultan Süleyman's beloved sister."

I am not the only one looking at Hatice. On a plush cushion on the dais sits Mahidevran, dressed in crimson, her neckline edged in fur, her eyes sharp. Even sitting at the far end of the room, I notice how stiff Mahidevran's posture is, her eyes focusing on Hatice. There is history here, tension. As she turns back to the room, she sees me. Her kohl-lined lashes narrow, menace oozing in my direction. She turns her attention back to the festivities though I get the distinct impression of a coiled cat waiting for the opportunity to pounce.

The festivities continue. I enjoy myself with Aleksandra and even some of the other concubines. We laugh and sway with the music; the heady atmosphere is too intoxicating to ignore. We feast on Turkish delights and giggle like schoolgirls at each other's funny quips. For a moment, I forget that I am far away from home—this moment could be anywhere, and I am happy to make merry for a time.

The tune shifts and three young women rise to dance. They spin with the music, their hips swaying as they perform an intricate play with veils that look like floating clouds—the dance would have made Salome proud. Applause rises in the room with each change of tempo.

Just as the music slows into something darker and more sensual, Mahidevran's voice rises above it.

"Katerina."

I look up slowly, feeling the weight of every eye turning to look at me. Even the musicians stop, waiting for the outcome.

"Come," Mahidevran says with the edge of a smirk. "Dance for us."

This is no invitation—it is a command meant to humiliate, a test wrapped in silk and smiles. But I have learned quickly here. You survive by appearing soft while being anything but.

I stand and move to the center of the room, walking slowly yet deliberately, as if the request is the most natural thing, though my heart is beating wildly in my chest.

I bow first to Valide Sultan, then Hatice, and lastly Mahidevran. Valide betrays nothing of what she thinks. Her face is stoic, though I catch the faintest curl of Hatice Sultan's lips—not quite a smile, but not disapproval either.

"It is a pleasure to dance for you, Mahidevran Hatun," I exclaim, purposefully showing her the due respect of her title as Lady.

The musicians begin again, slow and sultry. I close my eyes for a moment, remembering the music of my own time, of being on the dance floor in a nightclub, of letting go of all fears and inhibitions as the magic sweeps over me. I let my body move with the rhythm, graceful yet sensual and exotic; a dance not for Mahidevran, but for Süleyman. My hands tell stories, my hips suggest—gradually the room falls silent except for the haunting sounds of a flute and the soft slide of my slippers over the tiles.

Mid-turn, Mahidevran's voice cuts through again.

"Enough. It displeases me."

The music stops abruptly. My breath is high in my chest as I slowly lower my arms, maintaining my composure. The silence prickles with tension.

"You may sit," Mahidevran says, dismissing me with a wave.

Instead, I step forward with the grace of a courtier and bow deeply —first to Mahidevran, who does not mask her scorn, and then to Valide Sultan, who watches me with eyes sharp as glass.

"I thank you, Valide Sultan, for these festivities," I begin, my voice smooth and clear. "They have brought joy to us all. Your servant, Hürrem, is honored by your presence."

My proclamation rings through the chamber like a dropped pearl on marble. Mahidevran's lips part in disbelief, her eyes flare with rage. She stands so quickly, her gown rustles like storm winds.

"I find myself with a headache," she says tightly. "Good evening."

She brushes past me on her way out, her shoulder grazing mine with the barest, deliberate touch. I don't flinch. Once the door closes, the music begins again, light and joyful, and the festivities continue.

Later that night, a eunuch comes to my room with a summons from Valide Sultan.

The lamps in her chamber have been turned low, casting long golden shadows over the domed ceiling. A brazier burns softly near the wall, perfuming the air with sandalwood and cloves. The hush is absolute, broken only by the faint rustle of silk as I step inside.

I lower myself to my knees and bow, pressing my forehead to the carpet.

"Rise, Hürrem."

She says my name without hesitation. Not Katerina. Hürrem. It rings with weight now, spoken in the calm, assessing voice of the Empire's queen in all but name.

Slowly, I rise to my feet, eyes still lowered in deference. Valide studies me for a moment before gesturing to a cushioned stool near the fire. "Sit."

A eunuch serves sweet apple tea in small cups before fading away, closing the doors behind him with a soft click.

"I saw how you handled Mahidevran," she says at last. "You did not let her provoke you. I see you understand more than I gave you credit for."

I wrap my fingers around the warm cup. "She wanted a scene."

"And you did not give her one. That shows restraint. Cleverness." Valide pauses, sipping her tea. "Two things you'll need if you wish to survive here."

"You summoned me. Because of the dance?"

She smiles faintly. "I summoned you because you've stepped into dangerous waters. Mahidevran is the mother of a prince. I want to see if you understand that."

"I do," I answer slowly. "I think I do."

She studies me for a long time. "Süleyman is pleased with you," she says. "But favor is wind. It shifts without warning. A night— or two—means nothing."

I nod, accepting the words even as my heart protests.

Her eyes narrow, but there is something almost warm in her voice. "Be clever. Be quiet. Favorites come and go like the seasons. Only the woman who bears a strong son holds power."

My heart beats faster. A son. I nod again. "Yes, Valide."

"Do not be foolish with pride," she presses on. "You are favored now, yes. But the higher you rise, the more enemies you will have. Be cautious, speak little, and remember your place."

"I understand."

Valide studies me again, and something shifts in her eyes—approval, perhaps, or simply curiosity.

"You amuse my son," she says to my great surprise; he spoke to his mother about me.

"That is a gift in itself. But do not forget that you are one flower in a very large garden. If you draw too much attention, the gardener will prune."

I reply, my voice soft, "Thank you, Valide Sultan."

The elder woman rises, a signal that the conversation is over. I stand, bow once more, and back away, never turning my back, my heart pounding with the weight of the warning—and the opportunity it masks.

Outside, the halls are quiet. The night is thick with possibility. I, Hürrem, once Katerina, once nothing, now walk the path of something more. A favorite means nothing. But a mother… a mother can become a queen.

Chapter 15
The Fire Between Us

Life as a favorite of the Sultan moves to a new rhythm. My daily routine becomes one of strict preparation, refinement, and subtle performance. Gone are the days of scrubbing floors and stitching hems under the eyes of the older kalfas. Now, everything I do is in service to one goal: being prepared in case the Sultan calls.

My mornings begin in the hammam. My body must be perfumed, my skin smooth and hairless, my hair oiled and braided. It is a ritual not only of cleanliness but of readiness.

My afternoons are filled with refined lessons. Since becoming a favorite, the nature of my education has changed. I am now taught courtly etiquette. The correct form of greeting the Sultan's viziers—his ministers. The names of his sisters, and their husbands' titles and ranks. I learn to recite the poetry of Rumi and Hafez to please his refined ear. There are lessons in history, calligraphy, storytelling, and the games of backgammon and Mangala. And every day, my Turkish sharpens, flowing with greater ease and more refinement.

Evenings are times of leisure without idleness. Seamstresses show me the finest silks and tailor *kaftans* to flatter my figure and enhance my complexion. Aleksandra or other concubines tint my nails with henna and massage rose oil into my hands to keep them soft. At all times I am ready, the image of perfection, waiting to be called again.

The summons comes just as lunch is finishing. Melek Kalfa says loudly for all to hear, "Hürrem, Sultan Süleyman Khan expects you for dinner."

The twittering begins instantly. It is very common for a concubine to never be called again. That is not my fate. Jealous, envious eyes look at me. Not only am I summoned again to his chamber, but to dine with him—another rarity that further singles me out.

A thrum of nerves twitter inside me as I take the Golden Road. Dressed in crimson silk that clings like firelight to my skin, a shimmering gold veil conceals my face—though not strictly necessary in the harem, I want the ceremony of unveiling, so that Süleyman can discover me all over again.

I enter and bow, not falling to the ground, but the simple elegance of a curtsey, waiting, head lowered, demure. Süleyman gently takes hold of me, pulling me into him so that my head is angled upward. He caresses my face through the veil, then, almost urgently, uncovers and kisses me in one smooth movement. The kiss is deep, passionate—he sweeps me up in his arms, my feet momentarily leaving the ground. We stay in our embrace for a brief eternity before separating with soft laughter.

We wait for dinner on the garden terrace. It is glorious to be outside after months of near-complete confinement. Thick fur coats keep out the winter cold. The view is breathtaking, a tapestry of color and style. Süleyman takes pleasure in acting as my tour guide. He explains that Topkapi Palace sits at the tip of the peninsula of Istanbul, perched high above where the Golden Horn, the Bosphorus, and the Sea of Marmara meet.

The Bosphorus stretches out below like a glittering ribbon, its waters shimmering in the bright moonlight, dotted with the billowing sails of merchant ships as they glide across the strait. To the left, across the Golden Horn, Galata Tower stands proudly in front of distant homes tucked between cypress trees.

On the opposite shoreline, across the Bosphorus Strait, is Üsküdar province, the gateway to the Asian side of the Empire. Süleyman points out the Tower of Leandros, sitting on its own small islet, and his plans to rebuild it after it crumbled in an earthquake a decade ago.

Looking out to our right is the Hagia Sofia, standing like a sentinel, its great dome and pencil-thin minarets piercing the sky. From this height, the rooftops of Istanbul form a sea of red tile, the smoke of hearth fires curling gently into the air.

And beyond, the Sea of Marmara, its blue kissed waters rippling under the flight of gulls, tiny boats bobbing near the shore, their sails taut in the breeze, and distant vessels passing like quiet ghosts on trade routes that connect the Empire to faraway lands. Day and night, this corner of the world is a busy hub, and Süleyman is its guiding light.

The lamps in the Sultan's private chamber flicker like stars caught in brass cages, their golden light casting shifting patterns on the tiled walls and across the velvet cushions beneath us. The air is warm with the scent of jasmine and cedar smoke, and somewhere in the distance, the faint notes of a flute drift through the corridors, like a memory on the wind.

Low cushions are arranged around a bronzed circular tray, polished so brightly it mirrors the flames of the hearth. Steam curls upward from the dishes laid out before us, each prepared with care and precision. Grilled lamb, tender and fragrant with rosemary, glistens beside bowls of marinated olives and platters of fresh dates. Figs soaked in rosewater glimmer like garnets, their sweetness lingering in the air. There is jeweled rice flecked with pomegranate seeds, its spice a subtle whisper, and pastries folded into delicate crescents, their honeyed surfaces catching the light. A tall jug of sharbat, cool and golden, stands at the center of it all, shimmering like liquid amber.

We dine slowly, deliberately, savoring each bite as much for its flavor as for the quiet between us. The fire crackles softly in the hearth, and I feel its heat against my skin. Outside, the night settles over Istanbul, vast and eternal, but here, in this moment, time seems to pause.

We speak of everything and nothing—of poetry and philosophy, of the stars and the sea, of stories from our childhoods and dreams we have not yet dared to voice. His voice is low and thoughtful, and mine follows like a tide drawn to the moon.

"My father ruled with strength," Süleyman says, his gaze lost in the fire. "But strength without wisdom eventually collapses. I want to be a just and wise ruler."

I watch him for a moment, the shadows dancing across his face, the lines of thought deepening near his eyes.

"I think that wanting to be just is a good first step. We cannot achieve that which we do not want." I hesitate before continuing, not sure how smart I should be. "Socrates said that the only true wisdom is in knowing you know nothing."

"How is it that you know such things?"

I gulp from fear, but he looks at me as if I am a tasty morsel, something to be unwrapped slowly.

"My father was a priest," I reply, "a learned man." In truth, he taught history at Harvard—lessons that I review nightly in my thoughts, hoping they will serve me in this world.

"Tell me of your home," he asks.

After a long silence, I speak, answering him with as much truth as I dare.

"When I think of home," I begin softly, "I think of snow—soft and endless—falling in quiet blankets over the rooftops in winter, muffling the world until all that remained was silence and breath. I remember the breeze in summer, warm and playful, rustling the trees and carrying the scent of lilacs through open windows. The sound of church bells ringing at dawn—how they used to wake the world so gently. And my father's voice, calling me in as the sky blushed with evening light. I can still hear it sometimes in my sleep."

I pause, the memory catching in my throat before I continue.

"My mother's hands were always warm. Always moving. She braided my hair every morning, her fingers careful, loving. She pressed flowers between pages of her books, as though trying to preserve the beauty of fleeting things. I would sit and watch her for hours as she carefully arranged books on shelves, and I felt safe—anchored to something unbreakable."

A breath escapes me like a sigh.

"There were paintings on our walls—wild colors that seemed to move when the light struck them just so—and stone statues in the garden, softened by rain and years. There was music, echoing from the halls, clinging to the air like a memory that didn't want to fade."

My voice trembles then, barely a whisper.

"But more than anything, when I think of home… I think of being free. Free to run until my legs ached. Free to speak my thoughts aloud, without fear. Free to dream, and to believe those dreams belonged to me. That… that is what I miss most."

His brow tenses slightly. "Do you hate me for taking that away?"

"No," I answer without thinking. "You didn't take that away. The world did. You are only… rearranging the pieces."

Süleyman leans back, intrigued but uneasy. "And yet you smile."

"Because I know crying won't change anything. Nothing will bring back the world I lost. But perhaps… being useful will bring me peace."

He remains silent for a moment. Finally, he pours each of us a glass of rose sharbat.

"My mother chose you," he says. "She saw something."

I meet his gaze. "I hope not too much," I say, smiling coyly.

That makes him laugh. "Caution and boldness in the same breath," he says. "You are a contradiction."

"I am a survivor," I reply.

He leans closer. "Then tell me, survivor—if I were to go to war, what would you wish for me?"

I pause, then lift my chin slightly. "That you crush your enemies completely, so that no one dares touch your Empire again."

There is a flash of surprise in his eyes—then admiration.

"You are a singular woman, Hürrem." He stands then and extends his hand to me. "Come. Let us sit by the brazier. There is still time before the moon grows jealous of the firelight."

I take his hand, recognizing the look in his eyes. The time for talking has passed. By the fire, he strokes my hair as I lean into him, feeling his warmth, nearly purring at his touch.

"I am the moth, and thou art the candlelight, drawn to thee, I burn, and yet delight," Süleyman whispers to me. "*Muhibbi* is pleased with his muse."

"Who is Muhib…" I am cut off by his kiss. He picks me up and carries me to his bed, and all thoughts scatter to the wind.

Chapter 16
The Cost of Favor

The heavy doors to Süleyman's chambers close behind me with a hush. My slippered feet carry me through the corridor toward the harem. I feel weightless, transformed. The memory of his voice, the softness in it as he calls me His Hürrem, echoes louder than my footsteps. I am no longer the same girl who stumbled into this world. Now, I am the chosen one. His favorite. His beloved.

I sense a presence even before turning into the familiar hallway that leads back to the harem. She looms in a doorway like Marley's ghost—pale, silent, and burdened. Mahidevran steps from the shadows. She is fury given flesh, her face pale in the lamplight, eyes as cold as steel.

"You think one night makes you queen?" she spits at me. I dip my head, hoping to pass silently, not wanting a confrontation.

But she moves faster than I anticipate. Her hand strikes my cheek, open-palmed and cruel.

"You little snake," she hisses. "Do you think he loves you? You are nothing. A plaything. A novelty."

Another blow. Then another.

I do not fight back. Not because of lack of strength, but because I understand that if I raise a hand to her, I might win the fight but would lose the war.

My arms raised, I shield my face, but she strikes like a woman possessed. Stumbling back against the wall, my vision blurs, pain sparkles brightly behind my eyes. The sharp edge of a marble column catches my hip. Blood warms my lips.

"I should tear your eyes out," she sneers, grabbing a fistful of my hair. "He is mine. Understand?"

Before I can answer, her hand cracks across my cheek again. Then another blow, a fist this time. She seizes my hair and yanks me down, and I land hard on my knees.

The beating is intense. It takes every iota of self-control to remain immobile. When she is done, she stands over me—faintly, I can hear her ragged breathing, though I start to drift in and out of consciousness. She calls my name a few times, Katerina, telling me to stop pretending to be hurt. When I don't respond, she runs, her feet hitting hard against the floors in her rush to remove herself from the scene.

A door opens down the hall. Footsteps. Then gasps. Kalfas are upon me. Someone picks me up. The rest is a blur. I catch bits and pieces of their machinations as they consider how to hide this, how to make it go away. Very little of their calculations are in my regard—it is how to protect Mahidevran, the mother of the Sultan's only son.

They lay me in my bed and press compresses to my swollen face. My ribs ache. Blood trickles from my temple. The kalfas do not call for a doctor; they keep me tucked away like a forgotten thing.

"Rest Hürrem," one whispers. "It will pass. You must not speak of this. Not to anyone."

I spend the day in hiding, fevered and aching. But pain has a voice. And when Süleyman summons me, and I refuse, it is my silence that screams.

When the message comes that the Sultan has summoned me again, I turn my face to the wall and say nothing. The kalfa who delivered the summons shifts awkwardly by the doorway. "Hürrem Hatun, you must come. The Sultan waits."

But I can't. I won't. My body aches in too many places. My lips are split, my cheeks are swollen. The thin linen robe clings to bruises that are already turning the color of plum. It is not only my body that is beaten. They may call me a Lady now, but it is hard to forget that my well-being is worth less to them than Mahidevran's reputation—Hürrem Hatun, indeed.

"Tell him I am unwell," I whisper.

Silence. Then the soft slap of slippers retreating.

I remain curled in the corner of the room like a wounded animal. The harem moves around me, cautious, quiet. Whispers spread through the corridors like threads of smoke. Mahidevran has been seen with her clothes disheveled, hair wild.

Then I hear it. Boots. Not soft slippers. Not the scurrying steps of kalfas or the glide of eunuchs. Boots, heavy and deliberate. The door bursts open.

Süleyman stands in the doorway, his face carved in rage. Kalfas fall to their knees.

"Out," he says, his voice like thunder.

The kalfas scatter like startled birds. I rise unsteadily to my feet; one hand braced against the wall for balance.

He comes to me, at first in anger and then he sees me, his eyes sweeping my bruised face, the torn lip, the welt on my neck. He hesitates before touching my skin, then gently guides me back to sit on the bed.

"Who did this to you?" he asks, his voice low and dangerous.

For the briefest moment, I debate lying, thinking of the quiet warning of Valide: Only the mother of a son matters.

I shake my head in refusal.

When he speaks again, it is soft. "Tell me who dares to do this to my love."

I think of her hand in my hair, of the way she hit me, over and over. I think of his words, of his love. I burst into tears, shaking uncontrollably like a rag doll.

"It was Mahidevran," I say softly in between sobs.

His jaw clenches, his face darkens like a storm. He strides out of the room without another word. I hear him barking orders. When he returns minutes later, he lifts me into his arms like I weigh nothing, as if I hadn't just refused him, as if he hadn't waited for me in frustration. He carries me through the harem without speaking, his stride long and sure. Gasps follow us like ripples on water.

I rest my head against his chest, feeling safe in his arms.

"You will recover in my chambers," he says.

Back in his private chamber, he lays me gently on the cushions and calls for the court physician. Properly tended to at last, the physician gives me some medication that quickly makes me feel drowsy. I drift toward sleep.

Voices rouse me. I lie still beneath silk covers in his bed, aching, but safe, still half asleep. I hear Süleyman's voice from the adjoining room.

"She refused to come?" I recognize Ibrahim.

"I summoned her. She could not rise," says Süleyman. "I found her like that. I could have killed Mahidevran."

A pause.

"I love her, Ibrahim," Süleyman says quietly. "I cannot bear for her to be harmed."

Love. I close my eyes. My heart beats so loudly I wonder if he will hear it through the walls.

"What will you do with Mahidevran?" Ibrahim asks cautiously.

"I do not know," Süleyman murmurs. "But this cannot go unpunished."

I close my eyes.

In this palace of shifting sands and sharpened smiles, I have made an enemy of the most dangerous woman in the harem. But for the love of this man, I would risk much. He loves me, and that means everything.

Chapter 17
Enemies and Allies

I spend one week recuperating in Süleyman's chamber. I remain—morning, noon, and night—wrapped not only in silks but in his words, his laughter, his attention. He keeps the fire tended and shares stories to entertain me.

"Before the weight of the throne was mine, I lived in Manisa Province," he says. "I was a boy still, a prince, *Şehzade*, barely a man, and yet I carried the name of my father, Selim, and the shadow of my grandfather, Bayezid. Everyone looked to me as if I already wore the crown."

He pauses, and I see a flicker in his eyes—of memory or perhaps longing.

"Manisa is fertile. Gentle hills covered in olive trees, vineyards stretching to the horizon. The people are proud but kind. They knew I was learning—how to govern, how to command, how to temper justice with mercy. I would ride at dawn and hunt in the afternoons. There were nights I sat with the *kadi*, the judge of the province, to listen to village disputes. I learned more from those peasants and merchants than any vizier could have taught me."

He turns back to me, a smile forming as he continues, "I had my own Divan, my own court. It was the first time my voice carried real weight. I issued orders that mattered. I oversaw the building of aqueducts, a school, and a mosque. And I wrote—poems, prayers, thoughts… so many thoughts."

"You wrote poetry there?" I ask.

He nods. "That was when Muhibbi was born. The pen gave me freedom that the sword never could. When the palace walls closed in, the page opened. My solitude in Manisa taught me how to listen—to the world, and to myself."

His smile fades and shadow returns to his face.

"It was also where I first encountered ambition and betrayal. A single whisper in court could ruin a man. That was my first lesson: that even in beauty, danger grows."

His fingers brush mine, tender and certain. "I became a ruler in Manisa. But here, with you... I remember who I truly am."

He is unlike anyone I have ever met—sharp, curious, and passionate in equal measure. He listens when I speak, even when I stumble over his language. He asks about where I come from, and though I give only pieces, fragments of a world he can never understand, he does not press for more.

Instead, he speaks of the Empire, his desires for justice and conquest and of his fears—more than anything else, he wants to be a good ruler, he wants what is best for his people, he wants to remain true to himself and not become lost in the power of the throne.

The sky outside is darkening, painted in deep violets and bruised blues as the evening pulls its veil across Istanbul on our fourth night together. We sit huddled by the hearth. My body is still bruised, and I move slowly. Süleyman is tender, holding my hand, stroking my knuckles absently. He is distracted tonight.

"There will be war," he says at last, his voice low and steady.

I look up at him, his profile sharp against the twilight. "With whom?"

"King Lajos of Hungary. He is foolish and proud. He refuses to pay the tribute his ancestors agreed upon. My warnings were ignored. My envoys were killed."

He sets down his goblet with a faint clink and turns to face me fully. "The Kingdom of Hungary stands like a wall between my Empire and the heart of Europe. Its lords and bishops grow fat on gold while their peasants suffer. Their armies are poorly disciplined, but they cling to their old alliances with the Pope and the Holy Roman Emperor."

He looks into the flames. "I do not wish to fight for glory alone. But when a king defies the Sultan of the Ottomans, he must answer for it. If I allow one crown to spit at my feet, others will rise against me."

My father discussed two key battles of this time: The Battle of Mohács and the siege of Vienna. The first a resounding success, changing the borders of the Ottoman Empire, making them a force to be feared. The second, a failure, a demarcation of the limits of their expansion. I do not recall the years of each battle, though it is easy to conclude that Mohács came first; nor do I recall if he ever mentioned whether Süleyman survived these battles or if they were remarkable because they led to a change of ruler. I wish, not for the first time, that I had paid more attention to history.

"But Hungary…" I whisper, "it is far."

He nods. "Far, but not unreachable. Our armies are ready. My *Janissaries* are eager. The frontier *Beys* have long pleaded for war. I must ride east through the Balkans and meet Lajos on the field of battle."

I try to picture those endless plains where two mighty forces will meet: the clash of steel, the screams of dying horses, the banners torn by wind and fire.

"I'm afraid of what might happen to you in war… and of what will become of me without you." My words tremble with genuine fear.

Süleyman's voice softens as he looks back at me. "When I go, I will go for the Empire. Pray for me and I will return to you, Allah willing. But I will always ensure that you are protected. You are mine; no one will ever harm you again."

He takes my hand and presses it gently. He believes what he says, and I want to believe him too, though there are many ways to harm someone, and he cannot stop them all. I share none of this with Süleyman.

Instead, I ask whether foreign alliances might be helpful in his military campaign, and we spend the next few hours discussing the merits of each possible ally.

"You would make a fine vizier," he teases me. "But the Empire would never survive you."

On our last night—I am well enough to return to the harem and Süleyman has much work to do preparing for the campaign—he holds me close, his body warm against mine, his lips brush my temple, his fingertips trace poetry over my skin.

After gently making love, he murmurs to me in the dark. "My woman of the beautiful hair, my love of the slanted brow, my love of eyes full of misery ... I, lover of the tormented heart, Muhibbi of the eyes full of tears, I am happy."

I fall asleep in his arms; I, too, am happy.

On the seventh morning, just as the sun begins to stream through the carved wooden screens, he rises and crosses the room to his desk. From a small ebony box, he draws out a simple gold ring with a delicate emerald set in the center. He sits beside me and takes my hand.

"I made it myself," he says quietly. "Years ago. It has waited all this time just for you."

He slips it onto my finger.

"For my Hürrem," he says. "For the joy you bring."

Words fail me. I hold his gaze, trying to memorize the way he looks at me in this moment—as if I am not his slave, but his queen.

And when the time finally comes to return to the harem, I kiss his fingers before rising from the bed. My legs tremble. Not from fear— but from the terrible, tender weight of everything that has changed.

After a week that feels like time has stopped and stood still just for us, I step back into the harem and the weight of dozens of gazes presses into my skin. They look at me differently now. Their eyes are watchful, still edged with envy, but also something else. Respect, maybe, or fear. Some eyes glitter with jealousy, others with curiosity. But no one dares say anything to my face. Not anymore.

I move slowly, still a little sore from the bruises Mahidevran has left on me, but I hold my head high. The kalfas greet me with polite nods. Even the girls who used to mock me for my accent or my clumsy curtsey now avert their eyes.

Aleksandra catches my arm and pulls me aside into one of the smaller alcoves.

"He lost his mind," she whispers, grinning. "Screamed at Valide Sultan in front of everyone. Said if you were ever harmed again, heads would roll. Mahidevran hasn't been seen in days. They say she's been locked in her quarters under guard."

Süleyman's anger had been unmistakable, but this outcome is beyond anything I imagined.

"I didn't ask him to do that," I murmur, uncertain how deeply the game has shifted.

Aleksandra smirks. "You didn't have to. He has made it clear to everyone that you are his woman. You are Hürrem Hatun now."

How fleeting is success. A few days later, as I make my way down the tiled corridors of the Golden Road, ready to see him again, a shadow peels itself from a column. Ibrahim Pasha.

His arms are folded behind his back, his expression unreadable, his eyes hollow.

"A word," he says, stepping in close. The scent of sweat mingles with the incense floating in the hall.

I stop, heart thudding. He is too close for comfort, a brazen act of disloyalty.

"You've made quite the impression," he says calmly.

"It is not my intention," I reply, careful to keep my tone neutral.

He looks me over, sending a shiver down my spine. Then whispers, too softly, "Do not speak of Mahidevran again. Do not stir unrest in the harem. His Majesty has many duties. He does not need distraction."

His message is clear. It is not yet a threat—but close.

I pause before finally replying, "That depends on her".

He holds my gaze a moment longer, then turns and walks away without another word.

And that is when it sinks in: I am well and truly alone here. Aleksandra is a friend. But my only real ally, my only shield, is Süleyman.

I steady my breath and walk the last few steps alone.

Chapter 18
The Sun of My World

Melek Kalfa stands at my door, two younger kalfas in tow, their arms overflowing with a mountain of fabric. She keeps repeating that I am to leave the palace. My heart flutters hard in my chest—so much that I no longer hear her words. For those terrifying seconds, I believe I am being cast out. But then Aleksandra comes running in, breathless and giddy, her eyes wide.

"He's taking you with him," she hollers. "Outside the palace. No one does that. No one."

Her words finally sink in. I can hardly believe it. The royal family sometimes travels to other palaces, but a concubine—that is unheard of.

They wrap me in traveling silks, layers of pale green and ivory that move like water. A soft veil is fastened securely over my hair. My slippers are new, the soles untouched. A rush of nervous excitement pulses through me as I am led through the palace grounds and into the waiting carriage, drawn by four white horses whose harnesses are adorned with golden tassels and polished brass fittings. The carriage gleams beneath the early summer sun as though it has emerged from a dream. Süleyman is already seated inside, his expression unreadable until his eyes meet mine—and then his face brightens into a smile and any lingering fear dissolves.

The carriage is opulent, a decadent display of grandeur. Its wooden frame is lacquered in a deep claret red, the color of ripened cherries; it is trimmed with gilded filigree that curls into arabesques. Painted panels on either side depict miniature scenes—stylized gardens, peacocks in flight, and cypress trees that seem to sway with motion. The wheels are reinforced with iron and inlaid with delicate motifs; their creaking masked by the rhythmic jingle of silver bells tied to the horses' bridles.

A curved, arched canopy covers the seating area, crafted from rich velvet embroidered with golden thread and lined with silk brocade. The seat is wide and low, covered in soft, thickly woven carpets and layered silks. Plush cushions in royal hues of emerald and sapphire provide comfort. Heavy curtains are drawn shut for privacy, open just a sliver in the center to let in the light and allow me a glimpse of the countryside.

Small niches have been worked into the interior sides to hold perfumed sachets and rosewater flasks, and a small brass lantern hangs from the ceiling for nighttime travel. The scent of sandalwood and myrrh linger in the air. Along one side, a silver pitcher of water and a dish of sugared fruit has been placed in a small recess for refreshment during the journey.

The entire contraption sways with a slow rhythm as it bounces along the street, attended by soldiers on horseback who flank it like an honor guard, men in gleaming helmets and quilted armor, their sabers at their sides, banners fluttering gently as they move.

The city unfolds around us slowly; a place of domes and towers touched with gold. We pass by a market, and I catch a glimpse of children darting between crates, keeping pace for a time with our grand procession. The air carries the scent of salt, grilled fish, fresh bread, and blooming flowers. On the hills of the old city, minarets rise like spears of stone against the sky, and the great mosques glint in the light.

My mind wanders to my initial entrance into this life, the harrowing walk to the slave market, the overwhelming fear. But I banish those thoughts, refusing to let them ruin the excitement of this journey.

As we leave the walls of the city behind, the landscape changes, stone and brick giving way to rolling green hills, olive groves, and blooming meadows, dotted with wild poppies and yellow buttercups. Shepherds tend their flocks along the roadside, bowing respectfully as we pass. Farmers and traders move along the road with donkeys and carts, their curious eyes following the royal carriage.

We travel through the countryside, the scent of wild herbs and warm earth rising with each step. Birds dart overhead—sparrows, storks, and swallows singing in the fresh air. The roads are uneven but passable, lined with scrubby bushes, fig trees, and the occasional fountain where water trickles softly into basins of worn marble.

Gradually, the air grows fresh, and pine scented as trees close in around us. By midday, the carriage reaches a quiet clearing within a dense forest, where a grand tent has already been erected for us. This is no ordinary tent—it is the size of a small house, its posts wrapped in brocade, roof tall and pointed like a crown. Silk flaps, striped in deep red and cream, are tied open to let in the breeze. Inside, cushions are piled high, and a low table is laid out with platters of food—roasted meats, fresh cheeses, olives, honey-drenched pastries, and jugs of cool water and sweet sharbats.

We spend the afternoon walking together through the woods, hand in hand beneath a canopy of green. The light filters through the leaves in golden patches, and the sound of a distant stream murmurs nearby. Süleyman picks wildflowers for me, speaking softly of his youth in Manisa, of books and battles, of his plans for the Empire.

As the afternoon begins to wane, we return to our castle in the woods. The tent glows with warm candlelight. Cushions and carpets cover every inch of the floor. Gold and silver bowls overflow with grapes, figs, and pomegranates. Music drifts through the trees—someone is playing the flute, soft and melancholic; the effect is one of magic, a potent spell meant to enchant.

Süleyman and I sit close on plush cushions, sharing food with our fingers, giggling like teenage lovers, sharing our deepest secret desires. We talk about poetry, about the stars, about dreams. He recites verses to me, hand touching my cheek tenderly, the writings of his own Muhibbi. As I listen, a swell of tenderness ignites in my chest.

My heart burns with longing, O candle, like yours... I am the night, dark with desire, and you are my dawn.

We lie together in the tent, wrapped in one another's arms, listening to the quiet of the night, interrupted only by the rustling of the leaves and the chirping of insects. He whispers to me, his mustache tickling my ear, of his desire for victory, for peace, for more sons.

I face him, my eyes locked on his, caught in the tide of emotion between us. "More than anything," I say, "I would like to give you many sons."

He is quiet for a moment, then kisses my forehead. "Then may Allah bless us with one."

We make love—a passionate expression of hope, of commitment, and of our desire for one another—until we lie spent, entwined and contented. The last thought I have, just as sleep is gently pulling me under, is that my new favorite word is *Aşk*—I love Süleyman, with all my heart.

In the morning, he takes my hand and leads me down a narrow path through the trees, until the forest gives way to a secluded beach, the sand pale and soft beneath my feet. The turquoise water sparkles like molten glass, waves lapping gently at the shore. The Sea of Marmara stretches out before us, vast and glittering in the early sun. I stand at the edge, the breeze lifting my veil, and stare out across the water.

The wave of emotions that I feel suddenly is overwhelming. It has been almost one year since that fateful morning waking up on a beach just like this one. This world has its brutalities, and I have spent many hours crying at the injustice that brought me here. But now, I feel both hope and fear in equal measure.

As I turn to see Süleyman watching me, his eyes filled with warmth and longing, it is fear that wins—a deep and profound distress of losing him. Süleyman is my sun and moon, the stars in the sky, every color of the rainbow. Leaving him would break my heart. Tears trickle down my cheeks.

He wraps me in his arms and kisses me.

"I love you," I whisper. "You are the sun of my world."

His fingers tighten on mine. "And you are the fire in mine."

As the waves of the Sea of Marmara gently lap at the shore, a decision is made—perhaps more by the universe than by me, though I embrace it wholeheartedly.

"Süleyman, I want to be yours, in every way," I say, my voice full of resolve. "I want to be Muslim. I want to choose this path—for myself, and for us."

He looks at me for a long moment, the light of the sun gilding the edge of his turban. His expression is unreadable at first, then softens into something deeply reverent.

"You would take this path with me?" he asks gently. "Not as a demand, not out of duty—but by your own will?"

"Yes," I answer, without hesitation.

He steps closer, solemn now. "Then we must bear witness."

He turns to the captain of the guard standing nearby, a trusted man, and gives a brief command. The man approaches and stands at a respectful distance. Two more soldiers follow silently, taking their place to witness.

Süleyman removes his ring—his signet—and presses it briefly to his lips before taking my hand in his. His thumb traces slow circles on my palm.

"Hürrem," he says softly, "to become Muslim, you need only say with your heart and your voice: *Ashhadu an la ilaha illallah wa ashhadu anna Muhammadan rasul Allah.* 'I bear witness that there is no god but Allah, and Muhammad is the messenger of Allah.'"

He speaks slowly, clearly, and I repeat it after him. I say it a second time, and then a third.

The moment stretches between us as the sound of the waves lashes at the shore. Süleyman's gaze never leaves mine.

"From this moment, you are a believer," he says. "Your soul is clean. You are one of us. And now… you are mine. In this world and—if Allah wills it—the next."

I look out again at the sea, breathless, humbled and uplifted at once. He smiles at me. "My Hürrem. My joy."

Then, before the assembled guards, he kneels before me, kisses the hem of my skirt and raises it to his forehead, in the same way that I did on our first night together—a gesture of respect, protection, and affection.

As we walk back to the tent, my thoughts drift to my mother. I have made my peace that I will never see her again, though she will always be in my heart. Perhaps my voice can cross space and time to whisper with the wind. "Mother, I am happy, I am loved," I say inside my head, willing her to know my truth. I am not a believer, in Allah or any other, but it feels right and honest to embrace Him in this life. With fervent desire in my heart, I whisper to Allah, "Please give comfort to my mother and let her know peace."

We return to Topkapi as the sun reaches its zenith. The whole ride home, our fingers are twined, the beach a distant thought. I will no longer look back. That chapter of my life is gone. Only the future remains, in this time, in this place, with this man.

Chapter 19
A Fearful Season

The palace corridors are quiet, heavy with the stillness of impending departure. The torches flicker low, casting shadows that dance along the carved arches and tiled floors as I make my way to his chamber, heart tight in my chest.

Süleyman is standing on the terrace, past the open doors with their sheer curtains undulating slightly with the light sea breeze, gazing out toward the dark silhouette of the city and the glimmering waters of the Bosphorus.

He is dressed not as a sultan receiving envoys or holding court, but as a man preparing for a long road ahead. A finely tailored kaftan made of crimson-colored brocade flatters his silhouette, embroidered with gold and silver thread creating tiny tulips along the hem. His turban, carefully wound with white muslin, is adorned with a jeweled brooch. At his waist hangs a sheathed dagger, its hilt inlaid with turquoise, more symbolic than necessary in the safety of the palace, but a reminder that he is as much soldier as sultan.

There is a somber elegance to him. The man before me is both ruler and lover—imperial, unreachable, and yet, for the next few hours, entirely mine.

I bow low. "My Sultan."

He steps toward me and lifts my chin gently. "My Hürrem," he murmurs, my name soft on his lips.

For a moment, we simply look at each other, everything unspoken shimmering between us like moonlight on still water.

He takes me into his arms, wrapping me against him. I press my cheek to his chest and listen to the steady beat of his heart, memorizing it. In one sudden movement, he picks me up and cradles me in his arms. I look into his eyes and see the heart of this beautiful man. We kiss as he walks us to his bed. Hands fumble at clothes, a near desperation to feel flesh on flesh. We are crazed, wild, until eventually we lie spent, giggling at our own happiness.

"Pray for my return," he says suddenly, brushing a strand of hair from my face.

I try to keep my composure, but tears begin to cloud my eyes. "You must return to me. I am only complete when you are by my side."

"You have given me something worth returning to," he says, kissing my cheeks tenderly.

We stay in each other's arms for a long while. We do not speak of fear or longing. We do not speak of Mahidevran or the court or the dangers of the battlefield. We lie in silence, in the comfort of our love, until he leans down and kisses my forehead.

As I dress, he reaches for something on the table beside him—a brooch, shaped like a tulip, its golden petals wrapped around a deep red ruby. He fastens it securely to my chest.

"I made this for you," he says. "The image of my Empire for the Sultan of my heart."

My throat tightens. "I don't want you to go."

"Nor I. But the Empire demands it." His smile is sad and tender. "I will write to you," he promises. "And you will pray for me."

"I will do more than that," I whisper. "I will hold vigil every night, praying for Allah to be pleased with you. I will fast my devotion to give you strength on the battlefield. I will speak your name with every breath, so that the heavens never forget you. If blood is spilled, may it never be yours. If I must trade my peace, my sleep, even my soul for your safety, I will do so a thousand times over."

He studies me in silence, the flicker of torchlight dancing in his eyes. Then he reaches for my hand and presses it to his lips—once, reverently.

"If your prayers reach the heavens, then I will return from war untouched. And if they do not… I will still carry your devotion with me like armor."

His voice is low, but there is a tremor in it, something rare and unguarded. Then more quietly, "You speak like a wife, not a concubine."

A pause before he adds, "One day, perhaps, the world will see you as I do."

His hand lingers on my cheek before he steps back. "Go now, before dawn comes."

I take his hands in mine, kiss them and bring them to my forehead. "May Allah grant you victory."

At the door, I look back. Framed by the night sky, he watches me leave. This will be my memory of him for the coming months.

It is a beautiful May day, and yet I am chilled. Süleyman is leaving today. Our farewells were said last night, as the morning must be reserved for his farewells to the royal family—Valide Sultan, Hatice Sultan, and young Şehzade Mustafa.

The palace is quieter than usual, though beneath the stillness is a kind of tense hum, like a bowstring pulled taut. I would have liked to watch him mount his horse and ride out through the golden arches of the inner court. I would have liked to hear the thunder of hoofbeats fading down the marble road, the cheers of viziers and soldiers echoing through the courtyard, the proud music of war ringing in my ears.

But that is forbidden. That privilege, I'm told, belongs only to Valide Sultan—and to his official wives, of which there are none. Not even Mahidevran may stand at the gates.

And so I sit in silence, imagining the pageantry I am not allowed to see. I hold it in my mind like a memory that never happened: the flash of armor, the gleam of banners, the moment his eyes might have found mine one last time before he disappeared into the world beyond the harem walls.

I close my eyes and listen for hoofbeats, but all I hear is my own heart, steady and alone. Aleksandra sits with me, embroidery in hand, making pleasant conversation to distract me from my grief.

Later that day, Mahidevran emerges from her enforced seclusion. I see her in the garden courtyard. She stands at the far end of the tiled path wearing a dark emerald kaftan embroidered in gold. Her hair is bound in a thick braid coiled over one shoulder, and her eyes find mine instantly. The expression she wears is not one of shame or regret. It is pride. Defiance.

Fear pricks at my spine. The protection Süleyman has granted me has left with him. Though Valide Sultan remains, I know her loyalty is complex and political. If Mahidevran can find a way to strike at me without breaking the rules of the harem, she will. I avoid her gaze and turn away.

A few weeks later, I notice it—the fatigue after morning lessons, the lightheadedness during meals. My stomach twists at strange times. Certain scents in the hammam make me nauseous. Then, one morning, as I bend over to pin embroidery work to a frame, the dizziness overtakes me, and I collapse in a faint onto the marble floor.

When I wake, I am in the infirmary. The palace midwife, an older woman with gentle hands, offers me water and then begins a series of quiet questions. After a short examination, she smiles at me.

"You are blessed," she says softly. "You are pregnant, perhaps two months."

I sit up slowly, my hand drifting to my abdomen. My chest fills with something too wide to name as waves of emotions wash over me—terror, awe, joy, disbelief.

Valide Sultan summons me that same afternoon. I enter her chamber in silence. The room is scented with amber and cloves, and she sits beneath a tall lattice window, dressed in layers of silk and her jeweled crown glinting in the low light.

"I am told that you have news to give me," she says, her eyes narrowing slightly as she peers at me.

"I am with child," I say quietly.

She is silent for a long moment. Then, to my astonishment, she smiles. A true smile—not just political calculation.

"This is good," she says. "Very good."

She stands and comes closer, laying a hand gently over mine. "You must eat well. Sleep. Be cautious. This child will secure your place—if it lives."

Her eyes glint, not unkind, but hard with truth. "Do you understand?"

"Yes, Valide Sultan."

She steps back and nods once. "Good. Go rest. I will have the announcement made in the harem."

Fear, instantaneous and profound, rocks me to my core. "Mahidevran will kill me," I say, my voice trembling. "Must we announce it, Valide Sultan?"

"Do not be silly," she says, "Mahidevran will not dare to harm you. You carry the Sultan's child." She pauses, a thought, a doubt, creeps into her mind. "Be accompanied wherever you go," she adds, "just in case you feel faint again."

It is a clever way of saying that she is unsure of what Mahidevran will do, and a safe message for me to use to ensure that I am never alone.

The scent of roasting flour and butter drifts through the halls before the kalfas even say a word. I sit on my divan, trying to sew, but my hands tremble too much to thread the needle. In the corridor, voices rise—quick, excited, unable to be fully hushed.

"They're making *helva*! I heard it from the kitchen girls. Valide Sultan herself gave the order!"

"Mahidevran must be so pleased," says another.

I set down my embroidery, my heart pounding. It is tradition to prepare sweet helva when a great event is announced, especially a birth to come. The smell is thick now, buttery and golden, curling under my door.

For a moment, the world tilts on its axis. I press a hand to my stomach, not yet rounded, not yet visible. Inside, a tiny seed of life grows—Süleyman's child.

A wave of noise rises from the main hall where the women gather with laughter, exclamations, the clatter of trays. They have started distributing the helva—still warm, sticky, perfumed with honey and pistachio. Sweetness to mark a life not yet born.

I stand, smoothing my skirts, and walk to the main courtyard. Emine Hatun is there, leaning lightly on her cane. The harem girls take no notice of me.

"My lady Hürrem," she says, in a loud voice. The harem goes silent. "Valide Sultan sends her congratulations. The kitchen prepares helva for the harem... in your honor." She bows low, to me.

Gasps from the concubines. I am no longer just Hürrem. I am the mother of a possible heir. My hands rest on my belly. The child within me, no larger than a pomegranate seed, is already reshaping my life.

I catch Aleksandra's eye across the room. She grins openly and gives me a small, cheeky bow. Some concubines approach me, faces carefully painted in polite smiles.

"Congratulations, Hürrem," says one woman with a voice as sweet and false as syrup. "You bring honor to us all."

Another offers me a piece of helva on a delicate napkin, her hand trembling just slightly from the effort of hiding her resentment. "May your child be strong and beautiful," she says, though her eyes burn with envy.

Behind them, a few linger near the columns, whispering and pretending not to look at me. Their mouths twist around words I cannot hear, but it is easy to guess they are less than congratulatory.

Mahidevran is nowhere to be seen, but I feel her absence like a pressure against my ribs. I know she will hear about this soon enough, if she hasn't already.

I accept the helva with a small, dignified nod. I smile and thank everyone who offers me congratulations. Aleksandra comes to my side. "May your child be healthy and your birth easy," she says. I hug her, my only friend, and share with her the fierce joy burning inside me.

Mahidevran enters the courtyard. The harem parts like the Red Sea as she slowly approaches me—I get the distinct impression of a snake slithering toward its prey. Everyone holds their breath. Emine Hatun comes to stand by my side, a subtle reminder that Valide Sultan is always watching.

Mahidevran leans in, so close and yet not touching me, and whispers so that no one can hear, "I hope you die in childbirth."

Without another word, she turns heel and leaves. The collective sigh of relief is audible, her departure easing an unseen weight in the hearts of the concubines.

I remain in the courtyard for the rest of the evening, enjoying the joyful atmosphere, though my thoughts return to Mahidevran's comment and the implication that had never occurred to me.

Months pass; Süleyman's absence weighs on me, but his frequent letters help to ease my longing. Our child grows in my belly. I frequently return to those awful words. I had not realized what giving birth in this time might be like. No doctors, no pain relief, no modern medicine in case something goes wrong.

Women die in childbirth even in modern times, and in this time even a little thing going wrong can lead to disastrous results. I console myself in the knowledge that I am strong and healthy and try to push other thoughts out of my mind.

I follow Valide Sultan's instructions. I eat well, I rest, and I am never alone. From time to time, I pass Mahidevran in the corridors or the hammam. She sneers and makes snide remarks to her entourage that has them snickering behind my back. I do not rise to the bait. I remain regal, calm, and serene, knowing that I have Süleyman's heart, and soon, Allah willing, his son.

Chapter 20
A Star is Born

The city rings with joy. Even from the confines of the harem, I can hear cannon fire marking the victorious return of the Sultan. The harem is abuzz with celebration, bustling full of nervous, excited energy. Musicians play, concubines dance, sharbat is served after breakfast. There are no lessons today, no chores—it is a day of festivities and merrymaking.

But for me, the world narrows to a single point: his return. I sit in my chamber, dressed in a beautiful white gown, my tulip brooch pinned to my chest, waiting for his summons, counting how long it will take for him to see the royal family first, how long until he calls for his Hürrem.

The morning and afternoon trickle on. My heart sinks with fear that he has forgotten me, that his love has waned in his absence. Aleksandra does her best to calm me, but nothing can assuage the growing pain in my chest. Finally, Melek Kalfa appears at my door—Süleyman awaits my presence in his chamber.

I rise unsteadily from my seat, one hand presses to the heavy curve of my belly. My heart races. I nearly glide with joy down the Golden Road.

Süleyman's face breaks into a smile the moment he sees me. Without a word, he crosses the room and falls to one knee before me, his strong hands pressing reverently against my rounded stomach. His fingers spread wide, as if trying to feel every part of the child growing inside me.

"My Hürrem," he murmurs. His voice is thick with wonder. "My sun and my joy."

Tears blur my vision. I thread my fingers through his hair as he kisses the place where our child rests. He stands, wrapping me gently in his arms, mindful of my condition. His scent—leather, musk, and the spice of the road—wraps around me like a beloved cloak. I kiss him fiercely. Our fingers twine together. I lead the way to his bed. He kisses me, scents my neck, his fingers tracing the mounds of my swollen breasts. I pull at his shirt.

"Hürrem," he chuckles softly, "you are too far with child for what you seek." His eyes express his desire even as his actions urge caution.

"My pleasure is your pleasure," I whisper, as my hands begin to roam his body, seeking to remember the feel of him. He protests only once more and is finally lost to my caresses.

That evening, we dine together, a sumptuous meal eaten slowly in front of a bright fire. The lamps burn low and golden around us as he regales me with tales of his journey—how the mighty fortress of Belgrade fell, how the armies of Hungary scattered like leaves before him. He dances around the room, conjuring images of sword fights and mighty steeds charging into battle. I waddle after him, playing the role of Hungary never able to catch the army of the Ottoman Sultan. He laughs heartily at my efforts, and I pretend pout at my failure.

"The pain of parting is nothing to the joy of meeting again," I declare to Süleyman as we cuddle in front of the hearth, quoting Dickens.

"Has it been so awful without me?"

"Yes," I say, without hesitation. "Every moment without you is an eternity of suffering. Your son and I prayed every day for your safe return to us."

"My son?" He asks, "how can you be sure?"

"Because only a boy would kick me so fiercely." I grin at him as I say it. I cannot be sure, of course, but in my heart, I pray for it to be a boy. Only a boy provides security in this world.

Süleyman crouches down so that his face is against my belly. He speaks to his son in hushed whispers, of the Empire they will forge, of riding great horses together into battle, of the importance of always taking care of his mother. I listen, my heart swelling with pride and longing, savoring the rare, stolen hours we have together.

My Sultan is home, and I feel safe for the first time in months. We sleep tucked against each other, me propped up with a mountain of pillows, him curled up against me—even in sleep we are not willing to let the other go.

Süleyman has only been back one week when the first pains begin. They start early in the morning. I pay little attention at first, as I have been having them on and off for several days. It is deep in the night when I realize the cramps are not fleeting. They sharpen into something urgent and relentless. I am rushed to the birthing chamber, where the midwives gather like a flock of crows around me, their faces grim but determined.

The labor is long and brutal. The palace women said first births were hard, but no one has prepared me for this. The pain seems to tear me in half. I scream until my throat is raw. Sweat soaks my hair and dress; my body is wracked with tremors. Midwives wipe my brow, whisper encouragement.

The hours drag by, marked only by the drip of oil lamps and the pacing of anxious feet. At first, the midwives are confident, encouraging. But as night bleeds into morning, then afternoon and then into the next evening, the mood changes.

The midwives begin to exchange glances, silent and grim. Their hands, once sure and steady, now tremble ever so slightly as they wipe the sweat pouring off me and press cool cloths to my burning skin. They murmur prayers under their breath, soft invocations for mercy and strength. I drift in and out of fevered dreams. I think of my home, of snow falling on the rooftops, of my mother's voice. I think of Süleyman's hand on my belly, his words of love.

Valide Sultan arrives, moving swiftly into the birthing chamber, her robe trailing behind her like a shadow. She sits straight backed in a cushioned chair, her prayer beads slipping through her fingers bead by bead, her lips moving in silent prayer. Though she says little, her stern gaze does not waver from the bed, and her very presence makes the kalfas and midwives stand straighter, work faster.

As the sun climbs higher into the sky on the third day in the birthing chamber, gilding the windows with light, panic creeps in like a living thing. I writhe in agony, my hands clutching the sheets, my body trembling from exhaustion. I barely notice the world around me. All I know is pain and a desperate, ironclad determination to see my child born.

And then, at last, a wail breaks the heavy air.

"It's a prince!" cries the head midwife, her voice cracking with relief.

"*Mashallah*," I hear Valide Sultan express loudly from her seat as she heads to the door. She proclaims loudly that a prince has been born. Cheers rise from the harem corridors.

I close my eyes momentarily and say a silent prayer of gratitude. The baby is placed on my chest, slick and squalling, furious at the world. I look down at him, overwhelmed. The room is thick with the scent of blood and sweat. Midwives bustle quietly, cleaning the linens and tending to the fire, but I have no eyes for anything but the small bundle in my arms.

"My son," I whisper in awe. "My sweet prince."

He is the most perfect thing I have ever seen. My son, my son, I repeat over and over in awe. I count his fingers, his toes, brush the fine downy hair on his head with trembling fingers. I almost whimper as the midwives take him from me to wash and swaddle him. I watch like a hawk and only breathe fully when they return him to my arms.

The door opens quietly. I look up to see Süleyman enter, his eyes shining with unshed tears. He leans down and presses a kiss to my forehead. "I thought I would lose you." He stares at me for a moment longer, before reaching out to touch our son's tiny cheek with a reverence that makes my throat close.

"He is strong," he says, voice thick with emotion. "He will be a lion among men."

Süleyman leans closer, his forehead resting briefly against mine. "Hürrem," he murmurs, "you have given me a son. You have given me the future." I press my cheek against him, feeling the warmth of his skin and the weight of the moment settle deep into my soul.

Süleyman looks at me for a long moment, as if weighing a treasure beyond price. Then, bending low to kiss our son's brow, he whispers, "Mehmed. Your name is Mehmed."

The name ripples through the room like a blessing. The midwives, overhearing, bow their heads. Süleyman turns to his mother.

"We shall call him Mehmed," he says, his voice rich with pride. "Mehmed, our little conquering lion."

"A powerful name for our little Şehzade." Valide nearly purrs with delight.

I hold Mehmed against me, smelling the faint, milky scent of his skin, while sounds of the harem rejoicing in the distance drift into the birthing chamber. It is as if the whole world has turned sweeter, softer.

I clutch him to me, filled with a love so fierce it is terrifying. Süleyman kisses me again and murmurs that I should get some rest. I am terribly tired; I can feel a faint tremor creeping through me from exhaustion. The room empties, save for a handful of midwives who tend to Mehmed.

"Mother," I say in a hush, "I have a son. You should see him; he is so beautiful. Today, you have become a grandmother. Can you feel it?"

As I wait for the wind to bring her my message, I fall into a deep sleep, dreaming of my son and new hopes for the future.

Chapter 21
Mustafa – Part 1

I am ready to leave the birthing chamber. Mehmed is wrapped in a soft cotton swaddling blanket, sleeping soundly after nursing, a faint half smile on his lips.

Melek Kalfa is here to escort me back. We walk past the main harem courtyard. When I question her why we are not going through the courtyard to my room, she urges me patience. We walk deeper into the harem, beyond the familiar corridors, and into the part of the palace reserved for the royal family. Mahidevran Hatun and Hatice Sultan live here in their private apartments, with additional rooms for visiting sisters and future mothers of new princes. Valide Sultan lives a little further, down another corridor, near the section reserved for Süleyman himself.

We come to a large double door that opens in the center. As Melek places her hands on the two rounded handles to pull the doors open, she turns to me with a smile.

"Hürrem Hatun, as mother of a prince, you are part of the royal family. Welcome to your private apartment."

What lies before me is a symbol of my new status. I hand Mehmed to Melek Kalfa, leaving me free to roam and examine every nook. I feel nearly giddy with excitement, wonder and awe at the sights before me.

My new chamber is magnificent. It is vast with soaring ceilings painted in delicate blues, golds, and creams—a reflection of the heavens themselves. Sunlight streams in through tall, arched windows draped in sheer silk curtains through which I can see the Bosphorus, gleaming blue and alive, stretching toward the horizon. A heavy velvet curtain frames the outer edge of the window, pulled partially closed against the cold of the winter air.

The walls are paneled with polished wood inlaid with mother-of-pearl and intricate marquetry, each hand-painted with twisting vines and tiny blossoms. A thick carpet from Persia, woven with vivid threads of emerald, ruby red, and sapphire cover the floor.

Against one wall stands an enormous bed, canopied and curtained in embroidered silk the colors of ripe pomegranate. The bed is heaped with soft cushions and pillows, all stitched with patterns of tulips, carnations, and roses—symbols of beauty, prosperity, and love.

At the far end of the chamber stands a large commanding fireplace. Its hearth is wide and deep, lined with polished stone that glows golden in the flickering light. The mantel, carved from a single slab of white marble, is intricately adorned with delicate flowers. Within the vast hearth, a roaring fire dances wildly, its flames crackling, releasing the rich, sweet scent of burning wood mixed faintly with the subtle perfume of dried rose petals. The heat from the fire fills the chamber with a comforting, almost embracing warmth, banishing every trace of the chill from the stone walls.

The chamber is furnished with several sumptuous divans that line the walls, their long, low forms inviting both conversation and repose. Each couch is crafted from polished wood, dark and heavy, inlaid with delicate ivory designs of winding tendrils of vines, tulips, and intricate arabesques. The seats are deep and

137

luxuriously padded with firm cushions covered in thick velvet, dyed in rich jewel tones of royal blue.

Low gilded tables stand beside the couches, bearing delicate porcelain dishes of sugared fruit, roasted nuts, and sharbats cooled in glass carafes. Lanterns of colored glass hang from the ceiling above, casting a soft, jeweled glow over the entire room.

A small chest carved of cedar and bound in brass sits beside the divan, filled with my personal items—letters, scraps of poetry, small gifts from Süleyman. A delicate Qur'an stand made of rosewood rests on a low table, along with writing instruments—a reed pen, pots of ink, and fine paper.

The greatest marvel, however, is the balcony—a slender, graceful structure of pale stone, supported by carved brackets shaped like tulips. An intricate, lacy screen of gilded ironwork hides the balcony from prying eyes, while still allowing the view and breeze. Stepping onto it, I can see the silver ribbon of the Bosphorus glittering in the sunlight. The scent of salt and the chill ocean air remind me of home, different only by the mingling of the distant sound of calls to prayer echoing across the waters.

Small adjoining rooms open from the main chamber: one to serve as a private bathing room with a marble basin and copper ewers. A large nursery houses an ornate cradle of carved ivory for Prince Mehmed. The nursery can easily accommodate a small army of infants before feeling crowded. Another large room contains a divan and multiple single beds.

"For the concubines who will serve you," answers Melek, seeing the perplexed look on my face.

I will have concubines, here to serve my every whim, to care for Mehmed day and night, and to keep me company.

"Bring me Aleksandra," I say softly. "I wish to have her by my side."

Aleksandra, Mariia, Defne, and Handan arrive before dinner, eyes wide with amazement at the splendor of the rooms. They bow low. As Defne and Handan move about the room, tending to various tasks, Mariia goes to the nursery. I call Aleksandra to me. We dine together, and Aleksandra gives all the gossip from the past few days, everyone's reactions to the birth of a new prince—especially news of Mahidevran, who fainted in the harem after the announcement.

The next day, Süleyman comes to my chamber, leading Mustafa by the hand. A boy of five, he looks up at me with wary, cautious eyes. He is solemn and beautiful, with Mahidevran's dark hair and Süleyman's strong gaze. He touches my hands, tentatively, then reaches for my hair, twisting it in his little hands for a while; finally, he takes my face in his hands, bringing his head close, as if trying to see me better. I must have passed the inspection as Mustafa moves off and begins to explore his surroundings.

I call for Mariia to bring me Mehmed. Mustafa watches everything, eyeing the little bundle curiously.

"Come Mustafa," says Süleyman encouragingly, "meet your brother, Mehmed."

Mustafa steps close to look upon his brother. I move to sit on the floor to make it easier for him. He studies Mehmed, stroking his cheek delicately. He starts to talk to Mehmed, of swordplay and running through the gardens and important discoveries he made recently by the fountains. As he chats away the way young children do, Süleyman and I gaze at each other with wide smiles at the adorableness of Mustafa educating his new brother.

When it is time to leave, Mustafa kisses Mehmed and says very earnestly that he will have a sword ready for him so they can play together. As the doors close behind them, I can still hear Mustafa arguing with Süleyman, who is trying to explain that Mehmed will be too young for swordplay for a few years.

I laugh heartily for a while. Mustafa, despite who his mother is, is a beautiful child and I feel glad that Mehmed has an older brother.

Late in the afternoon, while Mehmed is asleep on a thick fur blanket on the floor near me and the concubines are in the hammam, Mahidevran appears in the doorway. She does not ask permission to enter. She simply sweeps into my room, her silk robes hissing against the tiles. For a long moment, Mahidevran says nothing—she stares at Mehmed with an unreadable expression. I struggle to sit up, wincing from the lingering pain, but alert and ready.

"Congratulations," she says, her voice low and cold, the faintest curl of disdain to her mouth. "But do not fool yourself, Hürrem. Mustafa is the heir, and he will be Sultan after his father. And when he takes the throne…" she glances meaningfully at the tiny form beside me, "the blood of his rivals will flow. That is the way of things. Remember it."

My stomach twists with fear and fury, my heart pounds in my chest. I wrap my arms protectively around Mehmed as if to shield him from the venom of Mahidevran's words, even as she turns and leaves the room without another word, the sound of her silk slippers whispering across the floor.

I sit on one of the low couches near the great roaring fireplace, Mehmed sleeping beside me, lost in thought. After many minutes, I realize Aleksandra is calling my name, her face troubled.

"Aleksandra," I say, my voice quiet, though the door is closed, and my servants are far. "Mahidevran said something to me... something about Mustafa... about killing Mehmed. What did she mean?"

Aleksandra's eyes darken, the playful spark she usually carries snuffed out in an instant. She looks around the room, almost instinctively checking that we are truly alone. Then she leans closer, lowering her voice to barely a whisper.

"It is... the law of the palace," she says. "An ancient tradition among the Ottomans. When a sultan dies, his sons—all of them— will fight for the throne. And the one who wins will kill the others."

I stare at her, stunned, struggling to find my breath. "Kill them?"

She nods solemnly. "It is called fratricide. Brother killing brother. It is meant to protect the Empire. To stop civil war. If a sultan's sons are left alive, they may rise against each other, and the Empire could fall into chaos."

I clutch my robe tighter around me, glancing at Mehmed, his tiny fists curled, his chest rising and falling with each breath. The idea of someone harming him—of Mustafa hunting him like an enemy—makes my stomach twist.

"Even a child?" I whisper.

"The law sees no age, only threat," Aleksandra says grimly. "To protect the throne, it does not matter if the brother is a baby or a man."

I press my hand to my mouth, my mind spinning. How could the Empire demand such a thing? How could a father ever allow it?

A thought crosses my mind. "You said that when a sultan dies, all his sons will fight for the throne. Does that mean it is not the eldest son who ascends to the throne after his father?"

"Older means nothing. It is the strongest who wins and survives."

Aleksandra reaches over and squeezes my hand. "It is cruel, but this is the way it is done, Hürrem. You must protect yourself. And you must protect Mehmed. No one else will."

For a long time, I say nothing. I only stare into the fire, the fierce, crackling flames reflecting the sudden new hardness forming in my heart.

"I will not let them harm you," I whisper to Mehmed, my voice trembling. "Not while I draw breath. You are mine. My son. My life."

Beside me, Aleksandra says nothing, but I feel her presence—a quiet, loyal shadow.

I turn to her. "I won't be helpless," I say, low but steady. "I'll learn. I'll watch. I'll grow stronger than any of them expect. For him."

Aleksandra touches my arm in silent agreement—the two of us, alone in this glittering, dangerous world. I understand now: the harem is not merely a gilded cage, or a contest for the Sultan's favor. It is a battlefield for the very lives of our sons.

So I will fight. I will smile sweetly when it serves me, bow low when it is wise, and I will never forget this moment. I will never forget what is at stake.

"That is why each woman is allowed only one son," she says.

I frown, confused. "What do you mean?"

She leans in, her blue eyes serious. "It is not only custom. It is to keep the peace. Imagine if a mother has many sons. Each of them would have a claim to the throne. They would fight each other—brother against brother—and the Empire would tear itself apart. One son means one heir. It is meant to limit the bloodshed."

I press a hand to my heart, hammering so hard my chest hurts. "But they still kill each other."

Aleksandra nods grimly. "Yes. Even with one son from each woman, when the time comes, they fight. It is... expected. It is said that a prince must do whatever it takes to seize the throne, that it is better for one brother to die than for the whole Empire to fall into civil war."

A coldness spreads through me, deeper than fear. "Better one brother than a thousand sons of the Empire," I whisper, recalling a saying I had heard among the kalfas. Aleksandra gives a small nod.

I turn my head toward Mehmed. He sleeps on, peacefully unaware of the heavy future already placed upon his tiny shoulders. My baby, my sweet boy. And then I think of Mustafa, a beautiful boy, and I make a silent prayer. Let it not be by my hand. Let this world not reduce me to child killer. I will protect Mehmed at all costs; I pray that fate resolves the war before blood stains my hands.

Late in the night, when the palace sleeps, I sit by the window, looking out at the Bosphorus, reflecting on this world—both beautiful and merciless. And I weep. I weep for Mehmed and the cruelty that he will one day have to overcome. And I weep for my love, my Süleyman, and the cruel tradition that will now keep us apart.

Chapter 22
Love Triumphs

The weeks after Mehmed's birth pass in a haze of sleepless nights and endless wonder. Concubines bustle around us, tending to the multitude of tasks required for the care of a newborn, but I insist on feeding him from my own breast and Mehmed is always hungry.

I spend hours gazing at his tiny face, committing every blink and sigh to memory. I still pinch myself that I have become a mother in this foreign world—a world that I will never leave even if a portal were to open right at my feet. Every morning, I sit on the divan facing a roaring fire holding Mehmed in my arms, taking in his scent, kissing his cheeks, humming a sweet lullaby.

When no one is around us, I sing to Mehmed. In hushed tones, I croon *Here Comes the Sun* from the Beatles or *Three Little Birds* by Bob Marley, songs my parents sang to me as a child. Tears well in my eyes, blending joy and sadness; how my parents would have loved being grandparents. I picture them holding Mehmed. The sight is odd, for I am always in Topkapi; they are here with me in this time, laughing with Süleyman, exploring the architecture of the palace, sitting cross-legged on the floor in front of the fireplace.

It is on one such morning of reminiscence in song, as the sunlight slants across the marble floor of my new chamber, that Valide Sultan pays us a visit, come to see her new grandson. She moves like a queen—regal, assured. I rise carefully from my couch, cradling Mehmed in the crook of my arm, and bow low, though my body still aches from the long labor.

Valide Sultan extends her hand to me, which I promptly kiss. "My grandson," she whispers, her voice warm with pride.

I render Mehmed to her as she settles herself on the divan. She rocks him gently in her arms, kisses his cheeks tenderly and whispers sweet words to him. I don't know why I am surprised that she behaves like a grandmother; I guess I imagine royalty to act differently, yet before me is Valide Sultan, the undisputed matron of the Empire, cooing to my Mehmed.

"He is a strong boy. He will be a warrior, Allah willing," she says, smiling broadly. Mehmed falls asleep in her arms, soothed by the gentle rocking motion.

She turns to me then, her face regaining its gravity.

"Listen carefully now, Hürrem," she says, "Prince Mehmed belongs to the House of Osman. Every breath he draws is now in service to the Empire."

I nod slowly, feeling the enormity of her words press down on my chest.

"You must dedicate yourself entirely to him," she continues. "Your time, your loyalty, your prayers. All must be for his raising. Nothing else matters now."

"I understand, Valide Sultan," I say, my voice steady, though in my heart I am angry that she is already claiming him for the Ottoman Empire.

Valide's gaze sharpens. "You must also prepare yourself. The Sultan is young and strong. It is his duty to call others to his chamber. You must behave with propriety. You must not question. You must not interfere. You are the mother of a prince, and I expect you to always act appropriately."

The words pierce deeper than any blade. I clench my hands together to stop myself from screaming.

"Yes, Valide Sultan." I say, recalling the vow to my son to do anything necessary to ensure his security. I had not realized that the cost was my love for his father. I bite back the tears that threaten to betray me.

She gives me a final approving nod before turning back to Mehmed. After a while, she hands him back to me and rises to face me.

"You have done well, Hürrem," she says, patting me lightly on the arm.

I cannot help myself from asking a question that has been burning since Aleksandra explained the policy to me. "Valide," I venture. She pauses, eyeing me cautiously. "I understand one woman one child and I will behave properly, but there is something that is bothering me."

"What is it, Hürrem?"

"Why has Mahidevran behaved as she has?" I ask. "She must surely have been given the same message."

Valide's eyebrows arch at my unexpected question. She takes a moment before answering. "Some women refuse to learn, no matter the cost," she answers, before sweeping out of the room, leaving the faint scent of rosewater in her wake.

Weeks pass. Süleyman visits often, coming to see Mehmed, sometimes holding him awkwardly in his strong hands. He is tender to me, caring. He starts and ends each visit with a kiss, on my cheek or my forehead. My heart breaks with every departure. He is oblivious to my suffering. He has a new son and is more content than I have seen him.

I dare not ask questions about whether he has called another concubine to his chambers, nor if he still loves me. Instead, I smile and laugh with him. And when he leaves, I sit by the window and weep.

Two months after Mehmed's birth, a message arrives that gives me hope. The Sultan has summoned me. I have dreamed of this since learning of the one child per mother tradition, and now I barely believe it to be possible that he will still want me. I am plagued by doubts. Nevertheless, I spend the afternoon in the hammam; I must be perfect tonight. My heart hammers wildly as I walk through the harem, past the guarded doors, into the familiar private corridor.

When I am ushered into Süleyman's chamber, I find him standing by the brazier, looking into the fire. He turns at once, and a smile breaks over his face—a real, open smile that warms me from within.

"My Hürrem," he says.

I fall to my knees, bowing low. "My Sultan."

He comes to me at once, lifting me to my feet, holding my hands between his. His eyes search mine, filled with something fierce and unyielding. He sweeps me up in his arms, holding me tight, and kisses me with a ferociousness that is breathtaking.

He sets me down gently and looks into my eyes, filled with tears.

"What is this, my love?" he asks, concern in his voice.

"I was told," I hesitate a moment, "that a concubine bears a son, and then... she steps aside."

He looks at me then, seriously. "No one dictates rules to me."

He strokes my cheek, softly, lovingly. He lets out a low laugh, pulling me closer. "Nothing, no one, will keep me from my beautiful red-haired lover."

His words strike me like lightning. A river of tears streams down my face. I pull him to me fiercely. He kisses my forehead, then my lips, and the world melts away to our passion. I am not just a concubine bearing a son for the Sultan. I am Hürrem, his lover, the keeper of his heart.

We kiss for a long while, reacquainting ourselves, reluctant to part. Later, Süleyman and I sit cross-legged at the low table, laid with silver dishes and bowls of every delight the palace kitchens can produce—roasted lamb with figs, sweet stewed quinces, pilaf jeweled with pomegranate seeds, warm bread brushed with butter and sprinkled with sesame. Fragrant steam curls from each plate, filling the room with mouthwatering aromas.

But I barely notice the food. All I see is him.

We talk about everything I have missed in the last two months. His concerns over this vizier's actions or that judge's interpretation of the law. Judicial reform is his top priority. He wants everyone to have clear rights that will ensure long-term stability and peace for the Empire.

"Injustice anywhere is a threat to justice everywhere," I say, quoting Martin Luther King Jr.

"Exactly," he replies, smiling. "You understand more than most men."

That is quite a compliment for a woman in this time.

He takes my hand in his and brings it to his lips for a kiss. "My beautiful Hürrem," he says, his voice rough with feeling.

I smile, feeling my heart bloom in my chest.

"Teach our son well, share your beautiful mind with him, and he will be the glory of the Empire."

His words send my thoughts wild. I have not considered how I should teach Mehmed—how should I use my modern education to help him secure his future.

I remain lost in thought as servants clear away the remnants of our meal and Süleyman moves to sit so close that our knees touch.

"I thought of you every night," he says, reaching out to tuck a lock of hair behind my ear. "When the cold bit into my bones... when the fires burned low... I thought of you, Hürrem. And it warmed me more than any flame."

I begin to say how much I have longed for him too, but he presses a finger gently to my lips. "No words," he says softly. "Tonight, I need only you."

He kisses me then, slowly, deeply, as if rediscovering something he thought he had lost. I melt into him, letting the love I tried to bury beneath duty and fear rise up and claim me.

Later, as we lie tangled together on the cushions, he brushes his hand tenderly over my hair and whispers, *Benim güneşim...*"— My sun.

I smile against his skin, thinking how strange and wonderful life has become. No longer the frightened girl from a faraway land, I am His Hürrem. Our love has triumphed, against all odds, against tradition—a bond that no one has the power to tear asunder.

Chapter 23
The Sun and the Moon

The mid-morning breeze drifts from the Bosphorus, carrying the distant scent of salt water and sunshine to my private terrace. I sit on silk cushions in the shade of a carved wooden canopy laced with climbing roses. This is one of my favorite places in the palace—my little garden of solitude and peace.

Aleksandra sits cross-legged nearby, peeling a plum, the juice already staining her fingers crimson.

"You look pale," Aleksandra says, glancing at me. "You haven't been eating."

"I'm too tired to eat," I murmur. "And it makes me feel sick."

Aleksandra raises an eyebrow. "Are you worried? Should I call for a doctor?"

My hand rests lightly on my belly. I turn my face toward the water, watching the sails drift lazily across the strait. I have suspected for several days now—the fatigue, the nausea, the strange fluttering in my stomach. "I have felt this before. The lingering tiredness. The way the smell of food turns my stomach. It feels like before... with Mehmed."

Aleksandra gasps, dropping the half-peeled plum. "You think—?"

"I think I might be pregnant."

For a moment there is silence, broken only by the call of gulls and the soft rustling of the breeze. Then Aleksandra springs to her feet.

"We must call the midwife. At once."

I give a small nod, still staring out at the glittering water. "Yes. But don't alert anyone else. Not yet."

The midwife arrives swiftly. She is a seasoned woman with silver-streaked hair tucked neatly beneath a white headscarf, and hands that have brought dozens—perhaps hundreds—of children into the world. She bows deeply before me before performing a discreet, experienced examination.

When she straightens, her face bears a quiet smile. "Yes, Hürrem Hatun," she says respectfully, "there is life growing within you."

I blink slowly, then laugh softly, overwhelmed by the surge of emotion. "Another child," I exclaim happily.

Aleksandra's eyes fill with tears, and she grabs my hands, squeezing them tightly.

The midwife bows again. "I will inform the palace physician discreetly. No one else will hear it from me."

"Thank you," I reply. "You may go."

As the woman departs, Aleksandra kneels before me. "Two children, Hürrem. You will be the mother of princes."

"Or a daughter," I murmur, one hand resting again on my belly. I cannot explain it clearly, but this pregnancy feels different from the first one. "And either way, Süleyman will know. Today. But first, I must see Valide Sultan."

Valide Sultan sits beneath a dome of stained glass, where the morning light paints colored patterns on the tiled walls. She sips from a delicate porcelain cup as I enter and bow deeply. She is not alone; Mahidevran and Hatice Sultan sit nearby, discussing their embroidery. Mahidevran nearly sneers at my entrance, then shifts position so that her back faces me.

"Rise, Hürrem," Valide says, watching me closely. "You come with urgency."

"I do, Valide Sultan, though I would prefer to speak in private."

"There is no need." She admonishes me sharply. Mahidevran and Hatice are now watching attentively, trying in vain to hind their smiles at my expense.

I stand tall, my hands folded calmly before me. "I carry the Sultan's child again."

There is a pause. Mahidevran gasps loudly. Valide's brows lift slightly, and then her face softens. She glances briefly at Mahidevran, then back to me.

"You are certain?"

"Yes, Valide, the midwife confirmed it this morning."

Valide sets her cup down. "Then the Empire will rejoice." She stands and approaches me, reaching out to touch my belly. "You do your duty well."

"I live to serve the Empire, Valide," I reply carefully.

Valide's gaze sharpens—perhaps she caught the sarcasm in my voice—but thankfully Mahidevran faints and draws all attention away from me. They barely notice as I back out of the room.

The palace corridors are hushed at this hour, the golden afternoon light filtering through latticed windows, casting patterned shadows on the polished marble floors. I walk with purpose, my emerald-green kaftan gliding behind me. My heart beats quickly in my chest—not from fear, but from anticipation.

As I reach the threshold of the Sultan's private chamber, I am met with a wall of silence. Ibrahim Pasha steps forward from the shadows, his arms folded, his expression unreadable.

"Hürrem Hatun," he says coolly. "His Majesty is not to be disturbed."

"I must see him," I reply. "I carry news for my Sultan."

Ibrahim's eyes narrow. He has never forgiven me for revealing Mahidevran's attack. "He is in council. Come back another day."

I try to step past him, but Ibrahim blocks my path. "I said…"

"Süleyman must hear this now," I interrupt. "I will not turn back."

"Are you deaf as well as shameless?" Ibrahim hisses, lowering his voice but not his scorn. "You may play your games with the harem, but you do not command the affairs of state."

Before Ibrahim can continue, a rich voice echoes from within.

"Hürrem?"

Süleyman's voice rings out clearly, like a blade slicing through silk.

Ibrahim stiffens. I smile brightly at him.

"Let her in," comes the command.

I meet Ibrahim's glare without flinching. His jaw clenches, and under his breath, he mutters something sharp—too quiet for me to catch, but clearly nothing friendly.

I step past him and enter the Sultan's chamber.

Süleyman stands by the open terrace doors, framed by sunlight, his eyes already on me. At once, his sternness softens. He holds out a hand, beckoning me to him.

I move to him without hesitation, and when our fingers touch, I bring his hand to my belly, pressing it gently there.

"I bring news," I whisper to him. "I am with child."

For a heartbeat, Süleyman is still. Then his hand curves over my stomach as if he might feel the child growing inside. A slow, genuine smile of joy flashes across his face.

"My Hürrem," he says. "The Sun rises twice in my sky."

Süleyman's hand lingers on my belly, his thumb stroking gently.

"You've brought me joy again," he says. "A child of love, not duty."

I can barely hold his gaze, overwhelmed by his reaction. I was expecting happiness. But this is something else. There is light in his eyes. Hope. Pride. Tenderness.

Then Süleyman turns toward the interior of the chamber. "Ibrahim!" he calls.

A moment later, the Grand Vizier enters, straight-backed and silent, though his mouth is a tight line. He stops when he sees me standing beside the Sultan, my hand still resting on my stomach.

Süleyman smiles as he addresses his closest friend. "Ibrahim. Rejoice with me. Hürrem is carrying another child."

Ibrahim bows first to his Sultan, then—after the briefest pause—to me. "May Allah bless the child with strength and wisdom," he says smoothly. "Congratulations to you both."

Though his voice is composed, I notice the faint flicker of something—restraint, perhaps, or calculation—in his eyes. But he straightens quickly, offering no further hint of dissent.

"Summon the astrologers," Süleyman says, still looking at me. "And have the court scribe record the date. This moment must be remembered."

Ibrahim inclines his head. "At once, Your Majesty."

As he turns to go, his eyes meet mine for the briefest moment. Civil. Controlled. And quietly wary. I will have to be very careful of Ibrahim in the future. I know he favors Mahidevran and Mustafa, but now I must fear what that favor means for my young prince.

I turn back to Süleyman to celebrate our moment together—the future will just have to wait.

Many moons pass and I am nearing the end of my second pregnancy when Valide Sultan surprises everyone with the announcement of festivities. The harem shimmers with candlelight and music. Heavy drapes cover the windows, blocking out the winter chill. Fires burn in braziers. Musicians play the oud while trays of sweet fruit, stuffed dates, and rose sharbat circle the gathering.

My belly round with child, I am guided to a place of honor near Valide Sultan. I recline on embroidered cushions of silk and velvet, my back supported by a gilded bolster. Aleksandra sits beside me, my constant companion. She has earned her place at my side.

Mahidevran perches across from me, dressed in deep emeralds and sapphires, surrounded by her small entourage, lips tight and eyes

158

wary. The concubines dance in pairs, swirling in their gauzy silks. Many more sit around the harem, darting furtive glances, sensing the tension between the mothers of the two royal princes.

Valide Sultan leans toward me. "You must be strong for your child. And you must show poise. All eyes are watching."

The festivities are enjoyable. Despite occasional cramps that remind me that my time is coming soon, I relax to the sounds of the music, eyes dazzled by the beautiful colors of the dancing girls.

Just then, Emine Hatun enters through the side door and bends to Valide's ear. "Süleyman has refused the red-haired gift you sent, without even seeing her," whispers Emine, though not silently enough.

Valide purses her lips. She gives a tight nod, but her eyes betray a flicker of sourness—as if she had tasted something bitter. Mahidevran catches the exchange too. Her jaw clenches. After a moment, she rises and excuses herself.

I understand now the reason for the sudden decision by Valide to host us this evening. She has secured another concubine with red hair to lure Süleyman away from me. And it has backfired. Süleyman did not even look upon her before turning her away, a clear message to his mother. I cannot be any happier than I am at this moment—one prince, another child on the way, and the Sultan of the Ottoman Empire has eyes only for me.

On my way back to my chamber a while later, Mahidevran blocks my path. "A beautiful celebration," she says sweetly, though her voice carries the chill of winter.

I meet her gaze with practiced serenity. "Indeed. I am grateful to Valide for such kindness."

Mahidevran's eyes drop to my swollen belly. "Enjoy it while it lasts. You may have won this time, but the Sultan's eyes will wander again."

Mahidevran tries to wound with words. "He will tire of your fire," she continues. "He will forget you and then you and I will be the same."

I offer a slow, controlled smile, my hand resting on my rounded belly. Süleyman is not forgetting. He is building a future, one with me at its center.

"You and I are nothing alike, Mahidevran." Her expression tightens at my words.

"And we will never be the same," I add.

She turns without another word and walks away, skirts whispering like silk serpents.

Two weeks later, I feel the pain begin—low, sharp, and undeniable. Within hours, I am back in the birthing chamber, surrounded by midwives and kalfas hurrying back and forth with hot cloths and bowls of water. Valide Sultan comes in briefly, offering prayers. Aleksandra stays close, wiping my forehead and whispering soothing words.

The labor stretches through the night and into the following afternoon. Just as before, tension mounts among the midwives. I grit my teeth and push through waves of pain, crying out to Allah to save me. At last, with a final gasp and shudder, the child is born.

"A girl!" the chief midwife exclaims, holding up the slick, wriggling bundle.

I collapse back, breathless and trembling, as the wail of my daughter pierces the room. Tears of joy spring to my eyes. I have brought life into this world. A daughter. A perfect little princess.

But beneath my joy, fear coils in my chest like smoke. A daughter. Not a son. I have failed my Sultan. I have not given him the heir he needs, the warrior prince he dreams of. Surely now I will be set aside, forgotten, replaced by another with softer hands and a stronger womb. There are always others waiting—smiling, watching, hoping for my fall.

I clutch my baby to my chest. She is warm and impossibly small. My heart already belongs to her, but I dare not let it show. Not yet. Not until I know whether this moment marks my rise—or the beginning of my end.

"A daughter," I whisper to Süleyman when he visits a while later. "I'm sorry. I know you wanted another son."

Süleyman comes to my side, brushing damp hair from my forehead. He kisses my brow and takes my hand in his. "We will have more sons, *Inshallah*. But tonight, I rejoice for my beautiful daughter. She will be as luminous as you."

"You are not disappointed?" I ask him.

"It is impossible to be happier," he answers, earnestly, smiling brightly. "Mihrimah," he says, gazing down at his daughter. "Sun and moon. A name worthy of her mother."

I look at my daughter, pink and perfect, swaddled and placed gently in my arms. My dismay at her arrival—the silent, shameful fear that I had failed—softens in the warmth of Süleyman's joy. He smiles as he gazes upon her, and in that moment, I realize she has already secured a place in his heart. Mihrimah. Sun and moon. My bright light in this dark and treacherous world.

I study her tiny features, her rosebud lips and delicate lashes. So small, yet already so precious. A girl, yes—but not a weakness. A daughter can be a power all her own. She will not wield a sword, but she will learn to move unseen through corridors, to listen, to wait, to speak when it matters. Just like her mother.

A quiet determination blooms in my chest. I will protect her with everything I have. I will raise her to shine brighter than all who would wish her dimmed. She will never know the helplessness I once felt. She will never beg for love or safety. She will command it.

She is mine. And I am hers.

Chapter 24
Tempus Fugit

The palace breathes with the quiet rhythms of family. My chambers, once a quiet refuge, now ring with the soft cries and laughter of children. After Mihrimah's birth, I bear Süleyman two more sons—first Şehzade Selim, then little Şehzade Abdullah. Each arrival brings me fresh joy, each child a blessing.

Süleyman dotes on his children, frequently summoning us all to his chambers. The evening meals are filled with conversation and the charms of family life—Mehmed whirling around the room with a play sword, Mihrimah reciting a poem she has learned, Selim clumsily grasping his spoon, Abdullah sleeping soundly in my arms.

Süleyman shares stories of his forebears, of distant lands and of empires past. These dinners are unlike anything the harem has seen before. A sultan, seated not with viziers and generals, but with his red-haired love and the children we have made together, speaking not of war but of stars, stories, and the future.

I live for these moments. The sight of my children surrounding their father, the laughter we share, the ease with which Süleyman's eyes seek mine across the table—it is more than I ever dreamed I could have.

Our nights together are filled with passion. Every touch enhances our connection, every kiss is another drop in a deep well. Far from growing tired of each other, our love is built up, layer by layer, into an impenetrable tower.

If life blossoms in my chambers, it withers in Mahidevran's. Once the proud consort and mother to the Sultan's eldest son, she now drifts through the palace like a shadow of her former self. Her visits to the harem are rare and stiff. Whispers follow her—of her bitterness and her isolation.

She clings to Mustafa's status with a quiet desperation, making her presence felt only through subtle slights and rumors that weave like smoke through the halls. But none of them stick. With each new birth, with each smile Süleyman reserves only for his joyful lover, Mahidevran's influence slips further from her grasp.

Her greatest humiliation comes not from my growing power, but from Süleyman's unmistakable declaration: no new concubines are to be sent to his chambers. The order spreads through the harem like wildfire. Valide Sultan herself has sent many to his chamber, more than one was young, beautiful, red-haired—and each girl has been refused at the threshold without so much as a glance.

It is an unheard-of command—a sultan who turns away new beauty. But Süleyman has made his choice. Not just of a lover, but of a companion. Many concubines are married off to viziers and other important men of the Empire. Many stay, enjoying the safety and luxury of harem life, happy to serve the Empire and care for the royal family.

It is late summer when the palace hums with tense preparation. The Hungarian crown has defied the Ottomans for too long, and Süleyman can wait no more. War is coming—swift, calculated, and inevitable.

Süleyman leaves Istanbul at the head of a grand army after bidding farewell to the royal family. Valide Sultan is greeted first, offering prayers to her son for a successful campaign. Hatice Sultan is next—she will be staying in the harem for the duration as her husband, the statesman Mustafa Pasha, will participate in the campaign. Süleyman nods briefly to Mahidevran as a courtesy, before hugging Mustafa to him, who begs again for the chance to join his father on the campaign. And finally, he comes to me. I take his hands, kiss them and raise them to my forehead, a display of respect. Mehmed and Mihrimah, though young, copy my lead. Süleyman looks at us with love in his eyes.

Though accustomed to longing by now, this departure cuts deeper. The world without him feels colder. My children cling to me, and I wrap them in the warmth of his promise of triumph and a speedy return.

From afar, news arrives in stages—crossing rivers, villages, and mountains before reaching Topkapi. Rüstem, the young stablemaster, delivers the letters from Süleyman, addressed to his beloved Hürrem, recounting the campaign's progress and expressing his longing. I read every letter many times, pressing each parchment to my cheek for even the faintest lingering smell of my lover far away.

Then comes news of a great victory: the Battle of Mohács. The Hungarian army has been crushed. King Louis II has fallen. The rain-drenched battlefield was strewn with broken lances and crumpled banners. The gates of Buda lie open to the Ottomans.

The victory is complete. The harem erupts in celebration. Drummers play in the gardens, sharbat is served, and the fountains in the main courtyard run pink with rosewater. Valide Sultan orders sweets to be distributed, and for once, even Mahidevran sits in silence. I say a quiet prayer for my father; the story of this famed battle was one of his favorites.

When Süleyman returns, he is not only a sultan, but a conqueror crowned by fate. And it is to me, glowing and round with our next child, that he comes first. He takes my hand, kisses it gently, and says, "As I conquer lands, you conquer my heart."

Time moves differently in the harem. Perhaps it is our lack of connection to the outside world that impacts our perception, perhaps it is the sameness of each day, blending seamlessly into weeks, months, and years without much thought.

As the years pass, my family grows even larger with the birth of Şehzade Bayezid. I have been here for seven years; I have four sons and a daughter. I frequently wrestle with concerns over how much to teach them about the modern world—just enough to give them an advantage without raising questions that have impossible answers.

My position within the palace has also shifted, from beloved consort to a woman of unmistakable consequence. No longer merely the Sultan's favored, I have become his confidante and his partner not only in love but in thought.

Süleyman, weary by court intrigue and the burdens of Empire, shares more and more with me—topics that are never spoken of outside of the confines of Süleyman's private chamber; it would be a great scandal should it be revealed. Women are simply not thought of as political allies. We dine together most nights and, after the children have been entrusted to my concubines for the evening and the silver trays have been cleared away, we linger long into the night, our conversations turn to matters of the state.

We speak of border negotiations, unruly governors, and European alliances. I use every bit of historical knowledge I have to offer insights, some of which are quite challenging to his world view. I have learned to read the language of diplomacy, to analyze personalities and predict the moves of rivals. Süleyman values my perspective, not because I echo his thoughts as do most of his viziers, but because I am willing to question him, to encourage him to think in new and unexpected ways.

I sometimes sit in the harem, reflecting on my life, on this world. I wonder if I am changing history. If I had not arrived, would there have been another Hürrem? I reflect on the multitude of concubines who have come and gone over the years—was one of them destined to become who I now am? These thoughts sometimes drive me a little mad. But then, I look at my children, at my Sultan lover, and realize that I don't care. They are mine and that is enough.

Chapter 25
Fear and Fever

A creeping dread is sweeping through Istanbul. It begins with whispers. A washerwoman collapses beyond the city walls. A market boy burns with fever; his skin blooming with sores by nightfall. In the fishmongers' quarter, entire families fall sick in a single night. Isolated cases give way to a greater and greater number of people becoming infected. Fear gives way to panic. Word travels faster than the sickness: the pox has returned to the capital.

Smallpox engulfs Istanbul like a silent wind—no fanfare, no warning, only fever and death. The city's pulse slows. Shops shutter early. Doors are marked with charcoal crosses. People avoid the mosques, the fountains, even the baker's stall. The smell of lye and vinegar clings to the streets. The sickness is insidious, spreading with alarming speed, infusing a sense of impending doom over the capital. Even birds flying too low over the courtyards seem ominous.

At Topkapi Palace, the mood turns from vigilance to dread. The harem's marble halls are scrubbed twice daily with rosewater and lime. Midwives and physicians spring into action, inspecting everyone in the palace on a regular basis, checking for fever, sores, any signs of the disease. When three of the kitchen boys fall ill, the Sultan makes the decision to move the royal family out of the city to a more secluded place—Kandilli, a hunting lodge on the Asian shore of the Bosphorus.

The inner courtyard of the palace is eerily quiet, save for the rustling of robes and the hurried footsteps of servants as they prepare for our departure. The children are swiftly gathered, and any trace of normalcy is abandoned for the sake of protection. Guards who would normally turn their backs in the presence of royal women now merely lower their gaze.

The entire family is on the move. Valide Sultan stands dignified, surrounded by her many attendants. Hatice Sultan, her husband Mustafa Pasha and her many children will be joining us, as will Ibrahim Pasha and his wife Muhsine Hatun and their young son. Mahidevran and Mustafa are waiting in the courtyard. I am told that several other viziers and their families will be joining us in our temporary exile.

A line of carriages waits. Horses snort, stamping the earth in protest. I climb into my carriage with trembling hands. Aleksandra sits beside me, gathering the children: Mihrimah, Selim, Abdullah, and little Bayezid. Mehmed and Mustafa ride with their father. Palace guards escort us, in ready defense should any danger present itself.

At the water's edge, a sleek boat waits in the shadows, tucked beneath an outcrop of trees, far from prying eyes. With almost imperceptible motion, the royal boat begins to glide away from the shore, cutting through the waters of the Bosphorus. The sound of the oars, dipping silently into the water, is the only noise that pierces the calm night.

The journey ahead will be brief, but the tension of uncertainty weighs heavily on the hearts of the royal family. As the boat moves further from the capital, the lights of Istanbul begin to fade into the distance, leaving only the vast, dark expanse of water and the distant murmur of the city behind.

Inside the boat, I hold Mehmed close to me, my hands trembling slightly. Süleyman sits opposite, young Abdullah on his lap, watching the horizon. Though we are moving in the dead of night, we both know that this is not a peaceful retreat—it is a forced flight from a threat that only reveals itself too late.

As the boat nears the Asian shore, Kandilli's silhouette emerges against the night sky—the Imperial Pavilion is a serene palace nestled among cypress groves, far from the crowded city, and our hope for safety in the face of devastation.

The children are separated into private chambers, each door guarded by two aghas to control who enters and who leaves. No longer allowed to play together, they are each given their own court physician, their own tutor, and mountains of books and toys to entertain them—a necessary seclusion for their protection. As horrible as it would be to lose a child, this disease can wipe out a generation of children and leave the Ottoman Empire devastated.

Mehmed, old enough to understand, puts on a brave face in front of his brothers. Mihrimah clings to me, begging not to be left alone. Selim tries to imitate his older brother, though he is more fearful and tears well up in his eyes. Little Abdullah, barely three years old, is quiet. He fails to understand the importance of the moment and begins to cry when the nurses take him from my arms. Bayezid, an infant still, is given over to his wet nurse for care.

In front of my children, I bear the separation with the composure of a queen, but inside, terror claws at my ribs. I am to be sequestered though I know that it is needless. In my time, smallpox has been eradicated, and I am fully vaccinated against

170

its deadly effects. I cannot, of course, convey this to anyone. And so, I blow kisses to each child and tell them to be brave.

The days pass with tense stillness. Birds sing in the gardens, but in the distance, the wind carries the far-off cries of a dying city. I sit in my room, day after day, reading passages from the Qur'an, praying for my children, my Sultan, his mother—day after day, I move down the list of people to pray for until I am praying for all the people of the Empire. Outside my chambers, the Bosphorus glistens in the sun, but it offers me no warmth, no peace.

Days turn into weeks, and I begin to smile again, to breathe more fully than I have since the start of this horrible episode. Then one morning, as dawn streaks the waters of the Bosphorus in shades of pink and golden yellow, news reaches me. Abdullah has woken with a fever. Despite all precautions, he has fallen ill. At just three years old, he is especially vulnerable.

I sprint from my chamber, ignoring the loud protest of the aghas in the corridor. Their attempts to stop me at the door to Abdullah's room are in vain. There is no power in the verse that can stop me from going to my child's bedside.

Abdullah seems so small. I sit at his side, gripping his little hand, whispering prayers into the curls damp on his forehead. The palace becomes deathly silent. Apothecaries come with the tools of their trade: cooling cloths, smelling herbs, amber beads, camphor, cloves crushed into warm poultices. They smear his brow with rose oil and burn sweet incense in the corners of the room to drive out evil humors.

Süleyman enters the room late in the night. Two guards stand on either side of him. He must not approach—the risk to the Empire is too great. He leans against the far wall, eyes watching as his son sleeps in fits and starts, his breathing shallow, rattling. The most powerful man in the realm stands powerless, mute, desperate.

As the days pass and Abdullah's tiny body is ravaged by fever and pustules, I break down, screaming at the heavens and cursing fate, my prayers have turned to fury. I beg the healers to do more.

"This is all you can do?" I snap at the eldest physician. "Where is your science? Where is your cure?"

The man lowers his eyes. "We are doing all that is known, Hürrem Hatun."

"All that is known," I cry, rising to my feet, my voice cracking. "What use is your knowledge if my son dies anyway? If I were born in a world where such fevers are vanquished, my son would be saved. He would be running down the halls again. There must be more than smoke and herbs and prayers."

I turn to the walls, as if time itself might hear me, my fists clenched at my sides. "If there is a world where a mother can save her child, let me go there! Let me trade everything—my jewels, my titles, my life—just to keep him breathing!" I rage against this time where there is no medicine to heal my boy.

Abdullah lies on a low mattress in a darkened chamber, surrounded by cool cloths soaked in rose water, their scent heavy in the stale air. His face, once plump with laughter, is now tight and pale beneath the blistering rash that spreads across his skin.

The pustules swell and burst, one after another, marking him with agony.

I kneel for days at his bedside, my hair unbound, my eyes hollow. My arms tremble as I hold his tiny, fever-slicked hand. His once-bright eyes flutter open, cloudy now, barely seeing.

"*Anne...*" he murmurs, the word a ghost on his lips.

"I'm here, my love. Your mother is here," I whisper, pressing my forehead to his. "You will get better. You will. I promise you."

Abdullah had been playful, chasing Selim through the marble corridors with a wooden sword and giggling so loud that even the kalfas had smiled despite themselves. Now, the quiet is unnatural. No laughter echoes through the corridors. No singing from the concubines, no clatter of trays or rustle of silks. Only silence, and the soft, wheezing breath of a child.

For three more days, we wait as the physicians come and go, repeating the same steps over and over. On the fourth morning, before dawn, Abdullah's cries stop. He lies very still, pale like a ghost, breath barely noticeable. Süleyman enters the chamber and stands rigid in the corner, his jaw clenched, his eyes rimmed red, his gaze fixed on the child's shallow breaths. The physician steps back, his silence an answer. All their efforts—herbs, poultices, charms, whispered prayers—have done nothing. The midwives look away, their hands wringing at their aprons.

When the end comes, it is so quiet it might have gone unnoticed. A last faint breath. A tiny hand slipping from mine. A silence too still to bear.

"No…" I scream. "No, no, no—Abdullah!" I pull him into my arms, sobbing into his small, still chest. I wrap my arms around his little body and weep, not like a woman of the harem, not like a concubine, but like a mother. "My son," I whisper over and over. "My little boy. My baby."

Süleyman folds into me, wrapping his arms around us both. He buries his face in my hair, his body shuddering with grief. "I am the *Padishah*, the Emperor of the world," he says hoarsely, "and I could not save my son." Then he turns away, ashamed.

I slam my fists onto the floor. "Why were we born in this cursed time? If I had the medicines they will invent one day, our boy would be saved."

Süleyman doesn't answer. There is no answer to give.

We sit like that for hours, until the fire in the brazier dims and the embers cool, and the boy's body is taken away, wrapped in fine linen, to be buried with princely honors. But no silk or ceremony can ease the breaking of a mother's heart.

The silence that follows is unbearable. It settles over me like a shroud, thick and airless. I feel like an empty shell, hollowed out by sorrow. I wander the halls like a ghost, unseen and unseeing, refusing to eat, refusing to speak. My body moves, but I am no longer inside it.

Each evening, Süleyman sits beside me. He does not speak. He does not try to lift the weight of my sorrow. His hand rests in mine—warm, real—but even that cannot draw me back. Between us is the bond of shared loss, heavier than any crown, older than any empire. We do not cry. We simply exist beside the wound.

In the weeks that follow, we return to Topkapi. Familiar corridors greet us like strangers. The echo of children's laughter drifts through the air, cruel reminders that the world has not stopped.

For a time, there is only grief too vast for words. A silence within the silence. The harem tiptoes around me. Servants avert their eyes. The musicians are dismissed. The fountains seem to murmur lament no one dares speak aloud.

But eventually, the palace begins to move on. It always does. Time does not pause for a mother's sorrow. In this time, as in all times, children die. And life, indifferent and relentless, must go on.

Abdullah is buried in the mosque near his grandfather, Selim I as the call to prayer rings out over the Bosphorus. I lay a small toy sword against a cypress tree in the palace gardens in my own private memorial.

One night, Süleyman comes to my chamber and takes my hands in his.

"He had your eyes," he says finally.

"He had your laugh," I reply.

We do not speak of war or state matters tonight, nor of the future. Only of a little boy who had been the brightest star in our world— and was now gone.

Chapter 26
A Solution to Grief

Grief settles in my chest like winter fog. Heavy. Lingering. Impossible to shake.

In the wake of Abdullah's death, silence haunts the chambers of the palace. My son, my sweet boy, is gone, and yet the world moves forward without him. The servants still bustle in the corridors, the concubines still whisper, and the call to prayer still echoes over the Bosphorus. But inside me, time has stilled.

I cannot allow it to consume me.

Abdullah has fallen to fate, and my heart feels broken. The physicians and imams have come with words of comfort; Süleyman holds me, whispering prayers meant to soothe my soul—but nothing will bring him back. My arms, once so full, feel hollow.

"I will not weep forever," I whisper. "I will not let grief make me useless."

At first, the work is modest—blankets here, a few silver coins there. But word of need reaches me faster than I imagined. A kalfa tells me of a poor woman who left a prayer at the palace gate, begging for medicine for her son. I send ointments. Another family, burned out of their home, receives warm cloaks sewn with care by women who once resented me.

In these quiet acts, I find fragments of peace.

One evening, Valide Sultan enters my chamber and watches as I wrap dried fruits in linen.

"You've turned yourself into a monument to duty," she says, one brow arched.

"I have nothing else to give," I answer.

She glances at Mehmed and Mihrimah, asleep on cushions beside the fire. "You have everything to lose," she says softly, then turns and leaves.

But I do not stop.

This mercy—this hidden thread of compassion—I will weave through the palace walls, from one hand to another, binding myself to my son's memory with every gift given, every mouth fed, every cloak sewn in the silence of my grief.

I understand Valide's point, that my children need me, that they are grieving their brother's loss and require the comfort of their mother. But I know two things that she, perhaps, ignores. First, is that I cannot give to my children what is frozen within me. My love requires oxygen to fuel it—it must be stoked back into life after being smothered by loss. The second is that good works soothe the soul, precisely the balm I need to recover. "The best way to find yourself is to lose yourself in the service of others," I say to myself one afternoon, remembering Gandhi's famous phrase.

And so, I continue. I use my own funds; it is easy to do good when it costs you nothing. There are few acts that I can perform as a slave—even good works are mostly closed off from me. But I will do what is possible with the limited autonomy offered to me.

One afternoon, I summon the Chief Eunuch who oversees the women's apartments. "Bring me bolts of fabric," I tell him. "Sturdy linen, cotton—whatever is cheap but warm. Enough for cloaks, shawls, and underclothes. And thread. Good thread and needles."

The eunuch, unsure, hesitates. "Shall I inform the Valide Sultan?"

"I have informed the Sultan," I reply, my tone crisp but calm.

Within a few days, baskets arrive at my chamber, filled with muted colors: oatmeal-colored wool, soft gray linen, coarse brown cotton. That evening, I call for volunteers among the concubines and kalfas. No one will be forced, though I have the authority to do so.

At first, only a handful appear—Aleksandra, Melek, Mariia, and three that I barely know.

"We will sew for the poor," I say, my voice steady. "For the widows who wait outside soup kitchens in winter. For the children who sleep with nothing on their backs."

Silk cushions are arranged in a circle, and the fabric laid out in neat piles. Aleksandra threads her needle beside me. Melek Kalfa lays out a pattern for a child's tunic. The others bend their heads and begin to stitch. The work goes slowly at first, but over time, rhythm settles in, cloth passing hand-to-hand, seams forming, fingers moving with purpose.

We meet once each week, always after the evening meal. Gradually, baskets are filled with hand-sewn items—simple cloaks, kerchiefs, warm undergarments, small slippers. The baskets are delivered by palace eunuchs to the soup kitchens of the nearby *Mevlevi tekke*. From there, they will be distributed among the poor.

Over time, more and more join the circle. And each week, I join them, not as their mistress, but as one of them. I stitch silently, my heart pouring into every hem and seam, spending hours stitching robes and cloaks. It calms my hands and gives purpose to my days. And every week, my heart feels a little stronger, a little more certain that it is worth continuing to beat.

On occasion, Mehmed sits beside me, helping where he can. Mihrimah hands out thread and pouts when her tiny stitches unravel. "Why must we do this, *Anne*?" Mehmed asks one evening, his fingers tangled in fabric.

"Because we have warmth, and others do not," I say. "Because we eat meat and honey, while others chew stale bread. Because mercy is the only gift that never runs dry."

The grief does not lessen, but it reshapes. In the quiet mornings, in the hush before the harem stirs, I sit by the window with my prayer beads, whispering supplications to Allah—for the strength to endure Abdullah's absence, and for Allah to claim no other of my children.

One such morning, after summoning Emine Hatun, I tell her with soft conviction, "I want a *hatim* read for Abdullah, from the lips

179

of someone who has memorized the Qur'an. I want every word to reach his soul."

Emine Hatun nods solemnly and arranges for a trusted *hafiz*, a veiled older woman known in the palace for her piety and learning, to be invited to the harem. With the permission of the Valide Sultan, a small chamber near the prayer room is cleaned and scented with rosewater and myrrh.

On the first day of the recitation, I wear a simple deep blue gown. I wear no jewels, only the gold ring Süleyman once gave me, now worn like a talisman of mercy.

I sit in a place of prominence, just to the left of Valide Sultan. Hatice Sultan joins us, as does Emine Hatun, Melek Kalfa, Aleksandra and a dozen or so other women of the harem. To my surprise, even Mahidevran attends, though she sits as far away from me as possible.

The hafiz begins the recitation.

The sound of the sacred Arabic verses fills the room, calm and melodious, each syllable a balm for my broken heart. I close my eyes. Aleksandra is quiet and reverent. Emine Hatun weeps silently.

I think of Abdullah, his laugh, the way he used to sleep with one foot sticking out from under his blanket, the warmth of his cheek against mine.

When the first *juz* of the Qur'an is complete, I distribute sweet dates, dried apricots, and spiced nuts to the women gathered— simple offerings, wrapped in silk and tied with golden threads.

"For his soul," I repeat. "And for yours. May your children be protected. May mercy fall upon us all."

Each day, the recitation continues. Each day, I prepare a small gift of food or coin to be distributed quietly to the laundry women, the cooks, the women who clean the baths—those who receive little and say less. I teach Mehmed to bow his head and offer a date to each of them with a smile and the words: "This is from the mother of Abdullah."

It is not grand. It does not bring back my son. But within the walls of the palace, within the boundaries of my confinement, I am building a sacred memory for my lost child. I pray that every verse will rise like smoke through the dome of the harem and into the hands of Allah.

Süleyman has been stalwart in his support during our time of mourning. At first, he is mostly silent, coming to my chamber, hugging his children to him, holding me tightly in his arms. But tonight, he summons me to him.

I arrive in his chamber in the evening. The fire is roaring in the hearth. Süleyman enters from the terrace, the cold air clinging to his robes. He sits on silk cushions, warming himself by the fire, and taps the cushion beside him, beckoning me to join him.

I look at him, waiting, but he stares into the flames.

"I heard about the cloth, the food, the coins," he says at last.

I keep my eyes down. "It is all I know to do."

He reaches for my hand. His fingers are still cold from the night, and when they curl around mine, I nearly break.

"I see him everywhere," I whisper. "His hands. His laughter. I wake sometimes thinking he is only sleeping."

He exhales, slow and deep, and leans closer. "I know. I dream of him too. In the garden, chasing butterflies."

I turn to face him, my throat tight with sorrow. "I begged Allah to spare him. I would have traded anything."

Süleyman brushes a curl from my forehead. "You gave him everything a child could know—love, warmth, joy. Even in a short life, he knew happiness."

We sit in silence, two parents mourning something no throne or crown could shield us from.

"He would be proud of you," Süleyman says softly. "You've given life to his memory. And the city, broken and reeling, breathes easier under your mercy."

I rest my head on his shoulder and let myself lean into his warmth. "I just didn't want the world to forget him."

"He will not be forgotten," he promises. "As long as we live, he lives in us."

The fire crackles low. Outside, the Bosphorus sighs against the shore. Within these walls, I am still a slave. But in this quiet hour—beside the man I love, and with my son's memory folded gently into my hands—I feel free.

Chapter 27
While the Lion Hunts

Süleyman is leaving me again. He is heading back to Austria with his armies, to face the stubborn Habsburg King, to thunder beneath the shadow of fortress walls. Mustafa is going with him.

Mahidevran has been strutting the halls of the harem like a peacock, preening in their midst, delighted with the attention, declaring before all that Mustafa is clearly the Sultan's favorite and heir.

She has spoken this declaration so loudly that the gods themselves have heard her—and they are not happy.

A few days before his departure, Süleyman gathers the entire harem in the main courtyard. From Valide Sultan to the lowest scullery maid, every kalfa and eunuch, all must attend. Mahidevran stands loud and proud, her hands on Mustafa's shoulders, reveling in his importance.

Across from her, I stand with my children, guiding each one as they bow to their father—except for my youngest, Cihangir, still in my arms, barely a year old, his tiny back already curved by the deformity he was born with.

Süleyman stands before his harem, turning his head, taking his time to examine all assembled. Many in the harem have never seen the Sultan so close; they stand, eyes averted, as if merely gazing upon him is difficult.

"Let it be known here," he begins, voice firm and commanding, "that which I declared before the Imperial Council this morning. While I ride to war, with the accord of Valide Sultan," he pauses to nod to his mother, "my Hürrem shall see to the order of the inner court. Her word is to be taken as my own. Let no man or woman question her place lest he question mine."

The silence that follows rings louder than the Janissaries' drums. No sultan has ever given such authority to a concubine. Valide Sultan extends her hand to me in front of all, a sign of her favor. I bow to her and kiss her hands. Whether she knew of the announcement beforehand, I do not know, but she is astute and seizes the opportunity to support her son publicly. Mahidevran looks white as a ghost.

"Mustafa and Mehmed," he declares, "shall accompany me on this campaign."

Süleyman smiles upon Mehmed who bows low to his father. Without another word, the Sultan leaves the harem, just as Mahidevran collapses to the floor in her grief. Shock ripples through the palace like a dropped stone in still water. But no one dares speak against him.

The days stretch long without him. The shadow of the Sultan lingers in the corridors—heavy in the hushed whispers of the concubines. As the weeks pass into months, and the echoes of that proclamation dim, I ensure no one forgets it. I am steward of his world, and I will not fail him.

Late one night, I pass by a group of eunuchs speaking softly in the courtyard. They stop when they see me. One drops his eyes and

185

murmurs a blessing. I do not need Süleyman's sword to rule the harem. I have his trust and that is sharper than any steel.

But I know better than to think I am safe. Problems will come, perhaps not today, but they will come before this is over.

Each morning, the aghas come to me with their reports: disputes among the concubines, shortages in the kitchens, theft in the spice stores. Today, it is the matter of a baker who has been found shorting the flour shipments to the palace kitchens.

"The man is under contract to the Valide," one of the scribes whispers, eyes lowered. "He's been paid through the end of the year."

"And he's stealing," I say plainly. "Replace the baker. The palace will not starve under my watch."

The scribes exchange glances. "Should we not wait until the Sultan returns?"

I look him full in the face. "The Sultan entrusts these decisions to me."

They do not ask again.

I meet regularly with the treasurer, Emine Hatun. We review the spending of the harem on silk and food, and the incomes of the concubines. Nothing must be amiss. I find that one silk merchant charges double that of another one.

"Is the silk of a better quality?" I ask.

"I do not believe so, Hürrem Hatun."

"Then, why are we paying her more than the local merchant?"

"She was chosen years ago by Mahidevran when she was still in Manisa with the Sultan, before his ascension to the throne. She is favored."

I debate with myself, very briefly, whether I should let this one lie. But I will not permit us to be taken advantage of.

"If she wishes to continue to deliver her silks to the palace, it will be for the same price as the other merchants," I command.

Emine Hatun scribbles down the new edict in her book of accounts before we continue our review.

Süleyman set aside years ago revenues from several Anatolian villages for my household and the children's tutors. Now I use those funds to buy blankets for the soup kitchens in Eyüp and thread for the embroidery workshops within the harem. I make sure the girls are kept busy—idleness breeds gossip, and gossip breeds discontent.

That evening, I write to Süleyman.

My Sultan,
The court is steady. The children are well. Mihrimah copies your verses, and Selim eats all the olives. Bayezid prays daily for your return, and little Cihangir clutches your ring at night. I act in your

name with care and gratitude. Return soon, so I may give this
burden back into your hands—though I bear it with pride.
—Your loving Hürrem

I seal it with the tulip and moon cipher, the symbol he designed
for me, the sign of my place not just in his bed, but in his world.

The women of the harem watch me differently now. Some with
awe, some with unease. I am not just the Sultan's beloved. I am
his voice, his chosen steward. His loyalty has lit a fire in me, one
that does not flicker.

Even my enemies bow—some with tight jaws, others with
trembling grace. I no longer walk behind the Sultan in his shadow;
I have become the shadow that moves ahead of him. And through
me, the court will blaze with his light.

I was expecting the crisis, which allows me to remain calm when
finally confronted by it. Sitting in Valide's chamber, we discuss
how to deal with a concubine found trying to sneak out at night.
The Sultan may have left me responsible for the harem, but
attempting to exclude Valide Sultan would have been a grave
mistake. I seek her council, asking questions, and often—though
not always—accepting her recommendations. I value her
experience even if I find it difficult to accept her thinking on many
topics.

I still when the sound of raised voices reaches the doorway. The
air tenses. Valide pauses mid-sentence as the interruption becomes
impossible to ignore. The door flies open. Mahidevran storms in,
her eyes blazing, forgetting all decorum.

"You have no right!" she shouts, the venom in her voice coiling around the silence. "You—slave girl, harlot—you presume to sit in his place? You were bought, not chosen by heaven."

Valide Sultan remains silent, face unreadable but not stopping her. I have no doubt Mahidevran has a long list of grievances against me, though I'm not certain which one in particular has caused her to lose her mind.

"This is the Sultan's will," I say, calm and even. "His seal is clear. I act under his command."

Mahidevran turns sharply to Valide. "You—mother of the Padishah—you will allow this woman, this usurper, to rule while your son is away? You disgrace your station."

Valide's eyes flicker from her to me. For a breathless moment, the room stands still and waits.

Then Valide raises her chin and speaks.

"You forget yourself, Mahidevran." Valide's voice is low and dangerous. "My son is the shadow of Allah on earth. He says this woman speaks in his name. His word is law."

Gasps pass from mouth to mouth. Even Mahidevran staggers back a half-step. For a moment, betrayal flickers in her eyes. She never imagined Valide would side with me. Neither have I.

Mahidevran sobs loudly and is half-dragged back to her chamber, muttering apologies and curses in quick succession. I'm pretty sure the curses are aimed at me. I hope for Mahidevran's sake that Valide thinks so too.

Later that night, Valide Sultan summons me back to her chamber. No attendants. No formality. Just us.

She pours the tea herself—an honor she has never offered me before—and watches the steam rise in silence.

"I spoke what I had to earlier," she says finally. "But do not mistake it for approval."

I meet her eyes. "I understand."

"You are clever. Dangerous, even. And my son... he loves you with a blindness I never thought him capable of." Her voice falters, then steadies again.

I say nothing.

She continues, "My duty is to protect the dynasty. Not my pride. Not Mahidevran. Not even my own wishes. So yes, I support you—because Süleyman wills it. And the court must see unity."

Then she looks directly at me, and her voice lowers like a blade sliding from its sheath.

"But know this—when his shadow fades, and your protection with it, the knives will come. From all directions. And not even the mother of princes will be safe."

"Shadows don't frighten me," I tell her. "I've walked among them too long to flinch. Now, I cast my own."

She says nothing more.

I leave her chambers and walk the halls alone, holding Süleyman's seal in my hand, as echoes of his declaration roll around my thoughts. Even the stones of Topkapi have ears. They will not forget me. I will not let them.

Chapter 28
A Slave No More

The scent of fresh bread carries through the stone corridors, thick with honey and warm milk. It is Mehmed's idea to bring the bread to the outer court. He saw an old man sitting beneath the fig trees near the palace gate, wrapped in a patched robe, his fingers blue from the cold. "He is hungry, *Anne*," Mehmed says to me. "He looks like he is disappearing."

That evening, I cannot stop thinking of the man—how many others sit outside these walls with no fire, no food, no name that means anything to anyone. I have all three: the Sultan's favor, his children, his ear. But what have I given the world? The sewing circle I established after losing Abdullah still sends baskets of clothing to the poor every week. But it is my will that keeps the circle alive. I have given nothing that will outlive me. And something settles in my heart like a pebble in a basin: a longing to give.

"I've been speaking with the Chief Eunuch about expanding the sewing circle," I say to Süleyman a few nights later. We sit alone in his private chamber, the lamps casting amber light across the marble. The lion pelt beneath us warms my bare legs, and the faint scent of musk clings to his skin after our lovemaking.

"If we have more fabric, we could prepare bundles for the dervish lodges in Galata and Eyüp before winter," I explain to him.

Süleyman turns his gaze to me, soft but alert. "You've already done so much," he says. "The tekke kitchens speak your name in their prayers."

"I want to do more," I reply. "Something to feed and house the forgotten. Let me use the money you give me for more than silk and jewels. I could set aside funds for bread and soap to be given each week."

He sits reclined against a velvet cushion, his eyes amused. "You want to be a patron now, my Hürrem?"

"I want to be remembered for more than the curve of my hip and the color of my hair."

He laughs, but there is affection in it. "You will be remembered, beloved."

"I want to be remembered for what I gave, not just what I was given."

He sits up slowly, the amusement fading into something else— something reflective. His hands, callused from sword training though softened by decades of ink and scrolls, reach for mine.

"You are generous. But generosity alone does not build a *waqf.*"

"A waqf," I repeat slowly. "Yes, that. A charitable foundation. Something lasting—something that will remain long after I'm gone."

Süleyman takes my hands and kisses them.

"Let me build a place for them," I continue, striking while the iron is hot. "A warm hall for the old and poor, with broth and bread, and a fire that never dies. I want to leave something behind that makes a difference in the lives of our people."

He looks at me then, seriously. "You've grown ambitious."

"I've always been ambitious," I say, smiling. "But now I have the means. You give me stipends, gifts."

He holds up a hand. "Gifts, yes. But they are still mine. You have no legal personhood, my love. You are still a slave. A slave cannot build mosques or soup kitchens. A slave cannot own land. She cannot endow a waqf."

The words strike like ice water poured down my back. After all these years, it no longer occurs to me that I might still be property. I sleep in the Sultan's bed. I am the mother of his sons. I wear garments sewn with silver thread. But in the eyes of the law, I am nothing. Owned.

I blink slowly. The word slave does not sit easily in my mind anymore. Not after all this time. Not after he has emptied his court for me, banished women for me, stood up for me against everyone.

Tears begin to blur my vision, head lowered, ashamed of the hungry ghost threatening to engulf me. I want for nothing, living in luxury in a time that many suffer lives of misery. And yet, I cannot help feeling the unfairness of my circumstance.

"It means this much to you," he asks, soothingly, stroking my cheek, "to help others with your projects."

"Yes, it does," I reply, holding my head high.

He remains quiet for a long time. I'm not sure what I was expecting him to do—say that he would do the projects in my memory, perhaps.

He stands abruptly, crosses the room and takes parchment and ink. His voice is calm but formal when he speaks as though delivering a decree to the court.

"As of this moment, Hürrem, the Sultan of my heart, is no longer my slave, but a free Muslim woman under the eyes of Allah."

I don't know whether to laugh or weep. I am free. The word flares through me like flame. I throw myself into his arms and kiss him— his brow, his cheek, his hands.

"Thank you," I whisper. "I will build them a hall, a bath, a fountain."

"You shall build as many as you desire," he says, kissing the corner of my mouth. "Let the world know your name."

I dance about the room, twirling like a schoolgirl. Aleksandra would scold me if she saw. But I don't care. My body belongs to me. My soul is my own. I can give in my own name. For the first time in twelve years, I think of my name. And the only answer is Hürrem.

In the days that follow, I float through the palace like a feather caught in an updraft. I visit the scribes. I ask questions of the Chief Eunuch. I send for architects. My mind races with possibilities: a mosque with my name, a fountain that sings to the weary, a kitchen whose smoke will rise in praise.

But joy is never allowed to last too long in a place like Topkapi. As is often the case, it is Mahidevran who yields the knife. To my surprise, Mahidevran was happy when she heard of my manumission. That should have been the clue that something was amiss.

"Süleyman has finally tired of you," she smirks, her eyes happy. She is nearly glowing.

"What are you talking about, Mahidevran?" I almost walk away from her without waiting for her answer, but her happiness makes me leery.

"He has freed you. Now he must take another woman," she replies.

I cock my head at her, not grasping her meaning. And then it hits me. I turn at a run, sprinting as fast as my slippered feet will carry me, Mahidevran's laughter echoing behind me.

I keep repeating over and over in my head. How could I be so stupid? Briefly, the thought crosses my mind that Süleyman must have thought of this and done it anyway—maybe he has tired of me. I push that thought away. No, he must not have realized.

I arrive outside his door, breathless. The aghas inform me that I must wait; several viziers are in with the Sultan. I wait, tapping my foot against the cobblestones. I pace, back and forth. Panic is rising by the second. Minutes feel like eternity. Finally, the viziers exit, bowing to me as they pass. I ignore them. My thoughts too scrambled for anything but the task at hand.

I enter in a rush. Süleyman turns to me, surprised to see me so pale.

"Hürrem, what is it? Are you ill?"

"Süleyman," I stammer, my voice trembling. "You freed me."

He smiles faintly. "Yes. And it pleases me to see your joy."

"But I am now a free Muslim woman," I push on, "and I cannot therefore share your bed. It is *haram*, forbidden."

He laughs then, full and deep. "Indeed, it is haram." He approaches me then, kisses my nose.

I look into his eyes and see only love. "Make me your slave again, Süleyman. I would rather be your concubine again than risk Allah's displeasure. Rescind it. I don't want it—my freedom. What good is it if I cannot be yours?"

He looks down at me, his face unreadable. Then he lifts me in his arms, my feet dangling in the air, and twirls us about his room.

"No. You will never be a slave again."

"Then what will we do?" I ask, my voice cracking.

He sets me down gently, folding me into his arms, kissing my cheeks, my lips. "You have made me happier than I dared dream. Fear not, my love. I have a plan."

"I don't understand," I say, looking into his face from inches away, fear betraying itself in my eyes. "What plan?"

He says nothing—only smiles at me, that infuriating, knowing smile.

"You will have to wait, impatient one," he teases. "Now go, Hürrem, my good Muslim woman."

If he had not been so loving, I might not have left. But I trust Süleyman—perhaps he had already realized his mistake and written to *Şeyhülislam*, the supreme religious authority for permission to take a free Muslim woman as a concubine.

I resolve myself to wait, though patience is not my best quality. I spend most of my time in my chamber, far away from Mahidevran and her cackling.

"Is it true?" Aleksandra asks me one night, tears in her eyes. "Mahidevran is telling everyone that you are to be expelled from the palace."

"I am going nowhere," I promise her. Though I assuaged Aleksandra's fears, mine still linger, and will until once again nestled in Süleyman's arms, warm and secure.

Chapter 29
Haseki Sultan

The wait is interminable. I stay mostly locked away in my chamber, venturing out in the gardens with the children, but staying away from the courtyard of the harem, where Mahidevran has been holding court since the announcement of my freedom, certain of her impending ascension.

Süleyman stays away for weeks. He is not gone from the palace; he is just keeping his distance. I send him notes, anxious for his plan to take effect, whatever it may be.

You look at me, then turn away,
What secret keeps your heart at bay?
If love still lives behind your eyes,
Why does your silence feel like lies?
Hold me, before the distance grows.

He writes back after each note with a single cryptic word: Patience.

It is a beautiful morning in late April. The breeze drifts in from the Bosphorus, cool and clean, laced with the salt of distant shores. That breeze—sometimes tender, sometimes sharp—seems to know secrets I do not, as if it had just come from Süleyman's side, and lingers near me to deliver a breath of him.

Melek Kalfa delivers the summons. "Hürrem Hatun, His Majesty requests your presence in the early afternoon."

I spend the morning in the hammam. After weeks of absence, I plan to be perfect for my love. I bathe until I am brushed smooth and perfumed in sandalwood and musk, a heady mixture preferred by Süleyman. I dress in his favorite, a lavish red gown with layer upon layer of silk interlaced with a deep crimson velvet. A red veil, pearls delicately woven into the hem, completes the ensemble.

I follow Melek Kalfa through the quiet halls. At midday, most concubines are at their lessons and the harem courtyard is empty. My slippers barely make a sound against the polished floors. I am led not to Süleyman's chamber, but beyond, down corridors that are forbidden to the women of the harem. Melek Kalfa is eventually replaced by the Chief Eunuch as we continue our journey out of the inner courtyard reserved for the Sultan's harem and into the outer courtyard, where viziers, ambassadors, and various court officials scurry about their tasks of administration of the Empire.

My heart beats faster with each step. I hold my veil to ensure discretion. We walk past an open garden, lined with janissaries, their white caps gleaming in the sun, to a domed building at the far end.

When the doors open, I nearly stop in my tracks. The room is soft with lamplight and the golden glow of candles. The scent of rosewater and sandalwood hang in the air. Small windows in the upper ceiling allow in little light, streams crisscross midair and pool in the center of the room.

There, at the center, stands Süleyman. He is dressed not in the casual robes of a lover, nor the armor of a Sultan, but in formal ceremonial garments. A deep emerald kaftan with gold embroidery wraps around him, and a tall white turban crown his head. He looks every bit the ruler of an empire.

But when he looks at me, I see only Süleyman. The man I have loved since the moment he first turned his gaze toward me. The man who has changed my fate.

To his left stands the Şeyhülislam, the chief religious authority of the Empire. An imam stands beside him, holding a small Qur'an in his hands. The Grand Vizier Pargali Ibrahim Pasha stands on the right.

Süleyman steps forward and offers his hand. "Come, Hürrem," he says softly. "Come take your place beside me."

The ceremony is brief, but every word hits a cord deep within me. The imam recites verses from the Qur'an about union, mercy, and love between husband and wife. He asks me if I consent to the marriage.

I lift my eyes to Süleyman and answer with my heart: "Yes."

A hush falls as the imam pronounces us man and wife, in the name of Allah, the Merciful, the Compassionate.

The witnesses, Ibrahim and the Şeyhülislam himself, sign the marriage contract. Süleyman offers the bridal gift. It is a symbolic sum, far more than any woman could ever need, a gesture of honor and respect.

He steps forward and cups my face through the veil. "From this moment, you are no longer Hürrem Hatun," he says. "I declare you Hürrem Sultan, the Haseki Sultan, my lawful wife."

Tears of joy gently trickle down my face. I smile through them. "Allah has heard the prayer I never dared to speak."

Ibrahim offers his congratulations to his Sultan, though I hear the insincerity in his words.

Şeyhülislam comes forward and turns to me. "From concubine to consort, by the will of Allah and the hand of the Sultan, you are now the honored wife of the Padishah. May your union be blessed, your heart steadfast, and your place among the righteous secured."

I bow to him. "I am most honored and pledge to dedicate my life to the welfare of our great Empire."

"*Inshallah*," he replies with genuine pleasure.

We walk back through the courtyard, smiling brightly with joy.

"Süleyman, this is more than I thought possible."

"There is no law that forbids a sultan from taking a free woman as his wife. It is rare. It has not been done in centuries. But I am the Lawgiver. If I choose to make you my wife, then it shall be so."

I have walked through fire to reach this moment, though I did not know it until this very second. I am no longer slave, nor even favorite. I am something no woman in this harem has dared to dream: wife to the Sultan of the Empire. But at what cost, I shudder to imagine.

"As happy as you have made me, I fear the result," I admit to Süleyman.

He takes my hand and kisses it. "Let them fear what they cannot stop. You have carried my sons. You have held my heart. You have served this palace with wisdom and fire. Why should I not honor you as you deserve?"

"I am yours, until my dying breath," I declare.

Süleyman pauses then. "And I am yours. But I warn you," he pauses to look at me, "your dying breath had better be far in the future. I expect much from my wife."

And with that one sentence, the world shifts again. He squeezes my hands, almost too hard, a fleeting look in his eyes that is hard to place—fear, perhaps desperation. It has not occurred to me that he genuinely needs me as much as I need him. My eyes fill with tears. Not of sorrow, but something heavier: gratitude.

We head straight to Valide's chamber. She is sitting on her divan, working on a complicated piece of embroidery. She looks at her son with love and a little apprehension. We have never stood before her together in all these years.

"Süleyman, what joy to see my son in the afternoon. This is unexpected."

"Valide, I have come for your blessings on this most glorious of days. I have taken Hürrem as my wife."

Valide doesn't immediately reply. The seconds tick on. I see the tightness in her jaw when she looks at me, the way she sits, stiff, her embroidery left untouched in her lap.

"I do not support this," she says, her voice low.

She lifts her gaze to him slowly, searching his face. There is silence. She stares at him for a long moment. Then her shoulders slowly lower, her voice softens—not with defeat, but with the heavy grace of a mother choosing loyalty over pride. Eventually, she lets out a long sigh and regains her composure.

"You are the Sultan. If you have chosen this path, then I will not be the one to stand in your way. History will judge you—but I am your mother. And I will stand beside you."

"That is all I ask," he replies, a little stiffly.

"Then may Allah bless your union. And may He grant me the strength to face the court when they hear of it."

And they will.

As Valide orders festivities to be prepared in the harem, Süleyman and I inform our children. They all bow low to their father, even little two-year-old Cihangir, and then kiss us both. Mihrimah is brimming with pride—you'd think it is she who has been married this afternoon.

Süleyman retires to his chamber with my promise that I will see him tonight. I have a whole world to face before then. In the hours to come, I will face the fury of the court, the whispers of the kalfas, the glares of the concubines.

The harem courtyard has been hastily decorated with freshly cut flowers. The scent of saffron and pomegranate fills the halls. Musicians play softly. The entire harem is assembled before I arrive.

Valide Sultan sits on a large divan in the center of the raised mezzanine. Hatice Sultan is hastily summoned and sits with her daughters to the right. Mahidevran and her entourage are comfortably seated just beside her. The right side of the mezzanine is replete with royals and their attendants, leaving the left side of the dais empty. In the rest of the hall, concubines sit at low tables, enjoying the festive spirit.

I enter the main hall, dressed in my red wedding gown, veiled as a bride. Mihrimah is by my side, looking like the Sultan princess that she is. Aleksandra stands a step behind, her eyes shimmer with emotion. We both know something immense is coming. My remaining concubines trail behind, heads held high. They have been loyal to me and now feel rewarded—they serve the wife of the Sultan, and as such, they too have been elevated.

I chance a glance at Mahidevran as I walk. She is cheerful, perhaps thinking this is my farewell dinner. I reach the center of the room and stop, so instructed by Valide. The music fades. Conversations cease. The harem holds its breath. They sense something is about to happen. Valide rises and walks to face me.

I bow to her, knowing what the next step will cost her pride. My entire entourage bows low to the Queen Mother. Her stern face softens at my show of respect.

The next moment should be engraved in the history books. Valide Sultan, in all her elegance, bows to me. Audible gasps rise like an army of bees, the air feels electric.

Valide makes her declaration, not in whispers but with the full authority of her imperial voice. "Hürrem Hatun, you are a free woman. Slave and concubine no longer." The gasps reach a crescendo. Undeterred, she continues. "And today, you have been elevated to legal wife of the Sultan. From this day forth, you are Hürrem Sultan. From this day forth, you are Haseki Sultan, the most favored, so declared by Sultan Süleyman Khan."

She steps forward and kisses me on both cheeks. "Come Hürrem Sultan and enjoy your wedding feast. Come sit by my side."

The harem erupts with a cacophony of conversations. The court is stunned. That Hürrem, the foreign red-haired favorite, has not only been freed but has become the Sultan's lawful wife. That a concubine, a slave, wears a wedding veil and stands beside the Shadow of Allah on Earth.

The walls of the palace, which usually echo with songs and laughter, now buzz with whispers like a nest of hornets disturbed. The implications slowly dawn on the ladies of the court—the Sultan has married me, now a free Muslim woman, thus elevating me above all others in his household, even the Valide Sultan herself.

I sit on the divan beside Valide. Mihrimah, Aleksandra, and the rest of my household take place of prominence on the left side of the mezzanine. Hatice rises with her daughters and bows low to me. I acknowledge with a smile and a seated half-bow.

All eyes turn to Mahidevran. Her face is hard, her skin gray as if all the blood immediately left her. There is a fine trembling in her hands. She rises slowly, painfully, and faces me. Her rage is palpable. And then Mahidevran loses whatever remains of her composure. She turns and flees, nearly slamming into the Chief Eunuch on her way out. Her entourage rises awkwardly, bows and rushes after their mistress.

The music resumes, though it can barely be heard above the chatter. I pick up snippets of the conversations.

"A wedding?" one of the older concubines mutters to another. "Not since *Orhan Gazi* has a sultan taken a legal wife."

"It must be sorcery," another suggests. "No woman seduces the sultan so thoroughly without enchantments."

"Poor Mahidevran," says a third, "she was saying just yesterday that Hürrem would soon be leaving the palace for good."

Gradually, dinner is served, lambs roasted on spits, trays of dates and spiced almonds, mountains of saffron rice, delicate desserts, rose sharbat.

After dinner, one by one, each concubine rises to pay their respects, curtseying to me—Hürrem Sultan.

And on this night, for the first time in my life, I lie beside my husband, not as a concubine, not as a possession, but as a woman chosen and cherished.

Lying in bed, his hair mussed from our lovemaking, the only light coming from a single oil lamp, casting flickering shadows across his face, he says quietly, "You are mine." He nudges his nose into the crook of my neck, scenting me. "And I am yours," he adds, barely more than a whisper.

It is not lust that binds us, not desire alone, but something more dangerous. Love. Partnership. History itself.

As we snuggle together, I think of all the women who have come before me. The silent beauties tucked into corners of the palace, remembered only in poetry or rumor. I think of Mahidevran, clinging to her son and the hope that he will sit on the throne after his father. I think of Valide Sultan, whose power will pass to me when her days are ended.

And I think of the world beyond these walls, the world I now have the power to change. From average American teenager to slave in a lost world, concubine, mother, I now stand as Hürrem Sultan, the legal wife of Süleyman the Magnificent, and the most powerful woman in the Empire.

Chapter 30
Mahidevran

It does not take long for the walls of Topkapi to echo with the news of our union. Whoever was not present for the wedding festivities is soon made aware. Not even the gilded latticework of the harem can contain such a fire. Whispers turn into tremors. A sultan has married his concubine.

Even the eunuchs tread more carefully than usual. Servants who had once mocked me in secret now bow deeply. I feel their eyes on my back wherever I walk, but none dare say a word to my face. The whispers do not stop. Some call me the Red Witch. Others whisper that the Sultan has lost his reason. But none of them can touch me now. In my hand, I hold the seal of my own destiny.

And wherever I go, I am announced as Haseki Sultan. I had not grasped the importance of the title until Emine Hatun explains that the Ottoman Empire has never had a titled queen, until me. This has become as much a part of my dynasty as the children I have given birth to.

Mahidevran has locked herself in her chamber most days. When she does emerge, she is dressed only in black, as though in mourning. Perhaps she is. Not for Süleyman—but for her power.

I should feel sorry for her, at least a little, even though she has done nothing but sneer and belittle me. Our wedding has shattered her. For years, she must have told herself that Süleyman's affection for me will wane as it has for others. But now, I am no longer a concubine. I am Hürrem Sultan, legally married, a mother of princes, and elevated above all others. The old order has collapsed. And Mahidevran, once the queen of this gilded cage, has been relegated to shadow.

But if I think for one second that Mahidevran is powerless, I am reminded that I have won but a small victory. The war is far from over.

Aleksandra comes running into our chamber one afternoon, breathless and excited. "Mahidevran appeared before Süleyman and asked for her freedom," she announces, between gasps for air.

"What? Has she been freed?" I ask, concern clear in my voice.

"Apparently, it took the Sultan about one second to answer her— he said no, of course, before telling her to leave his chamber."

I breathe deeply, conflicted feelings leaving in an instant. I may not like the institution of slavery, but at least Mahidevran will not be free to wreak more havoc.

"How do you know what happens in the Sultan's private chamber?" I ask, suspicion plain in my voice.

Aleksandra has the grace to look sheepish. "I heard it from Madga in the kitchens who heard it from the cook who heard it from the imperial taster who heard from the agha who was on guard duty when it happened. But don't worry," she adds hastily, "it is rare that news of anything that happens in there reaches our ears."

I glare at her for a second, just to show my disapproval, then smile, reassuring her that I am not mad. I was disabused a long time ago that anything worth knowing in the palace will remain secret.

"Apparently," she continues, "the fight after was spectacular."

"Fight? You said he told her to leave."

"He did, but she didn't leave," she adds. "She yelled at the Sultan. Can you imagine it? She must have lost her mind."

"And then what?" I am now fully immersed in the story. I know I should not encourage gossip, but it is the main pastime of the harem, and it is time that I should benefit.

"When he would not grant her freedom, she begged to be allowed to leave the palace."

I cannot believe it. "Mahidevran is leaving? Where will she go?"

"To *sanjak* with Mustafa of course. She was always going to leave Topkapi when Mustafa was sent to his province. It is custom."

The news hits me like a ton of bricks. I know that princes are sent to provinces to learn to rule, but I had not thought of the implications. Mustafa will learn to be a leader. Of course he must. He is still a threat. Poor Mustafa, he is actually a very sweet boy. That is only part of my fear. The custom for mothers to accompany their son is the other. I push that thought to the back of my mind. After all, I have many sons and I cannot accompany them all; and, I am more than just a mother, I am a wife.

Mahidevran is not content to leave without one final act. On the eve of her departure, she comes to me. She doesn't knock. She sweeps in, dressed in heavy purple velvet, her eyes lined with kohl. Her voice is steady, but her gaze is hateful.

"Congratulations," she says coldly. "A marriage at last. You must feel so proud. So secure."

I don't answer.

"You've won for now, Hürrem. But don't fool yourself. Süleyman is still sending Mustafa to Manisa. Do you know what that means?"

I do know what it means. Manisa. It had been Süleyman's province. It is the western province closest to the capital and the traditional post given to the heir apparent. In the event of the death of the sultan, the prince in Manisa will receive the news first and has time to rush to the capital and declare himself Sultan before other princes are even made aware—he also has time to issue a decree for their deaths before they know that the race is on.

"That is not a gift," she continues. "It is a declaration. It is the sanjak of the heir. The people know it. The court knows it. The soldiers know it."

I rise slowly to face her. "The Sultan loves all his sons. And the son who proves himself worthy will succeed his father."

Mahidevran's mouth twists into a sneer. "Mustafa does not need to prove himself. He is already the son they expect. You think your marriage changes that? You think your clever tongue and pretty smile have erased the laws of blood?"

"I think the Sultan chooses his heir, not the whispers of old women."

She steps back, breathing hard, as if I had struck her.

"You play at power like a child with a dagger. But know this: the moment Süleyman draws his last breath, I will take that dagger and slit the throats of your sons."

The air goes still, frozen by the vileness of her vow.

"All of them," she whispers. "One by one. I will drown them in their bath if I must. I will see them buried beside their bastard mother."

For a moment, neither of us move.

"Out," I scream at her. "Out, out, out!"

I watch as she glides from the room, her robes trailing like a shadow behind her. It is a shocking thing to say. I fall in a heap to the floor, tears streaming down my face, fear gripping my soul, my breath coming in great hiccupping gasps.

Her words leave a great wound. At dinner with Süleyman, I am silent, my thoughts far away.

"What troubles you, *güzelim*?" he asks.

"I am not feeling very beautiful tonight," I reply.

"Tell me then, what is troubling you?" he asks again.

"Mahidevran," I whisper. "She made a vow. That when you are gone, she will come for our sons."

His arms wrap around me, strong and sure. "Then I shall never leave you," he replies.

But we both know that even a sultan cannot keep death at bay forever.

I stay silent for a long time.

"I cannot punish her for words," he says at last. "Mustafa shall go to Manisa. But one act does not dictate the future."

And with that, he has given me hope. Nodding solemnly, I know better than to push for a promise that it is one of our sons who will succeed him. The rules of the Ottoman Empire dictate that it is the strongest son who succeeds. The ruler does not declare an heir. Manisa is a sign of favor, not a foregone conclusion. And our sons are still young, too young to be sent away.

This move tells me one thing—that the struggle for the future of the Empire has truly begun.

And so, I make my own vow, in the dark: I will build a fortress around my children—not of stone, but of loyalty, strategy, and power.

I will not let them fall.

Not to Mahidevran.

Not to anyone.

Chapter 31
The Harem of Hürrem

Spring slowly emerges from winter. The apricot trees in the gardens bloom with reluctant blossoms, and the sea winds carry the scent of salt and sorrow into the courtyards. Whispers sweep through the palace corridors like a tide no one can hold back. Hafsa Sultan, the Valide, is ill.

I visit her more frequently since Mahidevran's departure. She has never shown favorites—she has been neither kind, nor cruel. Her focus has always remained squarely on her son.

It begins with a cough—dry, sharp, and seemingly harmless. She waves it away with a smile, brushing off my concerned glance.

"Just the dust," she says, and we return to our afternoon.

We sit together in the sunlit alcove, embroidery in hand, golden thread looping through soft silk, our fingers steady even as our thoughts drift.

We speak lightly of the princes' studies, of their tempers and talents, of which young vizier might one day be worthy of Mihrimah's hand. She laughs, thinking of Mihrimah—strong, proud, certain to rule her husband one day—when comes another cough. Then another. She presses a handkerchief delicately to her lips.

At first, it passes quickly—just a moment, a pause in conversation. But over the days that follow, the fits become more frequent. They come suddenly, interrupting her mid-sentence, stealing her breath, making her grip her embroidery frame just a little too tightly. She insists she's fine, ever proud, ever dismissive, but I begin to notice the pallor in her cheeks, the way her shoulders hunch with the effort to hide her fatigue.

The room no longer feels as light. The fire is always stoked now, even when the day is warm. I catch her shivering under layers of brocade. Our conversations falter, replaced by silences she fills with coughing fits that stretch longer than before, leaving her breathless, eyes damp, and cheeks flushed not with health, but fever. Still, she smiles through it all. She is determined not to be a burden. But something is wrong, and we both know it.

By the third week, she can no longer leave her chambers. The court physician comes and goes with his head bowed, his silence a grim omen. Despite all the herbs, tinctures, and the prayers whispered in her name, Hafsa Sultan weakens with each passing day.

I enter her chamber one morning. The room is dim, lit only by the soft glow of oil lamps. The scent of rosewater and camphor hangs in the air. She lies against silken cushions, her skin as pale as parchment, her eyes hollow but watchful. When she sees me, a faint smile flickers across her face.

"Hürrem," she says, barely more than a whisper.

I approach slowly. "Valide Sultan."

"Sit with me."

I kneel at her side, careful not to touch her unless she wills it. But she reaches out, her fingers brushing mine.

"He will be lost without me," she says. "My son. My Süleyman."

A tremor passes through her voice, and her eyes glisten with something I have not seen in her before—fear.

"You must care for him. Promise me. Not as a wife to a husband, but as a mother to a child."

I take her hand fully, pressing it to my brow. "I swear it. As long as I live, I will guard him."

She nods, her strength spent. "Then I go in peace."

Three nights later, Hafsa Sultan passes away peacefully in her sleep.

The palace bells toll—low, mournful, unrelenting. Even the sky seems to bow in sorrow, veiled in thick clouds that dim the sun's golden gaze. It is as though the heavens themselves grieve the passing of the lioness of the Ottoman court. The Queen Mother is gone.

I weep, more than I expected to. In Hafsa, I found fragments of my mother, bits and pieces that reminded me of home. For the past fourteen years, she has been the only mother I had. And for the first time in too long, I think of her, my mother, Sarah. I wonder if she has died too, alone, questions left unanswered; my tears turn into a river, and the wound in my soul opens into a vast chasm of pain.

The harem grieves separately from the public, as it must. Within our veiled world, I order a month of mourning. There will be no music, no dancing, no laughter in the courtyards. The fountains are stilled, and the gardens trimmed back into quiet order. Life must wait. Now is the time for the dead.

Every archway is draped in black silk. The tiled halls, once vibrant with light and color, echo with the soft murmur of prayer and the shuffling steps of those who mourn. Eunuchs and concubines bow their heads as they pass her chambers, now sealed like a shrine. The scent of rosewater no longer lingers there—only the quiet emptiness of absence.

Süleyman says nothing for an entire day. He does not receive his viziers. He does not eat. He locks himself behind gilded doors, and I do not press him. But when he emerges at last, his face is gray with grief, his eyes bloodshot, his mouth drawn and silent. He moves like a man walking underwater, as if each breath is an effort. I have never seen him so broken. It is as though someone has carved away part of his soul and left him hollow.

He comes to me at last. He does not speak at first. He crosses the threshold of my chamber like a shadow, then collapses into my arms. Gone is the Sultan, the warrior, the ruler of empires. What remains is a son bereaved—a boy in a man's body, clutching at the only comfort left to him.

"She was the first to believe in me," he whispers against my neck, voice trembling. "The first to call me Padishah, even when I was just a boy trying to grow into my father's shadow."

219

I hold him as he weeps. My fingers thread gently through his hair. I whisper prayers—not just for Hafsa Sultan's soul, but for the grief clawing at his heart. He has always been my strength, the fire that lights my days and guards my nights. But tonight, I am his solace. I give him what he has so often given me: an unwavering presence.

Süleyman remains in his mother's chambers for hours each day. I do not ask what he does there. And every night, he comes to me—sometimes with stories from his childhood, memories of Hafsa's voice or her sharp wit, her pride in his victories. Other nights, we sit in silence, his hand in mine, the room heavy with everything unspoken.

She had been a pillar. A fierce, immovable force in his life, as constant as the moon and just as watchful. Though her judgments were often sharp, her love for her son was unshakable. She had raised him to rule, to conquer, to command the loyalty of men. And now she is gone.

As the weeks pass, color seeps back into the world. Slowly, almost guiltily, life resumes. The bells fall silent. Black is folded away and tucked into cedar chests. Musicians are summoned again after the evening meal, and laughter dares to return to the garden paths.

I miss her. We were never close by modern standards—that was not her way—but she gave me wise counsel. And though she opposed me often, it was never with malice. Even in her doubt, she protected me, and I think she came to see me as an ally and benefit to her son and the realm.

Now, with her gone, I feel the shift. The court has lost its center of gravity, and in its place, something uncertain stirs. But I do not show my fear. I wear my mourning with dignity and keep Süleyman steady, even as the weight of my own sorrow begins to settle. I am not only his comfort now—I must also be his compass.

Süleyman and I have just finished dinner when he calls the aghas at the door. They enter instantly.

"Summon Emine Hatun, Melek Kalfa and the Chief Eunuch," he commands.

I look at him quizzically as they head off on their errand. He arches an eyebrow up, his cryptic self when he has an idea that he is not ready to share.

The three enter his chamber, bowing deeply to their Sultan.

"From this day forward, Hürrem Sultan shall be the official head of the imperial harem." He pauses to wink at me. He is enjoying my surprise.

He continues, "She shall take residence in the late Valide Sultan's grand suite and assume all rights, responsibilities, and authorities associated with this role. Let it be known across the harem. Her will is law."

Thus, the Harem of Hürrem is born.

Within days, I move into the grand suite, with its domed ceiling painted with stars and its windows overlooking the marble courtyard. It had been Hafsa's private domain, filled with her memories and power. Now it becomes mine. I do not claim it with joy but with purpose.

The first act I undertake is to arrange rooms for my older children. Mehmed is given his own wing, worthy of my eldest prince, with a grand balcony overlooking the Hagia Sofia, and a series of suites to accommodate his every desire. Mihrimah receives my former chamber, the walls now adorned with poetry and maps. Selim and Bayezid are given private tutors and assigned their own apartments. Only Cihangir, still fragile in health and spirit, remains in the main chamber with me.

Then I summon the harem staff. Those concubines who have spent years sneering, whispering, and mocking me are brought before me. One by one, I dismiss them.

"The harem is a place of discipline, dignity, and unity," I say. "There is no place for cruelty here." They leave with their heads bowed, some in tears, others in silent fury.

Aleksandra, loyal and sharp, is appointed head treasurer. She has risen from a captured girl to a trusted steward, and I know she will guard the harem's finances as fiercely as I guard its soul.

Emine Hatun remains by my side as my advisor. Her wisdom, calm voice, and knowledge of court politics are invaluable.

With the harem under my control, I turn to the works that have stirred in my heart for years. I send letters to learned imams requesting Qur'an readings to be held weekly in the memory of Hafsa Sultan, open to all. I dispatch emissaries to the mosques, soup kitchens, and orphanages within Istanbul. Food, clothing, and coin are sent to the poor—all paid for from my personal funds, though I do so not in my name but in the name of Allah, the Most Merciful.

Mihrimah accompanies me in planning our first great waqf—an endowment for a hospital and school near the city walls.

"It must be for girls too," she says, her eyes bright with purpose. "They must learn, as I do."

I kiss her forehead. "Yes, my love. For the daughters of the Empire."

My days become full—meetings with the wives of state officials to expand the sewing circle or arrange for more donations to the soup kitchens, sessions with the stewardesses of the harem to review issues of discipline or the spending of the harem funds. I rise with the call to prayer and do not rest until the palace lamps dim.

But in the quiet hours of night, with Cihangir nestled close, lullabies drift from my lips in the language of my childhood. And I reminisce, thinking of the girl in chains—foreign, trembling, defiant. I remember the pain: of being torn away from my world, of hunger gnawing like a second soul, of the mocking laughter that followed me through the corridors like a shadow.

I remember Mahidevran's eyes, sharp as daggers, her voice like silk stretched over venom. Her threats, her slaps, the cruel games cloaked in ritual and custom. Every kindness was a prize. Every breath, an act of resistance.

Survival was not granted. It was seized—day by day, hour by hour—for a seat at the table, for the safety of small, beating hearts, for the right to dream.

And now I stand at the heart of the Empire.

The harem, once my prison, is now my throne. Its marble halls echo not with laughter at my expense, but with the footsteps of those who seek my counsel. The same walls that once loomed around me now rise as a fortress shielding what I have built. The same chambers that confined me now bloom with purpose, with strategy, with power.

The women who once turned their faces away now bow their heads—not in fear, but in respect. They follow me, not because they must, but because I have given them something to believe in: stability, dignity, direction. My leadership has shaped this place not in cruelty, but through vision. No longer a cage of silks and secrets, it is a court of strength, a womb of power—and I its unshaken center.

This is the age of Hürrem.

Chapter 32
Power is Power

The banners of war fly again in the courtyard, and this time, they point east—to the Safavid Empire. Süleyman prepares for a monumental campaign, his sights set on Tabriz and the glimmering city of Baghdad. He decides to take with him not only his most seasoned generals but also two of his sons, Mehmed and Selim. It is time, he says, that they see the reality of conquest—not just the pageantry of court life, but the blood, grit, and weight of the Empire.

Before his departure, we spend long hours in the serenity of my private chambers. The suite that once belonged to his mother is a place of comfort for him. Draped in opulent silks, the chamber is filled with the sweet aroma of amber and sandalwood, and the warm murmur of my voice soothes his war-hardened mind. But tonight, a different matter causes his unease.

"Ibrahim grows restless," he confesses one evening, lying with his head upon my lap. "He has become bold—too bold. Foreign envoys say he whispers that he is the shadow of my throne, as powerful as I am."

My fingers stroke his hair, calming him. "And does a shadow forget it needs the sun to exist?"

Süleyman looks up at me, his eyes dark and troubled. "He forgets much lately. His arrogance is blinding."

I say nothing more. I know that pressing the matter will only make him withdraw. But in my heart, I fear. Ibrahim's ascent has long been a threat not only to Süleyman's power, but to my children's future. He controls the military, and I do not believe that a coup to place Mustafa on the throne is unthinkable to him.

Süleyman makes one final decision before leaving the capital: he appoints Mustafa to oversee Istanbul in his absence. It is both a test and an acknowledgment. I see the danger in this decision. Ibrahim will be with Süleyman on the battlefield and Mustafa will already be in the palace. One single arrow will mean the death of all my children. This campaign fills me with dread like no other.

On the morning of their departure, as the morning sun pours into my chamber in soft streaks of honeyed amber, the family gathers to bid farewell. Süleyman is a grand sight to behold, a lion dressed in a crimson kaftan stitched with gold threads, layered beneath a fine leather vest adorned with his royal *tughra*. His turban is modest by court standards, yet still crowned with a single, magnificent emerald. In his presence, the chamber feels smaller, more intimate than ever.

Mehmed, now nearly a man, stands straight beside his father. He wears a shorter version of Süleyman's kaftan, tailored for movement, with a narrow belt bearing a ceremonial sword—his first. His youthful face is solemn, eyes bright with resolve. Selim lingers a pace behind, quiet as ever, wearing a coat of deep green brocade, the color of olives in the sun. He says nothing, but his gaze is fixed on mine, searching for reassurance.

My heart clenches at the sight of them. I open my arms, and both boys come to me. I hold them tightly, whispering prayers into their ears in turn—for protection, for courage, for safe return. I smooth

Mehmed's hair and kiss Selim's temple, my fingers lingering on their cheeks.

"You are my heart, both of you," I say, my voice thick with emotion. "May you bring honor to your father and return whole to me."

Süleyman approaches me then and bends to kiss me, not with hunger, but with reverence, his lips resting against my brow. I cling to him a moment, unwilling to let go. Süleyman turns back only once before leaving. His eyes find mine. In them, I see the love he will not speak in front of his children, and the weight he bears as father, husband, and emperor. I lift my hand, not to wave, but to give him strength.

Mustafa and Mahidevran return to Topkapi Palace later that day, and the old rivalries stir like embers catching wind. Mahidevran, emboldened by her son's new position, tries once again to resume her quiet war against me. She whispers in corners, tries to summon the old alliances among the concubines and the silent servants who once giggled at my expense.

But things have changed. Mahidevran returns to a united harem. The women of the harem now look to me not with fear or derision but with admiration. I treat them fairly, with kindness. I have improved their food, their rooms, their chances at future beneficial marriages. We host parties in the gardens, outside under the sun, unheard of before my rule. There are no more factions among the concubines. The harem of Hürrem is real—and it is loyal.

Mahidevran, for all her fury, finds herself alone. Despite my hatred for her, I ensure that she is treated with respect, as the mother of a prince. I will give to her that which she would never think of giving to me. A magnificent suite is prepared for her, sparing no expense for her comfort. Concubines are assigned for her care, more than are necessary. Festivities are hosted in her honor. And through it all, she sits sour and bitter.

Even Mustafa recognizes my care for his mother. Every request he makes of me is granted without question. I will give neither him nor Mahidevran any fodder for complaining to Süleyman.

I admit to enjoying Mustafa's company, while watching him interact with his brothers with caring and love. He teaches archery to Bayezid who remains bitter that he was excluded from the campaign—apparently my nine-year-old is more than ready for war. He spends countless hours with Cihangir, who treasures his oldest brother, looking at him with an adoration bordering on idolatry.

While the capital settles into its uneasy rhythm, the Sultan's army carves its way east. I read letter after letter, heavy with dust and the scent of campfires. In them, Süleyman recounts long marches through scorched lands, of traitors unmasked and cities surrendered. The campaign is grueling. Heat and disease thin the ranks, but still they press on. Tabriz falls swiftly, but Baghdad proves a longer fight. During a night raid by Safavid forces, the Ottoman camp is nearly breached.

Süleyman writes to me about Mehmed's valor: "Our son drew his sword with the fury of a storm. He led our defenses while I readied my guard. He struck down an assassin who had crept into the tent beside mine. In him, I see the fire of kings."

Selim, though less daring, proves shrewd in his observations. He notices weaknesses in Persian fortifications, and his tactical mind earns respect. Süleyman, in his letters, acknowledges both sons with pride but also with an eye for the future.

"Selim has no taste for blood," Süleyman writes, "but he sees the field like a chessboard. He understands placement, strategy, weakness in the enemy's supply lines. He'll be a fine general, in his own way."

Bagdad finally falls. Cannons fire over the Bosphorus in celebration. But the cold months are settling in and Süleyman decides to winter in the fallen city, while overseeing its reconstruction.

During those long months, I frequently sit under the stars, bundled in layers of furs to keep out the cold, wondering if Süleyman is staring up at the same sky thinking of his beloved far away. I receive a letter one evening, sealed with his signet and drenched in the scent of musk.

Throne of my lonely niche, my wealth, my love, my moonlight. My most sincere friend, my confidant, my very existence, my Sultan The most beautiful among the beautiful.

His words pierce my heart and fill it with love.

My Istanbul, my Caraman, the earth of my Anatolia. My woman of the beautiful hair, my love of the slanted brow, my love of eyes full of mischief. I'll sing your praises always. I, lover of the tormented heart, Muhibbi of the eyes full of tears, I am happy.

I weep, holding his letter to my chest as though it were him, as though the words could fill the silence of his absence. This is a poem that will be sung in whispers across the Empire.

As winter draws to a close and the early buds of spring emerge, I begin to breathe more fully knowing that Süleyman will soon be home. The long winter with Mustafa in charge of the capital and Mahidevran trying her utmost to stir unrest is drawing to an end. I should know better by now.

It begins with a cough, then a fever, then silence from Aleksandra's room. At first, I assume she merely needs rest. But by the second day, her breathing has turned shallow and labored, and sweat soaks through her pillows despite the cold touch of her skin. She barely has the strength to open her eyes.

Her life is too precious to me to entrust to the palace midwives. Though well-meaning, they lack the skill to treat more serious ailments. I request that the court physician be summoned.

One of the kalfas bows and rushes to deliver the message, but returns shortly after, face pale.

"Şehzade Mustafa has denied the request," she whispers. "He says the palace midwives are sufficient for treating a concubine."

That is all they see her as, a concubine, replaceable. Not the woman who has stayed loyally by my side since the beginning. Not the sister of my heart.

This is Mahidevran's work, no doubt. She is always watching, always waiting for my joy to crumble.

"Summon the Chief Eunuch," I order. "Now."

Moments later, the heavyset eunuch appears at the threshold of my chamber, bowing low.

"I need the court physician immediately," I dictate.

He hesitates. "With respect, I have received instructions from Şehzade Mustafa that the physician is not to be called."

I rise from my seat.

"I am the Haseki Sultan," I say, my voice like steel wrapped in silk. "I hold sole authority in the harem. You will do as I command—or it will be the last command you take in this palace."

His hesitation breaks. He bows deeper, turns on his heel, and disappears on his errand. The physician arrives within the hour.

He examines Aleksandra carefully, administers a bitter draught of herbs and oils, and stays by her side through the night. I refuse to leave her, holding her hand through every fevered dream, wiping her brow with rosewater cloths, and whispering prayers in the tongue of my childhood. She will not die. I forbid it.

The door to my chambers burst open just after dawn. Mustafa storms in, Mahidevran trailing behind him in veiled triumph.

"You had no right," he snaps. "You defied my orders. You went above your station."

I rise slowly, each movement deliberate.

"I have every right," I retort. "I am the Haseki Sultan. I am the power here. You may command the city, but the harem is mine alone."

Mahidevran steps forward. "Your pride will be your undoing."

"No," I say, staring past her to Mustafa. "Do not mistake kindness for weakness. If Aleksandra had died, it would not have been forgotten. Not by me. Not by the Sultan."

Silence stretches between us, taut as a bowstring. Mustafa turns without another word and sweeps from the room. Mahidevran glares, then follows. Only when the door has shut behind them do I allow myself to breathe.

That night, Aleksandra stirs in her sleep. She will live, and that is the only thing that matters.

When Süleyman returns in triumph, the court erupts in celebration. The campaign is a success. Baghdad is his, and Persian power has been checked. But more than conquest, it signals the emergence of Mehmed as a warrior prince. Süleyman brims with pride as he recounts how the crowds chanted Mehmed's name at the gates of Istanbul—the prince who saved the Sultan.

The feast begins at sunset. Süleyman sits on a wide divan, a long, cushioned seat raised upon a dais of polished wood. The divan is draped in rich brocade of deep crimson and gold, woven with tulip and cypress patterns, both symbols of eternal life and imperial power. His ceremonial sword rests nearby, its jewel-studded hilt glinting in the lamplight—a quiet reminder of the power he wields. Two palace aghas flank him. He is the eternal image of royal authority.

His position commands a view of his sons, his viziers and other important state officials invited to celebrate his success. A latticed screen partitions the women. I sit on my own divan, smaller yet still grand, overlooking Mihrimah, Mahidevran and the wives of our guests. The only sight we have is of the Sultan himself—the men mere voices in the background.

Over dinner, Süleyman recounts the journey in lavish detail. Before the gathering, he praises Mehmed openly. "He has my fire," he says. "But Selim has my foresight. Two sons. One sword. One mind. Allah has blessed me."

But amid this celebration, Ibrahim looms large. From his letters during the campaign, Süleyman laments that Ibrahim has grown colder and bolder, often meeting Süleyman's decisions with veiled critique. Even this night, Ibrahim dares to join Süleyman on the dais at the end of the meal, to personally salute each departing guest, as though he were sovereign.

We speak late into the night, as we often do. Süleyman trusts no one as he trusts me. And more and more, his words turn to Ibrahim.

"He was once my shadow," Süleyman murmurs. "Now he thinks himself a second sun."

I do not speak against him; there is no need. Süleyman is angry and sad, the two emotions pulling him in their separate directions. Ibrahim, the man who once swore loyalty with tears in his eyes has grown cold, bloated with power.

"He forgets his power is mine," he continues quietly. "I raised him from nothing."

I offer no reply. The silence between us is agreement enough.

Early one morning a few days later, Süleyman enters my chamber, his expression grim. He comes to sit beside me, heavy with sorrow.

"He is gone," he says flatly. "I had him taken in his sleep. He was buried before the dawn."

I lean into him, reaching for his hands.

"I loved him," he whispers.

"I know."

"I gave him everything," he adds, anger in his voice.

"And he forgot where it came from," I remark, as I kneel before him. "Empires must not be shared, my lion."

Süleyman looks at me then, unshed tears blurring his vision, but resolve etched on his face. "His power was never his own," he says. "It was borrowed from the man who just reclaimed it."

The court is lit ablaze with the news. Grand Vizier Pargali Ibrahim Pasha—Süleyman's boyhood friend, his confidant, the man who had once been called the Sultan's twin—is dead. Strangled in the palace while he slept. No fanfare. No trial. The Grand Vizier is simply no more.

Whispers flutter that I drove a wedge between them. But none dare speak such things aloud in my presence. The Sultan is grieving, and though I am the First Lady of the Ottoman court, I walk with a veil of mourning, not for Ibrahim, but for what he made Süleyman do.

Later, sitting in the garden, the wind tugging gently at my veil, the sound of the fountain splashing against the rocks, I whisper to myself, "He only lived as long as Süleyman allowed it. And he died the moment he forgot that."

With his death, a new chapter in the Empire is set to unfold, one where power and blood, love and loss, are inseparable.

Chapter 33
I Need More Allies

The winds of power are ever-changing in the palace, and though I am the undisputed matron of the harem, the currents shift once again beneath my feet. Süleyman is firmly in control of the Empire, having replaced Ibrahim with weaker leadership—not a good strategy in the long term, but necessary at present to reassert his hold on the council.

Yet danger remains as long as Mahidevran and Mustafa hold any influence. Though Mahidevran's last attempt to sow discord among the harem concubines has failed, I know that the harem is not the final prize. And Mustafa, governing the capital during his father's campaign, has taken well to the taste of authority. The need for loyal allies has never been greater.

Too many years have been spent fighting from behind silk screens, suffering Mahidevran's cruelty, the gossip of concubines, the quiet contempt of the court who still cannot stomach that a foreign slave has become the Sultan's legal wife. And though I have power now, it can be snuffed out in a second. What I need is a strategy that will endure.

I have watched Rüstem Pasha for years. First, as a rising star in the stables, where he commanded with quiet efficiency. Then as a tutor to my sons, including Mehmed and Selim, whom he had trained in discipline, languages, and the arts of governance and warfare. Recently, Süleyman has elevated him to the rank of vizier, an unusual honor for one so young. He is not beloved, but he has the ability to speak without revealing too much. Rüstem has proven himself capable, cunning, and—most importantly—

ambitious. And ambition, in the right hands, can be forged into a weapon.

One morning, I summon him to a quiet chamber off the library, away from prying eyes. He bows low, his eyes sharp as ever.

"I hope I am not intruding, Haseki Sultan," he says.

"Not at all," I reply, gesturing for him to sit. "You've always served the Sultan well. But I wonder, Rüstem Pasha, what more do you want?"

He does not hesitate. "I want to serve the Empire, and to rise as high as I am capable."

"A noble answer," I say, smiling faintly. "And if I told you I could help you reach those heights?"

His eyes narrow. He is cautious, wary. "Then I would be your loyal servant."

"Good," I smile at him. "That is very good."

I study him in silence. He is not handsome, not like the warriors of Süleyman's court. But he is shrewd, and ambition flickers in his eyes like a controlled fire. My plan takes form. Mihrimah is my secret weapon. I do not need a son-in-law for beauty; I need one for power.

I lean forward. "For I expect absolute loyalty from the man I permit to marry my daughter."

He pauses—but only for a moment. "Mihrimah Sultan is the light of the palace. An honor beyond words."

I nod. "You will protect her. And you will remember that you owe your life to me."

He bows deeply. "With every breath I draw until my dying day."

After dinner, I broach the subject with Süleyman. We sit together on the private terrace of the imperial suite, sipping pomegranate sharbat.

"Mihrimah is seventeen now," I begin. "It is time she wed."

Süleyman raises an eyebrow. "Indeed. I have considered it. I will find a noble match."

I place my hand gently on his. "I already have someone in mind. Rüstem Pasha."

He leans back, considering. "Rüstem? He is a capable man. But not of noble birth."

"Neither am I," I remind him. "He is clever, loyal, and devoted to you. He has served our sons, served you, and the Empire. More than any title, he has earned his place."

Süleyman looks into my eyes, and after a moment, he nods. "If Mihrimah agrees, then let it be so."

The next day, I bring Mihrimah to Süleyman's chamber—veiled and robed in soft lilac silk, the pearls in her hair trembling with each step. She bows before her father, and he smiles. She stiffens slightly at the sight of Rüstem Pasha standing in the wings. I cannot help but smile. Rüstem looks shaken—Süleyman must have rattled his cage quite a bit before our arrival.

Süleyman rises from his throne and smiles. "My shining star," he says fondly. "It is time to speak of your future. We have chosen a husband for you. Rüstem Pasha."

Mihrimah bows her head. "As you wish, my father." She is graceful as ever. The perfect Ottoman princess.

Rüstem steps forward and kneels in front of Mihrimah, kissing the hem of her dress. "I am deeply honored, Mihrimah Sultan."

But that night, she comes to me in my chamber, her hands trembling.

"I do not want to marry him," she whispers, her voice small. "He is cold. Calculating. I do not love him."

I embrace her. "Love comes in many forms, my daughter. I did not love your father when I first came to him. Love is born from respect, from alliance, from unity of purpose."

Mihrimah pulls back, her eyes fierce. "But why him?"

"Because we need him," I say. "We are alone, Mihrimah. One day, your brothers will be pitted against Mustafa—and he will not hesitate to kill them."

She shakes her head, tears in her eyes. "He would never. He loves them."

"I have no doubt of his love," I say softly. "I am asking you to become a kingmaker, the power behind the throne," I continue. "Mustafa will kill your brothers one day. You know this. He will have to. He will not share power."

Mihrimah protests. I understand her love for her half-brother. This is a hard lesson to learn.

"It is not Mustafa that I fear. Think of Mahidevran," I say finally. "Think of what she will make Mustafa do, or do herself in his name. If he rises, our family falls. This is not about love. It is about survival."

Tears well in Mihrimah's eyes, but she nods. "Then I will marry him. For you. For my brothers."

The day of the wedding is finally here. A grand affair of silks and silver that dazzles the court. Music pours from every garden and lanterns float into the night sky. The palace gardens are transformed into a spectacle of golden pavilions that shimmer beneath embroidered canopies. Perfumed fountains burble like laughter. Tables bend beneath platters of roasted meats, jeweled rice, sugared dates, and delicacies brought from every province. Peacock feathers and jasmine petals adorn the paths where the bridal procession will walk.

Istanbul itself seems to breathe in celebration. Musicians roam the streets, their melodies threading through alleys and squares. Acrobats flip through the crowds with effortless grace, and storytellers draw children close with tales of love and victory. Bonfires are lit on distant hills, and the roar of joy rises from the city like a blessing. Sumptuous feasts are laid not only for the court but for the people. This union is not just a family affair—it is an imperial celebration.

Dignitaries arrive from every corner of the Empire—governors, judges, foreign ambassadors—all dressed in their finest, bearing gifts that glitter in the candlelight. The court hums with approval, voices weaving praise and expectation like gold thread through brocade.

Mihrimah, regal and radiant in robes of emerald and gold, is the very image of nobility and grace. Her veil glows in the lantern light, and her eyes sparkle not just with beauty, but with resolve. She carries herself like a daughter of the Empire. Rüstem, proud and reserved, accepts the honor with measured dignity. Beneath his composure is something else—a tremor of awe, perhaps, at standing beside her.

The court praises the match with reverence. The Sultan's daughter has wed a rising star—a trusted voice in the Divan, a man destined for power. And though this marriage is political, it is also touched by something deeper. As their hands are joined, I see a flicker pass between them—a promise unspoken, but real.

It is a day the Empire will remember. And I, standing beneath the silk-draped archway beside Süleyman, watch our daughter step into her new life, knowing that she, too, will shape the future.

In the days and weeks that follow, I meet often with Rüstem, quietly pushing him forward, encouraging him to grow his network within the Council, to earn the loyalty of key administrators and generals. I begin hosting private gatherings in my chambers for the wives of influential viziers, foreign ambassadors, and religious authorities, where poetry and politics mingle under the guise of culture.

The harem, once a place of laughter and petty rivalries, becomes a hive of strategy. Aleksandra helps me manage funds for expanding soup kitchens and endowments in the city. Emine Hatun advises me on court dynamics, helping me avoid pitfalls and navigate rivalries.

And with each passing month, Rüstem's power grows. I am careful to seldom mention him to Süleyman. As much as he trusts me, I feel that he must learn of Rüstem's worth from other sources to solidify in his mind the worth of his new son-in-law.

In private, Mihrimah rarely speaks of her husband. She bears her new role with poise, fulfilling her duties at court and hosting functions with elegance. And in time, she, too, begins to understand the power she now wields. For Rüstem, despite his stern demeanor, does not make decisions without her counsel. And in me, Mihrimah has found a teacher in empire building.

With this union, I am forging a political fortress around my family. And though enemies still whisper in corners and plot behind closed doors, the harem of Hürrem now has a new pillar: Rüstem, loyal to his core, and bound by blood to protect my sons.

The Empire has witnessed a union. But I have forged an alliance, one that must now be encouraged, little by little, until my loyal son-in-law rises to the highest seat of power, sitting just below the Sultan himself.

Chapter 34
A Legacy of Light

"Although the world is full of suffering, it is also full of the overcoming of it," I express to Süleyman one night. He would never know of Helen Keller and how I admire her tenacity in overcoming adversity, but his world can still benefit from her wisdom.

"How do you wish to overcome suffering?" he asks earnestly.

"By building," I say boldly, "with your permission."

"May Allah strike down anyone who stands in your way," he chuckles and kisses me lightly on the nose.

And with that authority, I turn my gaze beyond the walls of Topkapi. No longer a mere figure within the harem, no longer the whispered object of concubines or the rival of the jealous Mahidevran, I now walk freely through the palace halls, a woman of power and prestige. The head of the imperial harem, wife of the Sultan, mother to his sons—and now, benefactress of the Empire.

For years, I have sent food and clothing to tekkes and soup kitchens. Now, with my status secure and my authority sanctioned by Süleyman himself, I can act openly and plan to do so with zeal. To further show his support, Süleyman presents me with a new litter, embossed with his own seal on each side, and a handful of guards at my permanent disposal.

I begin a plan for a large complex in Istanbul that will serve both the soul and the body. I summon architects, including the brilliant

Mimar Sinan. Together, we outline plans for what will become one of the great jewels of the city: the Haseki Sultan Complex. It will include a mosque, a soup kitchen, a school, and a hospital— all paid for by my own funds. I have been given a very generous income for years and I have been very frugal, amassing personal wealth to rival that of the richest in the Empire. It will rise beside the marketplace where the poorest gather, its minaret like a torch against the sky.

The harem watches my efforts with a mixture of awe and inspiration. No one has ever seen a woman move with such clarity of purpose. Servants who once laughed behind my back now bend their heads in respect. Even noblewomen in the court, wives of viziers and judges, begin to seek my favor, hoping to be included in my growing web of influence and benevolence.

Within Istanbul, architects are consulted for the construction of new bathhouses and fountains in the poorer districts. A soup kitchen is established, feeding five hundred people twice daily. Rare books are copied and ancient texts preserved for the generations to come. The sewing circle expands to include the wives of the city's elite, their hands stitching garments for the poor. My name, once spoken with envy, begins to carry gratitude among the women of the city. Each new day brings another soul to feed, another girl to shelter, another scholar to support.

Istanbul is not my sole target. Letters bearing my seal travel across the Empire—gracefully penned, deliberate in tone. In Mecca, a women's lodging is renovated under my patronage. In Jerusalem, funds are directed toward the restoration of a weary travelers' hospice. In Cairo, orphaned girls are given the chance to apprentice in embroidery and textile arts. Each act, quiet and far-reaching, extends the reach of my hand beyond the palace walls.

I even turn my gaze toward the West. With Süleyman's blessing, I send a carefully addressed letter to Venice—an invitation to Titian to visit the Ottoman court, to paint the beauty of Istanbul and capture our dynasty's grandeur. A living bridge between cultures, art as diplomacy. Should he accept, the story of our empire will enter the wider current of Renaissance Europe—an enduring legacy not only in stone and charity, but in oil and canvas.

Within the capital, the construction of my complex is a marvel. People come daily to see the work, to whisper about the Haseki Sultan who builds such things. A harem woman—a slave once—now funding a mosque. The idea is revolutionary.

Rüstem becomes my ear in the Divan. Though not yet Grand Vizier, he sits as one of the Sultan's trusted advisors. He reports to me in quiet conversations by the fountain, or in letters tucked within embroidery brought to the palace. He tells me who whispers against my sons, who questions my influence, who still dreams of Mustafa as the sole heir.

At home, I rule the harem with the firm hand of a mother. I have a grand palace built for Mihrimah and Rüstem just beyond Topkapi palace; Mihrimah is pregnant with her first child, and I wish to be close enough to visit. Selim, Bayezid, and Cihangir each have their own tutors and schedules of study and prayer. I review their lessons myself, hiring the brightest scholars to guide them. I decided long ago that my best gift to them was education, but an education steeped in the knowledge of this age and no further.

Most evenings, the family gathers for dinner. Süleyman reclines on cushions, listening as his sons recite poetry or debate philosophical questions. Sometimes Mehmed brings his oud and plays, a young man of both sword and song. Selim, ever clever with numbers and patterns, presents puzzles to solve. Bayezid, bold and fearless, recounts the fights he broke up among the palace pages. Cihangir, sensitive and poetic, sits beside me and quietly ask for my lap, though at ten years of age he is really too big.

These moments bring tranquility to my heart though I know that peace is a fragile thing.

As my complex nears completion, I invite Süleyman to walk the grounds with me. We walk slowly, arm in arm, guards standing at attention around the building site, the call of distant birds and the echo of chisels filling the air.

"You build cities, Hürrem," he says, pride and tenderness in his voice.

"I build homes, my Sultan," I reply. "For those who have none. For the women with no voice. For the children whose mothers are lost. For the sick who have no coin. If we do not feed them, who will?"

He stops and turns to me. "And yet, they call you ambitious."

I meet his eyes. "Let them. My ambition is not for gold, power, or even survival. My ambition is to leave the world softer than I found it. That is not sin."

He leans in and kisses my forehead. "If it be sin, then sin boldly, my love."

Back in the palace, the whispers against me finally fall silent. What once lurked behind lowered eyes and murmured greetings now gives way to genuine smiles and open acknowledgment. Even those who once feared me—those who scoffed at a slave's rise— have begun to admit that my works speak louder than any rumor. The web of lies spun to strangle me now unravels in the face of what I have built.

I am no tyrant, though the harem is ruled with an iron fist. Cruelty is not my nature—it was my teacher. The lash of injustice once tore across my own back; I have known what it is to suffer unseen, unheard. So now, I listen—truly listen— when concubines come to me with grievances. Their tears are not weakness. Their fears are not dismissed. The girls in training are guarded as fiercely as my own children, for I know the weight of terror that powerlessness brings.

Their education no longer ends with embroidery and court etiquette. I have opened doors once bolted shut. The concubines are taught arithmetic, poetry, the art of diplomacy, the history of the world beyond these walls. Knowledge is not just a gift—it is armor. With it, they may become more than ornaments or pawns. They may become women of consequence.

I sponsor dowries for those who prove worthy, and arrange marriages not just for love or convenience, but for strategy— placing trusted women into key households, building quiet alliances across the empire's spine. With every bond forged, every life improved, my reach is extended.

I write letters to governors and provincial administrators on the Sultan's behalf, planting seeds of loyalty—not only to him, but to me, and to the future I am shaping. When foreign ambassadors send gifts to the Sultan, more and more now include small tokens for me: rare perfumes, fine silks, carefully worded compliments. They know what it means to have my ear.

Each day, I work, not to wield power like a sword, but like ink—permanent, calculated, indelible. My tools are not armies or decrees, but persuasion and presence. I govern without a title, yet my influence flows like water through every corridor of Topkapi and beyond. I have become a political force not by demanding loyalty, but by earning it.

And at the center of it all is the man who rules the Empire—my husband, my beloved, my sun. It is in his trust, unwavering and public, that has cemented my place. With his name, I write. With his love, I rise. And with my own hand, I shape an empire that will remember not just the man who led it, but the woman who stood beside him—unyielding, unforgotten.

And yet, through it all, I remain true to myself. In the quiet moments with Süleyman, we laugh, and I dance in his chamber, barefoot and joyful. When Süleyman worries over political matters, I soothe him. When he doubts himself, I remind him of his greatness. I am his mirror, his compass, his moon.

In the intimacy of our nights together, he kisses me softly, whispering, "I have conquered lands, Hürrem. But you conquered me."

I smile tenderly. "Then I shall rule you gently."

Titian, the great master of Venice, finally arrives in the Ottoman capital, not as a subject of diplomacy, but as a guest of the court. He paints Süleyman in full imperial glory, every fold of his robe rendered with reverence. Süleyman is sceptic of getting his portrait painted, as idolatry is contrary to Ottoman values. But he agrees in the end, persuaded that a portrait will build alliances with Western kings.

Titian paints me, too—not in the shadows of the harem, but as I truly am: strong, veiled in silk, a scroll in one hand, a garden blooming behind me. His brush tells the world what words cannot. It is only a portrait, but it is also a message that ripples outward, stroke by stroke, color by color. Through him, the eyes of Europe see us—not as foes, but as rulers, thinkers, human. A message that will endure long after we are gone.

And so begins my true legacy—not just in palaces or politics, not just in monuments of stone, but in lives touched, minds awakened, and a world slightly changed by a woman who was once a slave.

My name is no longer Hürrem, the one who brings joy. It has become Hürrem, the one who carves stone, feeds the poor, and cares for the orphans and widows of the Empire.

From slave to Sultan's wife. From prisoner to protector. I am building something that cannot be torn down. And I'm not finished yet.

Chapter 35
The Shadow of Ambition

Summer in Istanbul unfurls like a silken tapestry, each thread woven with light, scent, and song. The Bosphorus shimmers beneath the sun's golden gaze, its waters rippling with ferries and fishing boats while seagulls wheel and cry above. The air is rich with the mingled aromas of roasted chestnuts, blooming jasmine, and salt from the sea. Cypress trees sway gently in the palace gardens, their shadows dancing across marble courtyards. Minarets pierce the blue sky, their calls to prayer echoing in the warm air like a lullaby. In the evenings, the city glows with the flicker of lanterns, musicians play in hidden courtyards, and the breeze carries the promise of stories not yet told.

Yet for Süleyman, no amount of sunshine can brighten the shadow that lingers in his heart. The grandeur of his conquests and the splendor of the Empire weigh less on his mind than the deepening unease over the one who had once filled him with pride—his eldest son.

Sitting on his terrace one night after dinner, I look at Süleyman, whose eyes are heavy with thought.

"What troubles you, my love?" I ask him, calling him out of his reverie.

"There are echoes that bother me greatly," he responds. "I am told that Mustafa has visited the Janissaries."

"Mustafa has spent years training with them, it is normal that he should visit their barracks," I reply. I have already heard the whole story from Rüstem, so I know to tread carefully.

"I am not objecting to the visit itself, but the Janissaries are said to have chanted Sultan Mustafa. Even that transgression I could bear, for we do not control the hearts of others. What troubles me is that multiple accounts prove that Mustafa did not stop them. He encouraged them; he held court, not as a prince, but a sultan-in-waiting."

"You are the Padishah. No son, no matter how beloved, stands equal to the shadow you cast."

He smiles faintly, but there is no warmth in it. "It is not just the Janissaries. I have received letters, Hürrem. Not just whispers, but written words. Reports on secret meetings. Courtiers bending the knee to my son as if I am already dust in my tomb."

Süleyman is visibly upset. "Mustafa is a loyal prince. I cannot imagine that he would be so bold," I declare, to salve his worry.

"Do not defend him," he snaps. "There is no excuse for such behavior."

Silence falls between us, thick and brittle.

"You are correct, of course." I keep my tone soft, ignoring his rising anger.

He gives my hand a gentle squeeze, his silent apology wrapped in the gesture. I push the conversation no further. Süleyman will have to act. He stays silent for a long moment. Finally, he exhales.

"Loyalty is not only declared; it must be proven, again and again," he muses, more to himself than to me. "I will summon him back. If he harbors treachery, I will know."

"And if he does not, then you give him the chance to prove himself."

Though I would rather let the rumors marinate a while longer than give Mustafa the opportunity to clear his name, my response is supportive. Let it never be said that I behaved badly, even toward my rivals.

Messages are sent, and within weeks, Şehzade Mustafa arrives in Istanbul with his retinue. Mahidevran sweeps in, draped in silks and jewels befitting a queen. She even dares to wear a crown on her head and demands that she be announced upon entering the harem courtyard.

Süleyman keeps himself busy. He shares with me that he is deliberately avoiding meeting Mustafa. He wants to destabilize him, keep him waiting, off guard.

Mustafa uses his time to visit his brothers. I see them laughing in the gardens, practicing swordplay. Even Cihangir joins in as best he can—the brothers crouch low so that Cihangir can swat at them with playful aggression. It warms me to see them. In my secret thoughts, I feel bad for Mustafa. He is cursed to have a scheming mother who, I fear, will be his downfall.

The day is bright. A formal reception is being held in the harem gardens. We are all present, even Mihrimah and Rüstem with their young daughter. We mingle in the shade of blossoming jasmine trees, drinking sharbat. The reunion between father and son begins with warmth and affection. Süleyman embraces Mustafa, congratulates him on the pregnancy of his favorite, and reminisces on the goings on in Manisa. But tension simmers beneath the surface.

Süleyman nods to an attendant who rings a gong, inviting everyone to be seated. Süleyman seats himself on his throne, a sign of how seriously he views the situation. A divan is set for me to sit on his right hand. The remainder of the family sits on plush cushions in two long rows on either side of a narrow garden path.

In an unprecedented move, Süleyman declares loudly, "In the name of Allah, the Merciful and Just, and for the preservation of the order of my realm, I command that all members of my household, high and low, by blood or by bond, make plain their loyalty to me, their sovereign. Let there be no doubt, no shadow of division, for the strength of the state lies in the unity of its house."

Without hesitation, I rise to kneel in front of Süleyman and declare, "In the sight of Allah, the All-Seeing, the All-Just, I, Hürrem, your devoted servant and lawful wife, kneel before my sovereign and my sun. My heart, my voice, my every breath I pledge to your name. I vow loyalty to you alone: in thought, in deed, in faith. Wherever you command, I will go. Whatever you entrust, I will guard. And whosoever dares threaten your legacy or the future of your house, I shall rise against them. Let Allah bear witness to this vow, now and for all my days."

He extends his hand, which I kiss. After me, comes Mehmed, proudly declaring his loyalty to his father. Child after child comes forward and kneels before their father. Rüstem is particularly eloquent, evoking filial piety. Mustafa is next.

He kneels before his father and bows his head. "In obedience to Allah, I pledge myself to you, my father and my Sultan. Your will is my path. Your glory, my cause. In your light, I find purpose. May I always be worthy of the trust you have placed in me."

I glance toward Süleyman and sense his unease—a silent dread that the rumors may be true. There is nothing about Mustafa's speech to elicit such fear, and nothing to dispel it either.

If Mustafa has failed to quell his father's angst, Mahidevran adds fuel to the fire. She approaches Süleyman with a sharp gleam in her eyes. With barely a bow, she declares, "By His will, I stand before the father of my son. I have always honored the dignity of this household, and I now live to see our son raised in your image."

Süleyman stands abruptly. The palace holds its breath.

Mahidevran, bitter and emboldened, cannot hold her tongue. "It is well," she says with feigned grace, "that Mustafa has returned to Topkapi. It has been too long since the heir apparent was allowed his place in the court."

The words echo through the gardens like a slap. Mahidevran has made a fatal misstep. Süleyman's gaze hardens.

255

"You are dismissed," he says, rather cryptically, and leaves without a backward glance.

I wonder if Mustafa realizes the impact of his mother's temerity.

At nightfall, Süleyman summons me. I find him pacing, his fury coiled tight like a snake. The doors have barely closed behind me when he strikes.

"She dares to name him my heir," he booms. "To speak it aloud, as if my death is already written. I cannot allow such boldness."

He moves like a man haunted—torn between the love of a father and the duty of a sovereign. I wrap my arms around him, willing him to be calm. After several tense minutes, he softens, collapsing into my embrace, drowning in his rage. I kiss his lips, using our love to anchor him, to salve what his conscience will not yet name.

Eventually, he sleeps.

But I remain awake beside him, my eyes open in the dark. My thoughts run like blood beneath still waters.

Something broke today. Not with thunder, but with the whisper of inevitability.

What comes next will not be swift, nor clean. It will gather in silence, like storm clouds massing over the Bosphorus.

And when it breaks, there will be no shelter.

Chapter 36
The Heir Apparent

The day wakes serene and golden. Sunlight streams through open windows, a warm breeze blows in from the Bosphorus. But in the quiet, Süleyman paces like a man pursued, his mind clouded with anguish.

In the week since the disastrous display in the garden, Süleyman has remained confined to his chamber. He has refused to allow Mustafa to leave the capital; but neither will he answer his son's request for an audience. I spend my days handling the affairs of the harem and my nights soothing the pains in Süleyman's heart.

"He is too popular," Süleyman murmurs, his voice heavy with fatigue. "Every time he walks through the streets, crowds gather. They call him the next Padishah. Some even call him the living lion of the Empire. He does not deny them. He does not correct them."

I do not immediately answer. This decision must come from him. I am not afraid of being accused of influencing the Sultan; that is inevitable. I am afraid that Süleyman will resent me in the future if I push him to a particular action.

I rise then and go to him, placing my hand upon his chest. "He is your blood, Süleyman. But he is also Mahidevran's son. And you know better than I how tightly she clings to her dreams."

He does not flinch. "Mahidevran cannot sway him alone. But others may try. The more powerful he becomes, the more he risks being turned into a banner for the ambitious."

"He would not rebel," I say softly.

"But others may rebel in his name," he replies, a grim look on his face.

And now, I understand his fear. It is not only about Mustafa. It is about the shifting tides beneath his feet. The Empire is large, and a young, charismatic prince could become the rallying point for anyone discontented with the long shadow of Süleyman's rule.

"He has done nothing yet," Süleyman says, almost to himself. "And yet I feel the tremors in the earth."

"What will you do?" I ask, in a tone as neutral as possible.

He walks to the small table near the window, where an unfurled map lies in wait—Anatolia stretches across the parchment like the hide of a hunted animal. He stares at it, tracing the line from Amasya to Manisa with a fingertip.

"He cannot remain in Manisa. Proximity to the capital makes his influence too dangerous. I will reassign him."

My pulse quickens. Silence hangs heavy in the room, filled only by the distant cry of gulls and the rustle of garden leaves. The room itself holds its breath.

"Yes," he says finally. "Mustafa will go to Amasya."

For the first time in weeks, Süleyman smiles. The weight of indecision lifts from him. He comes forward to kiss me. Happiness returns to his heart. We dine together and our discussion now moves to other topics, mundane husband and wife chatter. We lie together, a calm and sensuous moment, and Süleyman drifts off into a deep sleep, a slight smile still lingering on his lips.

The decision finally made, Süleyman wastes no time in making the announcement. There is no proclamation, no ceremony. Just a decision—a single stroke of Süleyman's pen—and the entire Empire trembles beneath it. A decree is sent to Mustafa informing him while Süleyman and I breakfast together in his chamber. His soul is light, and he makes me laugh with his stories.

A fury begins to rage outside the doors to Süleyman's apartment. Mahidevran is outside yelling like a banshee, the palace aghas trying in vain to remove her. Süleyman stands. I begin to stand but he stops me with his hand.

"Let her in," he says, voice loud and clear.

Mahidevran enters, face twisted, eyes wild.

"You betray your own blood! You send my son away from his birthright," she hisses.

Süleyman's face is a storm. "Mustafa is not being punished. Amasya is not exile. It is a post of importance. But it is farther from the capital, farther from whispers and plots."

"If there are any whispers, they come from that witch," she says, pointing to me.

Süleyman meets her eyes steadily, his voice holds no hesitation. "The Empire watches Mustafa. He is the son of the Sultan, but he is also dangerous. He gathers men like storm clouds gather thunder. If the world whispers, perhaps it is because they see the truth."

"And who will go to Manisa?" she yells at him.

He does not look at me as he replies. "Şehzade Mehmed will go to Manisa."

The name falls like a stone, its implications rippling through the room.

"You raise Hürrem's brat in the place of my Mustafa?" she asks, incredulous.

"Enough, Mahidevran. Your place here has always been as the mother of my son. Not as my wife. Not as my counselor. Your tongue has cost your son his inheritance, not I, not Hürrem. Your ambitions have pushed my prince to become too bold, too proud."

Her anger collapses into grief, and she leaves weeping loudly.

Mustafa is being moved. After years in Manisa, the prince once called the heir apparent is reassigned to Amasya, far to the east. Amasya is no disgrace—it has housed princes who later ascended to the throne—but Manisa has always been the jewel, the province closest to Istanbul, the proving ground for the future sultan. And my Mehmed is its new governor.

It is a death knell and a coronation in one. I had not asked for it, not even in whispers. The timing, the execution, those come from Süleyman alone.

"Thank you, my Sultan," I kneel before him, kissing the hem of his robe.

"Our son is brave. Kind. The soldiers speak well of him after the Persian campaign. He has proven himself. The people love him. He is ready. Let the Empire see the Sultan's favor."

He kisses me on the forehead before continuing. "It is high time that our sons learn to govern. I will send Selim to Karaman. Our two eldest sons will serve the people, and in time Bayezid will join them." He looks at me then, reassuringly. "Do not fear, my Hürrem, you will have leave to visit them whenever you choose."

As I return to my chamber, I breathe a sigh of relief. Not only for my sons, who will take their rightful place in the line of succession. Not only for Mustafa, who is now sidelined. But for me. Every mother has accompanied her son to sanjak. Without exception. But I am not like every mother.

There will be no sanjak for Cihangir. Ruling a province is a precursor to ruling the Empire, and Cihangir is excluded from the race. I will have to find other pursuits for my youngest son.

Mustafa received the decree in silence, but word spreads quickly of his shattered composure. Servants speak of a goblet flung across the room, of his mother pacing like a caged lioness. But when he appears again in public, his face is carved from marble. Not defiant. Not humbled. Just unreadable.

261

I am expecting Mahidevran when she storms into my room. There was little doubt in my mind that she would come.

"You have poisoned his mind!" Mahidevran spits out, waves of anger flashing across her face.

"The Sultan makes his own decisions, Mahidevran."

She takes a step closer. "Do not play innocent with me. You and your pet Rüstem whisper in his ear. This was your doing. I too have heard rumors—secret meetings, mountains of gold leaving the palace. You lie! I see your game. One by one, you'll destroy all who stand between your sons and the throne."

I stand, calm and composed. "The Sultan favors Mehmed because he has earned it."

I am certainly not going to explain to Mahidevran that those meetings and mountains of gold are for charitable works. She would not believe me even if all the poor of Istanbul were to stand before her and chant my praise.

"You think this is over?" Mahidevran hisses. "One day Süleyman will die, and my son will return. And when he does, your sons will be the first to fall."

"Then I must pray for a long life for the Sultan," I say with chilling calm. "For the sake of us all."

We stand in silence, the weight of our animosity as heavy as the shadows cast by the courtyard's colonnades.

"You think this ends in Amasya?" Mahidevran whispers. "I promise you, it ends in blood."

Before the next call to prayer, Mahidevran, Mustafa and their household depart for Amasya. This is not the end. The war is only getting started. But it is already too late for caution. We have stepped onto the stage of history, and the audience is watching.

I inform Mehmed and Selim the next day. Selim takes the news with ease. He is calm tempered, controlled. He rarely betrays his thoughts. My Selim is a strategist and knows better than to reveal his inner workings aloud. Mehmed is ready. I see it in his eyes, the same fire that burns in his father, tempered by compassion and sharpened by purpose. At first stunned, then proud, then serious.

"I won't fail you," he says.

I kiss his forehead. "Do not think you have won, my son. You have only stepped into the arena. The real battles lie ahead."

He bows to me, understanding more than I realized.

Before their departure, Süleyman holds a grand feast for his sons. We gather in the Sultan's apartment, musicians playing gently in the background. Mehmed and Selim, dressed in full imperial regalia, stand proud before their father.

"My sons, you leave the safety of these palace walls and step into the weighty world of duty. You are not mere princes now—you are governors of my Empire, shepherds of its people, and symbols of its future. Rule with justice, not pride. Listen more than you speak. Know that your name carries mine, and your conduct reflects the throne. Be heirs worthy of a great legacy. Each of you is a mirror of the sultanate. May Allah the Merciful and Just guide your hands, steady your hearts, and keep envy far from your path."

Mehmed and Selim stand tall before their father, eyes full of hope for the future. "I will serve you in all things, my Padishah," they say, in near unity, before bowing low to their Sultan, the images of princely perfection.

The future begins to shift, like sails catching an unpredictable wind. I feel the weight of it pressing against the edges of our lives. My legacy stands at the heart of the great storm ahead. All that I have built—all that I have fought for—now teeters on the brink of change.

The storm is no longer gathering. It has begun. I pray for the strength to guide us through the tempest, to hold the helm steady until we reach the far shore. For what lies beyond may be greater than all that has come before… or it may rise to undo us all.

Chapter 37
The Light That Faded

The wind is cold this morning. Early November brings with it the first sting of winter. Although the fire is roaring away in the hearth, spreading its warmth throughout my chamber, I sit bundled in furs, unable to shake the chill in my bones.

Emine Hatun is relaying news about the construction of my new soup kitchen near Eyüp, when Süleyman enters, a grim cloud hovering over him, eyes tear-stained. Without a word, Emine Hatun backs solemnly out of the chamber as Süleyman kneels before me. His eyes wide with unspeakable sorrow, his hands are shaking badly. He hands me a letter, bearing the mark of the Manisa palace—Mehmed's seal.

He does not need to say a word.

"No," I croak, my voice raw and trembling. "No, no, no!"

My voice rises with each syllable until it cracks the air. My knees buckle beneath me. I crumple to the floor, a screech tearing through my throat as I clutch my chest.

"Not my Mehmed. Not my lion," I howl.

Süleyman tries to steady me, but I shove him away, blind in my grief. My hands beat against his chest, but he endures it, pulling me back into his arms, holding me tightly even as I fight him with everything I have left.

"It was sudden," he chokes. "A fever," he adds between gritted teeth. "He... he called for you."

A sound rises from me that is no longer human—a howl so piercing that birds flee the trees.

"I cannot breathe without him," I sob, collapsing fully against Süleyman, clawing at his robes like a drowning woman reaching for the surface. "He was mine. Mine."

"Ya Allah," I cry, lifting my face to the ceiling as if I could crack the sky with my voice. "Swallow me whole! Take me with him! Take me to the heavens! Let me die beside him!"

I rage and snarl and gnash my teeth, tearing at my dress as I dig deep grooves into my skin until blood wells up, and still I do not stop. The pain is too deep, the sorrow too much.

Süleyman grabs my wrists, but I thrash against him, striking him with my fists, sobbing so violently that I can no longer see. I scream into the emptiness that has swallowed my son, pounding at the only solid thing left—Süleyman's chest—until my strength is spent and my body quakes with exhaustion.

We sink together onto the cold marble floor, a tangled heap of grief, a single knot of raw nerves, exposed and wretched. My forehead presses against his, our tears mingling. There is no palace, no empire, no titles, no crowns—only two broken parents cradling the memory of a boy who once laughed in these halls. A boy who will never again return.

Süleyman buries his face in my hair. "He was brave, our Mehmed," he says. "And kind. The Empire has lost a first among princes."

Süleyman whispers the details of the letter to me. The fever that took Mehmed lasted but three days. The physicians claimed it was sudden and natural, most likely smallpox. I cannot accept such simplicity. My Mehmed was young and strong. The physicians are wrong. The signs were not there—no rash, no pustules. No, I do not believe them. My mind sees the truth.

"She did this," I hiss, eyes red with fury. "Mahidevran. She said she would destroy all of my sons. She vowed that their blood would flow. Now—now she begins."

Süleyman stills beside me. "She would not dare…" his voice trails off, thought unfinished.

Evening after evening, Süleyman returns to my chambers, his face tight with sorrow. Mostly, we do not speak. We simply sit side by side and watch the sun sink behind the palace walls. Some nights, Süleyman stares at the letter again and again, searching for some hint, some clue that this had not been a simple illness. His sorrow has no bounds.

One night, he finally asks, "Do you still think she did it?"

"Yes. But not by her hand. There are always those willing to serve a bitter woman."

Süleyman sighs. "I've ordered an investigation, quietly. If there is evidence…"

"There won't be," I cut in. "Not with someone as clever as Mahidevran. She is careful, calculating. We have other sons; she will not stop."

He nods slowly, resting his head against mine, grief settling between us, heavy and raw.

The following day, Emine Hatun tries to soothe me, but there is no comforting my soul. I sit at my writing desk, hands shaking as I scratch out a letter, each word seething with venom. I cannot bury him in silence. She must know that I will not forget, nor ever forgive.

What have you done to my Mehmed? May Allah look into your soul and see the depths of hell. I swear upon his grave you will not see peace, not while I breathe. I will pull heaven down to avenge him.

I seal the letter with my own signet and give it to Emine. "Have this delivered to Mahidevran by a trusted servant. Have him look into her face when she reads it."

Black cloth hangs from the palace gates. Dervishes are asked to chant for the soul of the fallen prince. Süleyman orders a month of public mourning. Mosques are told to hold prayers daily. The city mourns with its sovereign. Markets quiet, and storytellers speak only of Mehmed's virtues: his learning, his kindness, his swordsmanship, the way he protected the weak and wrote poetry in the evenings. But no words can mend my broken heart.

I haunt the palace like a dark ghost, insubstantial, inconsolable. Even my beloved Cihangir cannot comfort me, though he sits quietly by my side for hours, his eyes shimmering with tears.

I have Mehmed's daughter brought to the palace—just a month old, still so small, so new. I take her in my arms, press my cheek to hers, searching for some trace of him in her warmth, in the scent of her skin. But he is not there. Only silence. Only the ache he leaves behind.

"You will be safe here," I whisper to her. "And you will remember your father. We all will."

That night, sitting alone in Mehmed's old study, breathing in the scent of parchment and ink, I trace the edge of his favorite calligraphy quills. I remember teaching him his letters when he was barely walking, the way he giggled when I called him my "little vizier."

I weep again—silently this time, for I have made a decision. I enter Süleyman's chamber with a soft knock.

"You must send Selim to Manisa," I say, my voice no longer that of a grieving mother, but of a woman who remembers the stakes. "If Mustafa is allowed to return, it will mean the death of our other sons."

Süleyman nods slowly. "Selim is already packed. He leaves at dawn."

My vision blurs. Süleyman gathers me close, trying to hold the pieces of us together. We sit as we had after Abdullah's death, two parents bound not only by grief but by responsibility.

"Mehmed would have made a fine sultan," Süleyman says, his eyes fixed on nothing. "He reminded me of my father. But Selim—Selim is clever. Quiet. Patient. He may yet surprise us."

"I only fear his heart," I reply, "which is softer than Mehmed's ever was."

Süleyman leans over and kisses my hand. "He has your heart. And my ambition. Between the two of us, perhaps that is enough to make him a worthy ruler."

I summon Rüstem to my private chamber while Selim is still on the road to Manisa.

"I will need your eyes in Manisa," I tell him. "Selim must be protected. The snakes will rise now, sensing blood in the water."

He nods. "I will place only my most trusted men around him. Not even air will pass between them without my knowledge."

I grip his arm. "And if anything happens to him..."

"I will know before it does," Rüstem says. "And it will not happen."

Though my grief remains a living thing inside my chest, I force myself back to the rhythms of life for the sake of my other children and grandchildren who need me, and the Empire's women who depend on my works. I order a new soup kitchen to be built in Mehmed's name and a fountain where travelers can rest and drink. I fund Qur'an recitations in the prince's honor throughout the month of mourning.

But in the quiet hours of the night, holding my granddaughter and pressing kisses into her hair, I know that part of me has been buried with Mehmed. He was my star, my firstborn son, and my brightest hope for the future. Now, the road ahead is narrower and more treacherous.

Süleyman takes me to the mosque just after dawn, when the city is still hushed in the pale light of morning. The litter carries us slowly through the empty streets of Istanbul. My Sultan says little on the journey, his expression unreadable beneath the deep fold of his turban. I sit beside him in silence, my hands folded tightly in my lap, wrapped in the same black silk worn since the day the news broke my world.

When we arrive at the mosque, I lift my eyes to the minarets, a beautiful structure, elegant and solemn. The dome rises like a shield to the sky, circled above it by birds whirling and diving.

The scent of incense and cedar meet us as we step inside. In the corner stands the tomb, draped in a rich green cloth embroidered with gold. A silver crown rests at the head of the sarcophagus, "so that all may know he was first among equals," answers Süleyman to my unasked question.

I kneel before the tomb, pressing my forehead to the edge of the marble, reading the inscription below. *Most distinguished of the princes, my Sultan Mehmed.*

"My lion," I whisper. "You were the best of us. Rest now."

Süleyman kneels beside me. "He is with Allah, the Merciful and Just. He is at peace."

I nod, unable to speak. Tears slip silently down my cheeks. "Thank you," I say to him softly. "For bringing me."

He bows his head slightly. "You are his mother. This place is yours, too. You may visit as often as you please."

I glance back one last time. "He was not just mine," I say. "He was ours. And the Empire's. May his name never be forgotten."

And with that, we step back into the world, side by side, beneath the gaze of the heavens.

Chapter 38
The Gathering Storm

The palace is not the same after Mehmed's death. My son's absence is a hole in the very stones of Topkapi, an echo of laughter that has not returned. The air itself seems dimmer.

In every corner, I imagine him—practicing swordplay in the courtyard, bent over calligraphy in his study, chasing his younger siblings with a grin that breaks my heart to remember. His tomb in Şehzade Mosque is a beautiful one, adorned with the finest *Iznik* tiles, its dome high and brilliant like the boy who now rests in its hall. But nothing can replace him. Not for me. Not for Süleyman.

Word reaches me that Mahidevran read my letter. The tension between us now stretches like a taut wire across the Empire. The death of the favored son has left a void, and in its wake, old rivalries rekindle with renewed fervor.

Sitting in my chamber one morning, light filtering through the latticework, casting intricate patterns on the floor, a letter lies open on the table before me, its contents as sharp as any dagger.

I weep for every mother who loses a child. But perhaps Allah reclaims the arrogant first, before they poison what is sacred.

Mahidevran's words are a calculated affront, veiled in piety but dripping with malice. My hands tremble as I read them again, the insult igniting a fire that grief has only dampened temporarily.

I summon Rüstem Pasha, my trusted ally and now Grand Vizier of the Empire.

"She dares to mock my pain," I seethe. "This cannot go unanswered."

Rüstem bows his head. "Her words are cruel, Haseki Sultan. But perhaps we can use them to our advantage."

"Explain," I demand.

"Let her reveal herself further. Those who speak in shadows often stumble when brought into the light."

And thus, I agree to wait, to give Mahidevran enough rope to hang herself. She is not as smart as she thinks she is. She is proud and arrogant and will soon make a mistake from which she cannot hide.

On the surface, nothing changes. Time marches on. There are no attempts on Selim's life. He proves himself a worthy governor, settling local disputes, building a new mosque in Manisa in honor of Mehmed, expanding my soup kitchen program to his province. The people are slow to love him, but he earns their respect.

Bayezid is sent to sanjak in Karaman, Selim's first province. He is less focused on governing than on running through the countryside hunting for bandits, though he does that very well. He still has time to prove himself.

The winds from the east carry more than dust and the breath of distant wars. They carry whispers, venom cloaked in silk, and treason folded into parchment. I feel it—an unease in the palace air, like the stifling pressure before a summer storm. There is a shift in the eyes of some concubines, a stiffness in the backs of once-obedient eunuchs. These are the faint tremors that precede the earthquake.

Mahidevran has begun to move.

Amasya, once her quiet place of exile, has become her nest of vipers. She has made herself indispensable to her son. Şehzade Mustafa loves her fiercely and listens more to her each year. In the shadows of that distant province, where she is both adored and feared, Mahidevran begins to spin her web anew. I have long expected it.

I first learn of her activities from Emine Hatun, who arrives breathless one morning with word from the outer courts. "Letters," she whispers. "Dozens of them, my lady, unsigned."

"To whom?" I ask, though dread has already risen in my throat.

"To many," Emine says. "The Janissaries, the dervishes, even a vizier. Someone is buying loyalty with gold and promises."

Of course she is. I do not need her signature to know her tactics—she has always been the sort to let other people fight her battles. With Mehmed dead and Mustafa still strong, still beloved by the army, she sees an opportunity. With each coin she sends, each word of poison she pens, she builds herself a court of sympathizers, a shadow palace of whispers and discontent.

I will not stay idle. I have eyes in the barracks and ears in the halls of the Divan. When word reaches me that a group of Janissaries have refused a new command—citing loyalty to the true heir—I know Mahidevran's influence has already crossed dangerous lines.

"I doubt that Mustafa knows anything of this," I say aloud to Rüstem during one of our strategy meetings.

"Then he is a fool," Rüstem replies coldly. "And perhaps he not only knows, but sanctions, encourages."

"He is still Süleyman's son," I retort.

"That did not save Ibrahim."

It is true. Ibrahim once sat at Süleyman's side and believed himself untouchable. But in the end, even he had fallen. And now his body rots in an unmarked grave, a warning to those who overreach.

Süleyman is not blind to the unrest. He summons me late one evening, and I find him in his chamber, alone but for the fire flickering low in the hearth.

"Sit with me," he says. "There are things I must know. Things I think only you will say."

I sit beside him, close enough to feel the weariness in his limbs, the grief still etches lines into his brow. "What burdens you, my lion?"

"Mustafa," he says. "The Janissaries still speak his name in the barracks. They refuse orders from Rüstem. There is talk of revolt—small, disorganized—but dangerous."

"Then crush it," I answer simply.

He turns his face to me, and I see the pain there. "I can crush a few Janissaries. But discord is growing in many places, too many to be spontaneous. If I crush them all, I am seen as a tyrant. If I do nothing, I risk my Empire."

"Then only crush one," I offer, hastily adding to avoid misunderstandings, "Mahidevran."

"She has not the power for this," he replies. "I must find the true culprit."

I sigh. The greatest fault of men in this age is failing to recognize that women can be just as dangerous as they are.

I touch his hand. "Then let the truth do your work for you."

He studies me. "Explain."

"Someone is bribing officials. Someone is sending letters. Choose someone you trust to find the source."

I hope he will choose Rüstem, but the truth will out no matter who is given the assignment, as long as they themselves have not been bought.

Rüstem informs me the next day that he has received the commission and authority to question anyone he chooses.

While he is busy with the outside world, I work on the inside one.

I have been aware for a while of discord within the harem when once there was none. That cannot be a coincidence. It takes weeks. Aleksandra, still head treasurer and one of my most trusted allies, uncovers the trail first. Gold disappearing. Concubines fighting in the hammam. Eunuchs smuggling in letters. We work together, Emine Hatun, Aleksandra and I to compile a list of every person within the harem who is suspect.

Rüstem is a brilliant investigator. He tracks down every letter sent to the Janissaries, the dervishes. He compiles his own list of names—traitors to the Sultan who choose to follow the prince. He questions everyone. Eventually, one name emerges again and again: Vizier Cemal Pasha, a man who has always seemed more interested in his own advancement than the laws of the Empire.

Rüstem corners him in the Hall of Petitions with a squad of guards. It is not a subtle move, nor is it meant to be.

Before the Divan, Cemal Pasha confesses to the Sultan. Mahidevran has sent him bags of coin and letters sealed with her own ring. He has arranged for her messages to be delivered to sympathetic soldiers. He has withheld intelligence reports from the Sultan. Süleyman, his face carved from marble, listens attentively and does not speak until the end.

"She would bring the Empire to its knees to raise her son," he says softly, dangerously. "She forgets who built the Empire in the first place."

Our response is three-pronged. I dismiss everyone in the harem suspected of being complicit. There are wails and cries as concubines are forcibly ejected. They will be given no advantageous marriages. They will simply be exiled.

Rüstem is harsher. Janissaries are flogged in their barracks until their blood flows into the sand. This is the best way to ensure future obedience.

Süleyman has Cemal Pasha beheaded, his head placed outside the main gate of Topkapi to rot in the summer heat. He sends an imperial warning by letter to Amasya—any further acts of sedition will be met with blood.

Mahidevran, ever proud, denies the accusations in a long and venomous reply to Süleyman that he reads to me late one night. She calls the confession a fabrication, blames me—of course—and Rüstem, and anyone else who has ever breathed the air of my favor.

But Süleyman has heard enough. He exiles Mahidevran—she is never again to set foot in the capital. She is never to leave Amasya without his written permission. Every guard in Amasya is replaced with guards loyal to him, to keep watch over the disloyal son and his scheming mother.

The tension does not vanish—the court is not so easily calmed—but it lessens. The Janissaries, shamed by their association with the traitorous vizier, return to order. The harem, once divided, is now united once again behind me. And my children, though scarred by their brother's death, are safe. For now.

Sometimes, in the dark, when the palace is quiet and even the lanterns outside flicker low, I still imagine Mehmed. I see him in my dreams, laughing on the steps of the Şehzade Mosque, calling out to Selim to hurry, always impatient, always leading the way.

I will never stop mourning him. But I will not be destroyed. Not when I still have sons to protect. Not when the Empire still needs me. Not when the shadow of Mahidevran still lingers, hungry and dangerous, waiting for the day Süleyman closes his eyes forever.

She will not take the future from me. I have lost a son. But I will not lose the war.

Chapter 39
Mustafa – Part 2

The Empire has grown quiet in the years following the death of Şehzade Mehmed. Though the palace still bustles with ceremonies and the eternal rhythm of court life, a heavy silence has settled beneath the glittering surface. Rumors about Mustafa have not faded. Whispers pass between servants, scrawled letters are exchanged between courts, and foreign ambassadors watch with sharpened interest. Many believe that the Şehzade in Amasya is merely waiting for the right moment to make his move.

I know better. Or rather, I fear worse. Süleyman has grown cautious with age and increasingly consumed by uncertainty. We have spoken often of Mustafa in recent years, our private conversations cloaked in candlelight and suspicion. Though Süleyman never openly accuses his son of treachery, he has become more reticent about his future and more withdrawn from his past.

War erupts again with the Safavids. Their rebellion is bold, their alliances more dangerous than before. Süleyman resolves to lead another campaign east, though age weighs upon his shoulders and slows his step. Still, the imperial tent is packed, the Janissaries prepared, and his household sets out once more to follow the happenings at the edge of the Empire through letters.

Süleyman discusses the campaign with me late into the night. And when he forgets a detail, I remind him of it with gentleness. Selim will accompany him on the campaign as will Cihangir, not to fight of course, but to give our youngest son a chance to be of use to his father—though his health is poor, he badly wants to contribute to the esteem of the Empire.

Before departing, Süleyman issues orders to Mustafa: remain in Amasya. The message is clear. His presence is not required. His loyalty will be tested not in battle, but in obedience. "The Janissaries love Mustafa too much," he explains to me. "I will not add fuel to the fire."

I see the written order with my own eyes, my heart clenching at the implication. This is not merely a military campaign—it is a game of dynastic chess, one Süleyman can no longer delay.

In many ways, he is protecting his eldest son. I have no doubt of his love for Mustafa. It is Rüstem who explains to me another reason for Süleyman's fears. "A crownless coronation," he says. In modern terms, a coup d'état.

Rüstem Pasha, as Grand Vizier, will lead the war effort. He rides ahead, as winter gives way to spring, to defend the Empire against Safavid raids. He writes to me nearly daily. I read each of his reports carefully, my fingers trembling only once, when he speaks of letters intercepted between Mustafa and provincial commanders. Nothing seditious—yet. But the air smells of ambition, and ambition has a cost.

By early fall, Süleyman leaves the capital with a large contingent of Janissaries and frontier *Beys*. Cihangir, too ill to ride his horse, accompanies his father in a gilded carriage, his personal physician staying close in case of need. Selim will join them in camp.

Just weeks into the campaign, a letter arrives in Süleyman's tent. It bears the seal of Mustafa. The prince writes of a plot. He claims that the Sultan is in danger, that he has intercepted information suggesting an assassination attempt. He has no choice, he writes, but to ride to his father's side, with his own personal guard. It is not defiance—it is loyalty.

Rüstem writes to me that Süleyman read the letter in silence. The parchment trembled in his hands. His viziers waited, holding their breath. He adds that Süleyman did not respond right away, instead, he called Rüstem to his side, asking his opinion.

"I told him," he writes, "that there is loyalty, and there is ambition. The difference is in timing."

Rüstem is not the only one who writes to me. Süleyman sends me frequent letters. In one, the words grow slanted and heavy with emotion.

I do not sleep. The stars above my tent blink like the uncertain eyes of destiny. My soul is unsteady, Hürrem. I have heard Mustafa is coming. Not alone, but with the full might of his personal army. The men love him, chant for him. I fear what it means. I fear my own blood.
—Süleyman

Thus, before an official reply could be sent, Mustafa arrived. He rode at the head of his own army, his standard flying in the wind. The dust of Anatolia still clung to his clothes. The men he brought were loyal to him alone, veterans of his governorship, soldiers who had long whispered his name in place of the Sultan's.

Süleyman saw this and understood. Mustafa may have believed he was offering his strength to protect his father, but to the Sultan it looked like a coup unfolding before his eyes.

The imperial tent was readied. The guards took their places. Süleyman issued the order. When Mustafa entered the tent, bowing low before his father, the bowstring was pulled tight. In moments, the prince lay dead.

I learn of it all in a letter, penned by Süleyman.

The courier delivers two letters to me, with instructions to place them personally in my hands and not those of any servant. The first, from Süleyman, is short and heavy with grief.

My Hürrem,
The stars of my life grow dim. Mustafa came to me in arms. I had no choice but to defend what I have built. It is done.
Pray for me.
—Süleyman

The second letter, from Rüstem, is longer, more analytical. It details the events with a tactician's eye. It offers no regret, only confirmation that the act has preserved the Empire.

I sit with both letters clutched in my hands, my fingers trembling.

After all these years, the fears and attacks, the worry for the safety of my sons, it is over. I did not ask for this; I never connived to make it a reality, though I have known that this was always going to be the outcome. Mahidevran made sure of it.

The news strikes the palace like a storm. Concubines gasp behind curtains. Eunuchs whisper in doorways. Mustafa—the beloved—is dead. Strangled by his own father's command. But grief is a bitter vine, and it wraps tighter still.

A month after Mustafa's death, I receive another letter. It is from Manisa, but not from Selim. It is a palace courier bearing a message from the physicians: Cihangir has succumbed to illness. His curved spine has long caused him pain, but the heartache of his brother's death broke something deeper.

Sitting for a long while, with the parchment letter resting in my lap, the words blur beneath my fingers. I read it only once, and do not need to read it again. My darling boy—so sweet, so fragile. He had been born into pain, lived with it like an old friend. From the moment I first held him, the fear of losing him took root in my heart. My poor Cihangir.

But knowing does not soften the blow. When Mehmed died, I screamed until my throat bled. I begged the heavens to take me instead. I broke in ways I thought could never be mended. But with Cihangir… something inside me simply folds away. Quietly. As if the world dims, and I decide not to resist.

I whisper his name only once. "Cihangir." Then silence.

I do not weep. My grief settles like a stone at the bottom of a well—deep, cold, unreachable. There is nothing left in me to wail with. I have spent those tears on Mehmed. He was my joy, my future. Cihangir was my heart, yes, but a heart already cracked, always a breath away from breaking.

I withdraw for three days, speaking to no one, sitting silent in candlelit rooms. I have prayers said in every mosque and food sent to the poor in his name. It is the only way I know how to move forward.

A letter arrives from Mahidevran. The handwriting is sharp, angular, like the edge of a blade.

You have taken my son. But Allah is just. And now yours is taken from you as well. Did you know? Cihangir is dead. He loved his brother so much, he could not live without him.

The letter smells faintly of rosewater. I tear it to pieces with my bare hands. For all the suffering this war has caused, the only bright side is that I never have to speak to Mahidevran again. There is nothing left for her. Her power died in a tent. Even her only grandson was executed by strangulation a few days after his father. There can be no opportunity for future rebellion.

Süleyman returns to the capital weeks later. Together we visit the chamber where Mehmed lay, his tomb crowned with a sultan's turban. A symbol of what might have been.

Süleyman reaches out and touches the stone. "He should have ruled after me," he whispers.

I take his hands in mine. "He rules now in paradise."

A long silence passes. At last, Süleyman speaks. "I have no joy left in war."

286

It is a strange thing to say for a man still at the height of his power. But I understand. He has buried four sons now—one by fate, one by force, one by grief, and one by his own hand.

The palace sits silent. The capital, too, has hushed. The Empire's greatest family has been torn by sorrow. In that silence, I make a vow. I will not let the storm consume what remains. There is still an Empire to protect. And so, the wheel of fate turns once more.

Selim, my remaining son of strength, is returning to Manisa. He leaves with quiet eyes, burdened by the ghosts of his brothers. I stand on my balcony whispering into the wind, "Please stay alive."

Chapter 40
The Last Light of the Harem

It is spring again, the season that always reminds me of Mehmed. The palace is quiet in the early morning, the kind of golden silence that only comes after a storm. I sit alone in the garden outside my chamber. The breeze carries a promise of warmth, a fragrance of blooming jasmine, as soft as the voice of a child just learning to sing. My body is older now, but my spirit is strong. Stronger than I ever imagined it would be.

When the first letters arrive detailing their growing conflict, I feel as if the earth has shifted beneath me. Disputes over territory, protocol, loyalty. Bayezid is too proud, Selim too cunning. The old fears come back. I know how rivalries end; I have seen it in Mahidevran's eyes for years, felt it when I sent Mihrimah into a political marriage. And I see it now, in the tightening web of messengers and rumors. Süleyman tries to hide it from me, but nothing in the world can mask the tension, the tremor that has begun to spread through the palace and now rattles even my bones.

Only Selim and Bayezid remain. My sons. So different. I have loved each of my children like the moons of my soul, but time and ambition have stolen so many of them. The Empire, once so full of promise, is now a quiet place. I am haunted by memories and shaped by survival. Mehmed, my golden boy—his death still lives in my bones. And Cihangir, my gentle one, whose crooked back carried the weight of the entire family's sorrow. Now, these two sons circle each other like wolves in the night, drawn to blood and legacy.

Their rivalry has grown with the years, like two suns vying for the same sky. What once had been brothers play-fighting in the gardens has become sharp letters sent from distant provinces, hidden messages, and rumors whispered in the corridors. It has not yet become war—but the scent of it hangs in the air, pungent as smoke before a fire.

The whispers reach me from every corridor of Topkapi, from every vizier and servant alike: Bayezid is growing too bold, too defiant. Selim, newly emboldened by Süleyman's subtle favor and his own ambitions, is no better. The two are not merely vying for their father's notice; they are preparing for battle. I will not lose another son.

I summon them. Not just them, I summon the entire family—the favorites, the grandchildren, Mihrimah, Rüstem, all of them.

I have not done such a thing in years. They have grown into men, rulers of their own distant provinces. But I am still their mother. I am still the woman who bore them, who held them against my chest as they cried. I have lost too many children. I cannot let another of my children die.

They arrive three days apart. Selim comes first, looking every inch the prince—calm, composed, robes tailored to his aging figure. He kisses my hand, bows before me, and sits at my side with a weary grace that reminds me of his father.

Bayezid arrives like a storm, all fire and wounded pride. His eyes are darker now than I remember—perhaps with grief, perhaps with rage. He does not bow as low. He embraces me tightly. I smell dust and the tension of campaign life on his shoulders.

We sit in my great chamber, its walls newly tiled to bear verses of the Qur'an and Süleyman's own poetry. I have a concubine bring tea, and I dismiss her. It will be only us.

"My sons," I begin, my voice steady though my hands shake slightly. "You are both strong, you are both wise, you are both beloved to me. And yet you would undo each other."

Selim looks away. Bayezid scowls. They sit on opposite sides of the room, almost as far away from each other as is possible while still being in the same space. I watch them, my hands folded, my thoughts like lightning.

"Enough," I say, before either can speak. "I will not see the Empire turn its own blood to ash."

The chamber falls quiet. I sit a little straighter despite the ache in my joints. My heart beats with purpose.

"I have buried too many sons. I will not bury another."

Neither speaks.

I turn to Bayezid. "You have your father's fire. And your brother, he has your father's crown. This does not mean he stole it."

Bayezid looks at me, face dark with passion. "Am I to bow to Selim? I have governed well. I am beloved."

I rise from my seat. My knees ache, but I stand tall. "You must relinquish your claim, Bayezid. Selim will succeed your father."

Bayezid's face goes pale. "Why? Because he flatters better?"

"Because I say so. Because your fight will destroy us. Because your brothers are dead and I will not bury another. Because if you do not let go, you will become like Mahidevran. Bitter. Alone."

Tears fill his eyes, but he does not argue. He turns away, trembling.

"Bayezid, I know your heart. But if you take one more step down this path, the only thing you will inherit is death."

He looks at me then. And I see it—the fear in his eyes.

I reach out and take his hand.

"I beg you, my son," I whisper. "Relinquish your claim. Let Selim ascend. Do not do this for him. Do it for me. For your brothers who are buried. For the daughters who will lose fathers, and for the Empire that cannot survive a war of princes."

Bayezid remains silent.

Selim finally speaks. "I do not seek his death. Only peace."

It is the right thing to say. And yet it feels rehearsed. I close my eyes for a moment, remembering the days when all my sons were boys with ink on their fingers, when the only rivalry was for my lap.

"You must not forget," I say quietly, "that the blood you spill is your own."

Later that evening, Bayezid approaches me privately on my terrace. The sun is dipping low, casting everything in a soft golden glow.

"I will go back to my province," he says, "and there I will remain."

"And you will not fight against your brother?"

"As long as he does not fight against me," he replies.

"And you will write to your brother to affirm your loyalty?" I ask.

He hesitates. "If he gives me no reason to doubt his sincerity."

I can push no more. "You will stay here longer. I barely know my grandchildren. I wish to meet them all properly. In a few days, after I have rested, we will meet in the rose garden."

The following day, it is Selim who comes to me.

"Do you love me?" I ask.

"More than life," he replies without hesitation.

"Then give me your pride. I am not asking you to love your brother. I am asking you to let him live."

He looks away, blinking hard.

I reach for his hand. "Promise me you will not fight."

"I can only promise if Bayezid does not raise arms against me."

It is a fair answer. I cannot ask for more.

"You will be Sultan," I say, clearly, firmly. "I believe it. Your father believes it. But you must be good. You must be wise. You must remember your brothers and carry them with you, always."

He says nothing for a long time.

Then, "You believe I am worthy?"

"With all my heart," I answer truthfully.

He kneels at my feet. "I will not fail you."

And for once, I believe him.

Peace, that fragile, delicate bird, has settled on the edge of my garden.

It is a bright day, the sun high above Istanbul. The domes of the mosques shimmer in the light, the breeze smells of salt and blooming roses, and the birds sing louder than they have in weeks.

The garden is full of cushions and carpets. Musicians play their delicate harmonies. Platters overflow with figs and honeyed dates, lamb in fragrant spices, delicate sweets in the shapes of stars.

My children gather. Mihrimah, resplendent in green silk, her eyes wise and sad and full of strength. Selim and Bayezid sit at opposite ends of the circle, but there is no hostility between them. Not today.

Not on the day their mother has summoned joy.

Süleyman sits on his grand divan under a canopy, as handsome as ever. He is dazzling in a kaftan of deep blue with embroidered tulips in real gold yarn. He is smiling and laughing as grandchildren surround him. He kisses their heads as they run past, trying to steal his sweets, though there are mountains of them on the low tables set along the garden path.

I sit on my own divan, my fingers wrapped around a silver cup, my lap warm with the weight of a sleepy grandchild. I smile more this day than I have in years.

And as the sun passes overhead, I imagine them. My lost boys.

Mehmed, tall and strong, standing at my right. Cihangir, delicate, eyes sparkling, leaning against my shoulder. Even Abdullah, who had barely known the world, dances among the roses with the laughter of a child who never knew sorrow.

I whisper their names to the wind.
Mehmed.
Cihangir.
Abdullah.
My darlings. I see you. I remember.

The wind curls around me, kisses my cheeks, ruffles my hair.

And in my heart, I thank Süleyman. Not for power, not for position. But for this day. For this family. For this fleeting moment of peace.

I look out over my family. My Sultan, the sun of my heart. My three surviving children, spouses and favorites in tow, and thirteen grandchildren, from Hümaşah, Mehmed's now teenage daughter, to babes in arms and others yet to be born.

"It is enough," I whisper.

It is enough.

Let it be written in the stars: this is the harem of Hürrem, the era of a mother's will, the peace of the Empire won not only by sword—but by love.

Chapter 41
The End

I have known for some time now. Long before anyone else dared whisper it. The ache in my bones that will not ease. The heaviness in my chest each morning, as though my heart must drag the weight of all the years behind it. The illness is beyond healing. My body, which has borne six children and held its own through decades of palace intrigue and war, is beginning to fade.

I have lived long. Longer than I ever dared to dream. I have loved deeply and been loved by a man who could conquer empires, yet looks at me still as though I am the only treasure in the world.

But even treasures crack with time.

I am no longer the slave girl who arrived in this world, frightened and confused. No longer the firebrand who defied Mahidevran, the harem, the world itself. I am Hürrem Sultan—consort of the Sultan of the World, the first Haseki, mother of princes, builder of mosques and hospitals, patron of scholars, lover of poetry and beauty.

Aleksandra stays by my side as the doctors come and go. Their whispers trail me like shadows. They bring their tonics—bitter and warm—and speak soft, practiced reassurances. I smile, but I know they cannot fix what has begun inside me. Whether it is my heart, my blood, or simply time, it is not theirs to mend. It is something only Allah understands.

I am dying.

Lying in my bed, surrounded by silk and softness that once meant luxury, all I crave is warmth—from the arms I love.

Süleyman sits beside me, his hand wrapped around mine. He reads our old letters aloud, his voice catching in places he thinks I don't notice. But I hear everything. He reads the letters I wrote during his campaigns—filled with longing, wit, devotion—and his replies, gilded in verse and tenderness. Sometimes he pauses to stroke my hair, now silver at the temples. At other times, he simply watches me as I breathe.

"My beloved," he reads. "I count the days until your return. The sun does not rise for me in your absence."

His words. I remember that letter. I remember my reply, aching with longing, yearning for his touch. It feels like yesterday.

His tears fall then, soft and quiet, landing on my skin like a blessing. I never thought I would see him weep. Not like this. Not for me.

There is so much I want to say. About the girls who held my hand in the slave market. About the first time I saw the Bosphorus, a shimmering golden-blue expanse that reflects the heavens. About the children I bore, each one a jewel in my crown. About Mehmed. About Cihangir. About my Mihrimah, and my grandchildren, whose laughter echoes through these halls.

At last, now that the journey is ending, I want to share the truth with Süleyman, to tell him of my world, to explain to him the future that lies ahead, and express my deep love for my parents, for whom I have never stopped yearning.

But my lips are tired. The words hover, just out of reach.

I close my eyes and think of the bright summer day last year, when all my children and grandchildren were gathered. I remember the sunlight dancing on their faces. I see the outlines of those I've lost—Mehmed standing just behind Selim, Cihangir's delicate hands on Bayezid's shoulder, my little Abdullah so full of life. I see them all. My loves. My legacy. My life.

He strokes my hair, his fingers reverent, as if I am something holy. I look at his face, lined now with time and sorrow, and see the boy who was once a prince. The man who made me a queen. The father of my children. My sun.

"Süleyman," I whisper. My voice is barely there. "I have loved you every day... for almost forty years. I would not trade a single day."

My breathing slows.

"If I had been born a man," I whisper, only breath now, "I would have conquered empires. But I was born a woman... so I conquered you."

My eyes flutter closed. I am not afraid. I am grateful.

The pain recedes like a tide pulling back into the sea. I hear Süleyman still whispering, but the words no longer matter. His voice is the only sound I want to carry with me.

I think of Allah, the Merciful, the Just. I think of all He gave me. And I offer one last silent prayer—not for myself, but for those I leave behind.

"Hürrem," he says.

I breathe in.
I breathe out.
And the world goes black.

Chapter 42
Rebirth

Gasping. That is the first thing. A great heaving breath, as though I have been holding it for centuries. My lungs burn and then open, greedy for air, for life. My eyes flutter open, and I blink against the light—clean, white light, pouring through wide windows I do not recognize. My body feels... light. Whole. I sit up slowly, unsure of what will meet me, of what world I have entered.

I am in bed. A wide, soft bed with white linens. Not the brocade of Topkapi, not the scent of rosewater and incense, but the sterile, fresh scent of detergent and lavender. My fingers grip the edge of the duvet as I push myself up and notice the smoothness of my skin. The stiffness of illness is gone. I move my hands slowly, testing each finger. Then my arms. Rising, my legs are strong beneath me, my spine straight, my chest free of pain.

Walking barefoot to the mirror across the room, I stare.

A stranger. A girl with bright eyes and flushed cheeks. Hair the color of burning copper. I am her again. Not the woman aged by sorrow and time. Not the matriarch of an empire. I am nineteen again, the age when I first looked into Süleyman's eyes.

Am I in heaven?

My fingers reach to my face, tracing the line of my jaw, the fullness of my lips, the curve of my cheekbones. I whisper aloud, just to hear my own voice: "Am I dead?"

The room answers with silence.

I turn. It is a modern apartment, glass and steel, books stacked on shelves, a single framed photograph on the nightstand. I cross to it. A picture of a city skyline—tall buildings, a great harbor, ships docked far below. Boston. My mind knows it. My soul does not.

I open the closet. Jeans. Dresses. Blouses. Sneakers. The clothing of another life.

Am I reborn?

I reach for the robe on the hook and slip it on with trembling hands. I turn my wrist over and bring it to my nose. Sandalwood. Still there. And underneath, the warm musk of a man—my Süleyman. My breath catches in my throat.

Has it all been a dream?

No, the grief is too real. The love, the children, the betrayals, the victories. That cannot be dreamed. But here I am, standing barefoot in a modern room with traffic honking distantly outside and the glow of morning spilling through sheer curtains.

The memories rush in, colliding as they try to settle into place. They are jumbled, confused—a tapestry of images that do not belong together. A veil over a subway. A minaret behind a glowing screen. A cradle and a cardiac monitor.

Past and present spill into each other like ink across a map—boundaries lost, names bleeding into unfamiliar lines.

The date on the clock beside my bed glows red, sharp, cruel in its certainty. No time has passed. Yesterday was yesterday. And yet it wasn't.

It is too much. My mind cannot hold it all.

I step outside onto the balcony. The warm July breeze rushes past, tugging at my hair, cooling my cheeks. Below, the city bustles with life—cars honking, people walking fast, voices in every direction. It is different from Istanbul. Fresher, in some ways, yet also more oppressive. And louder. Harsher.

I sit in the small metal chair and weep.

For Süleyman. For Mehmed, Cihangir, and little Abdullah. For Mustafa, Selim, and Bayezid. For Mihrimah. For the palace and its endless corridors. For the women I left behind. For the power I held in my hands and for the blood on them, too.

I weep for myself. And when the tears stop, I rise.

I walk slowly through the apartment, touching everything. My bookshelf—cluttered with paperbacks, books on philosophy and great works of history. I run my fingers over a dog-eared copy of Plato's *The Republic*. The irony makes me laugh under my breath. A potted monstera sits in the corner, too large for its ceramic pot. I remember nurturing it, watering it every Saturday.

The kitchen still holds the scent of cinnamon. Did I bake something last night? There is a pan with remnants of apple crisp on the counter. I taste it. Too sweet. I always make it too sweet.

I step into the shower pondering the nature of time. I baked an apple crisp last night. I held the hand of my beloved Süleyman last night. Both cannot be true. And yet, the apple crisp exists, and I can still feel the rough hands of my Sultan caress mine.

I dress myself. There are no concubines here to help me. I peruse my closet. No silk gowns, no veils, no velvet wraps. I put on jeans and a T-shirt. Everything feels constricting. I put on running shoes, not silk slippers. I grab a jacket and find my wallet and phone sitting on a small table by the door. What an odd concept, a cellphone.

Picking it up, my heart thunders in my chest. Instinctively, I dial. Two rings and she answers.

"Hi mom," I say, tears streaming down my face, a flood of emotions overwhelming me. "No, everything is fine. I just wanted to hear your voice." She chats away pleasantly. A smile so wide threatens to bruise my cheekbones. "I'll come for dinner soon," I add, before signing off.

I crumble to the floor, torn by conflicting feelings, engulfed in a battle of pain and happiness. Each life wraps my heart in twisting vines of love as my mind struggles to comprehend the metaphysical world.

Feeling dizzy and lightheaded, I struggle to rise and head to the kitchen sink. Cold water refreshes me and clears the cobwebs. Before I can overthink it, I open the door and step into the hall. The familiar beige carpeting. The elevator still creaks as it descends. The lobby smells like detergent and old heating vents. When I step outside, the city hits me all at once.

The sky is painfully bright. The air is heavy, not like the clean sea air of the Bosphorus. The scent of gasoline, food trucks, and blooming trees clash in a strange harmony. People pass briskly, heads down, faces impassive, staring at glowing screens.

I walk up Newbury Street toward Mass Ave. The sidewalk is uneven in places; the cracks filled with pebbles and debris, caught in the heat like forgotten crumbs of the city. Cars rush past—horns, engines, voices. It feels overwhelming. Everything moves faster here. The noise digs into my skull. Istanbul had been loud, yes—but this is a different kind of noise. There is no rhythm to it. No call to prayer. No market song. Just the roar of the modern world.

I cross into the Back Bay and turn onto Marlborough Street, passing an old townhouse I have always admired. I remember looking through its windows once, imagining myself living in it.

I keep walking until I hit the Boston Common, following paths my feet know even as my mind reels. The grass is wet—it must have rained last night. Ducks waddle through puddles. Children chase each other around the statue of George Washington. The wind blows harder here, curling around the bronze horse.

I sit on a bench in front of the great statue, pulling my knees up to my chest, looking at the trees and their long, gnarled branches. I try to understand what is happening to me.

Have I truly lived and died in another world? Have I ruled an empire from within silk curtains, whispered into the ear of the most powerful man on earth? Have I borne six children and lost three? Have I loved and been loved?

My hands tremble as I open my phone. There it is. My name— Katherine Elizabeth Dubois. My photos. A picture of me at the beach last summer with friends. We had been drinking iced coffee, our feet in the sand.

Is this the dream? Or the other life?

I push on, needing to walk, giving myself time to think. A bookstore—Brattle Book Shop. My favorite. I press my palm against the glass. Inside, the morning light warms the old wooden shelves. A girl inside is shelving a display of poetry books. My thoughts turn to the scrolls of Süleyman's poetry, verses he composed for me.

Tears prick my eyes.

On Hanover Street, I pause outside a small restaurant, Carmelina's, where I worked briefly last summer, just for three weeks before I'd quit to focus on school. I had scrubbed dishes, waited tables, listened to arguments over wine and steak. I remember laughing with the dishwasher, Jorge, who taught me how to curse in Spanish.

I wander into the Seaport, drawn by the smell of the sea. This is not the Bosphorus. It lacks the deep tang of salt and fish and history. But it stirs something in me all the same. The wind is strong here, and I let it whip my hair around my face. I close my eyes and for a moment, I am back in his arms.

Süleyman.

Had he been real? Had I invented him from longing? Had my mind, overwhelmed with the constraints of this modern world conjured a fantasy of love and purpose?

I walk into a café by the harbor. It is crowded with laptops and headphones and quiet conversation. I order a coffee. The barista smiles.

"What's your name?"

I open my mouth. "Hürr—"

I stop.

"…Katherine."

He scribbles it on the lid.

I sit by the window, watching the boats drift in the harbor, touching the hot lid of my coffee cup. The name stares back at me.

Katherine.

I'm unsure whether to be happy or heartbroken.

And then I hear it.

A couple nearby, speaking softly in Turkish. And to my shock—I understand. Clear as if it were my mother tongue. They are talking about the storm rolling in from the east, about the ferry schedule, about the food truck they like at the edge of the market.

Tears fill my eyes.

I cannot explain it. I do not know if it is a dream, borne of snippets of knowledge. But in my heart, I am still her. Still Hürrem. No matter the time, the city, the body—I have not forgotten. I close my eyes and whisper into the wind that comes in off the water.

"I love you, my sun. Every day. Always."

Chapter 43
My Obsession

There are moments when reality seems to slip, like silk through fingers. Life has taken on an eerie silence after my reawakening. I try to settle back into the rhythm of my modern life, but I feel like a ghost drifting through time. Something has shifted in my soul, as though I have lived and died and now wander somewhere in between.

I find it hard to doubt that I was once Hürrem Sultan. The memories, the emotions, the scents and textures of my past life are too vivid, too embedded in me to dismiss. Yet I know that it cannot possibly be true. My subconscious has played a horrible trick on me, creating a world so real that my heart aches with longing.

I open my laptop with a trembling hand, blinking at the harsh blue light of the screen. The hum of the fan sounds alien to my ears, like the buzzing of some mechanical insect I had forgotten ever existed. My inbox contains dozens of messages stacked like unanswered questions. My latest bank statement, random newsletters, university notices. I click slowly, uncertainly, as if expecting something to leap out at me from behind the subject lines.

A notice from the university catches my eye. Course Registration Now Open for Fall Term.

For a moment, I just stare. Course registration. That used to mean everything—jockeying for seats, comparing schedules with friends, planning coffee breaks between lectures. It feels like a lifetime ago.

I click through. The portal opens to a clean, impersonal interface. "Select Your Classes." My cursor hovers over the fields like it belongs to someone else. I can feel my breath hitch in my throat. What am I supposed to choose? What matters anymore?

Philosophy—I took a seminar on ethical paradoxes and argued with a professor about whether intention could outweigh outcome. It all feels like wind now. I scroll further.

Literature—Victorian novels, modernist poetry. I wrote papers on the death of the author and the semiotics of dreams. All of it feels thin to me now. Ghosts with ink for bones.

And then I see it.

HIST 224: Empire and Legacy—Ancient Rome to the Ottomans
HIST 301: The Age of Suleiman the Magnificent
HIST 257: Women and Power in the Islamic World
HIST 310: Memory and Monument—Imperial Architecture
HIST 199: Great battles of the 16th century

My mouse clicks of its own accord. One after the other, I register for all five. My heart beats faster with each confirmation. Registered. Registered. Registered.

I stare at the confirmation page. My reflection stares back at me in the black border of the screen—young again, but with the eyes of a woman who has seen children born and buried, wars declared, love lost, kingdoms shifted. The girl in the screen is not a girl at all.

I whisper to her, "Well, if this is insanity... let it at least be educated madness."

Something in me tingles at the sight of those class titles, even as I resist the urge to write to the university to correct the spelling of Süleyman's name. It isn't hope—not exactly. It is hunger. A deep, gnawing ache to know everything I already know. To prove myself right. To find the fissures in history's smooth surface and dig into them, looking for myself.

What if they call Hürrem a manipulator? A seductress? Will I recognize myself in their words—or will I be erased, distorted by the fiction that created the world in my mind?

I want to read every footnote. Every biased chronicle. Every love letter etched in time. The screen fades to idle, and I touch the trackpad to wake it again. I cannot bear to lose the image of those names: Süleyman. Hürrem. Selim. Bayezid. I am going to learn my life from scratch.

I begin keeping a journal. I fill pages each day with thoughts, recollections, and questions. My handwriting grows frantic, looping wildly as my thoughts outpace my hands. I sit for hours by the Charles River, staring at the water, imagining the Bosphorus, hearing echoes of the calls to prayer calling out over domes and minarets.

"I was her," I whisper to the wind one afternoon. "I lived, loved, ruled."

I know it is a lie, but it is a lie that refuses to fade, a lie that my mind believes to be true.

Every morning, I wake with a gasping breath, half expecting to see Süleyman beside me. Sometimes I can smell the faint trace of him on my skin—that musky scent of leather, sandalwood, and myrrh. My dreams are always of Topkapi. Sometimes I walk its halls with bare feet, feeling the chill of marble beneath my toes. Other nights, I watch my children run ahead of me through a flower-filled courtyard, their laughter rising into the sky like birdsong.

One afternoon, I enter the Brattle Book Shop, the familiar bell jingling overhead. I wander the shelves like a sleepwalker. My fingers trace the spines: history, politics, biographies. Ottoman Empire.

I freeze. My eyes scan the titles. And there, among them, a book calls to me. *Empress of the East: How a slave girl became queen of the Ottoman Empire.*

My breath catches in my throat. I pull it from the shelf. On the cover, a painting—a woman with red hair, richly dressed, eyes both cunning and kind. I see myself in the image, different, yet similar.

I stumble to the back corner and begin to read. The words are familiar. Uncannily so. Not a perfect rendition of my other life, but how could it be. The harem is closed to outsiders, a world unto itself. But many of the stories are as I remember them, the stories of Hürrem, a young girl captured and sold into slavery, chosen by Sultan Süleyman, mother to princes, adviser to the throne, builder of mosques and charitable foundations, diplomat and strategist. My hands tremble.

I begin studying everything I can on Ottoman history. Reading like a woman possessed. Harem culture. Islamic politics. I comb through book after book. The deeper I delve, the more astonished I become. So much matches my memories. The smallest details are correct—the courtyard layouts, the exact position of the harem baths, the intricacies of court politics.

I'm not crazy. Or, if I am, then history itself conspires with my madness.

I read some of my letters to Süleyman, still preserved in archives. Of my rivalry with Mahidevran. Of Mehmed's tragic death in Manisa. Of Mustafa, executed in Süleyman's tent. Of my beloved Cihangir, who followed his brother into death.

And then Selim. My son. Sultan Selim II.

He reigned after his father, though not without struggle. There was war with Persia, unrest in Anatolia, intrigue in the court. I read about Bayezid's rebellion, his defeat and the execution of his sons. I weep for my boy. My headstrong Bayezid. The fierce light in his eyes. I begged him to yield. He did not listen. And now, all of it confirmed. Written in pages printed long after my death.

One morning, while reading a biography of Süleyman the Magnificent, I see a portrait of him, ascribed to a follower of Titian. My heart clenches. His eyes. That half-smile. It is him. My sun.

I press my fingers against the image and whisper, "You remember me, don't you?"

The next page describes the Sultan's final years: his loneliness, his retreat from the pleasures of court, his turn to faith and solitude. It says he became almost monk-like, writing poetry of grief and longing, never smiling as he once did. It describes how, in his final campaign, he kept a worn letter from Hürrem close to his heart.

I break down in great sobs.

"You mourned me," I sob. "Even after death."

I begin to find my way back to Hürrem through ritual. I light candles each night and place them by the window. I whisper prayers in Turkish, my tongue recalling words it has never known in this lifetime. I begin to wear red again, her color—vibrant, proud, defiant.

Walking the streets of Boston, I feel like a woman reborn and yet exiled. I stroll past Trinity Church and remember the Hagia Sophia. I cross Commonwealth Avenue and imagine the procession of court eunuchs on their way to fetch me for a summons from the Sultan. The modern world is loud, indifferent, blinking with electric eyes. I feel too tender for it. Too ancient.

In the shop window of another bookstore—Beacon Hill Books— I see a copy of *The Sultan's Favorite* in the window. It is a fictionalized account of Hürrem's life. The story is embellished, full of court intrigue and spicy seductions. But the bones of it is true.

Yet no one can know how it truly feels. To have been in love with the most powerful man in the world. To have carried his children and fought for their survival. To have lived in the gilded cage of the harem, rising to its highest tower.

I turn to the internet, finding forums of historical reenactors and Ottoman enthusiasts. I create an anonymous account under the name "K. of Istanbul" and begin to post long, detailed narratives. I write in the first person, recounting my memories. People assume it is elaborate fan fiction.

One user replies, "Your writing is so vivid, it's like you were really there."

I smile. "I was," I type, and hit send.

In the weeks that follow, my obsession grows. I chart the fall of Bayezid, my once-beautiful son, headstrong and brilliant. I read of his rebellion and eventual execution by Selim—my own choice of successor. My heart breaks anew.

"Forgive me," I say into the night. "I chose peace over you."

I read of Selim's reign—The Drunkard, they called him. But he ruled, just as I wanted. He carried my bloodline forward. That was all I had hoped for. He fulfilled my final request.

Online, I begin learning about the Sultanate of women, a phenomenon where some consorts, mothers, sisters and grandmothers of the sultans of the Ottoman Empire exerted extraordinary political influence that lasted from 1534 to 1715.

I laugh then. A real, deep laugh that makes my shoulders shake. I started an era. For the first time since waking up in Boston, I feel joy.

On my way home one afternoon, I pass by a small Turkish café and stop in for tea. The man behind the counter says, *"Selam, nasılsın?"*

Without thinking, I reply, *"Çok iyiyim, teşekkür ederim."*

I sit in the corner, sipping my tea, watching the world move around me. No one knows who I am or was. But I remember. I lived as Hürrem, now I live as Katherine. I carry both. I honor both. I am both.

Outside, the wind moves gently through the trees. Somewhere in it, I swear I hear Süleyman's voice. It is time to go home.

Chapter 44
The Istanbul Trip

Istanbul is calling me home. With only two weeks before the start of school, I check online and book tickets for the flight leaving tonight. I hastily pack a bag, grab my passport and head to the airport, too excited to wait. Every step is a step closer to my beloved.

The plane tilts as it descends and I see Istanbul again. Soft tears well in my eyes. I see the domes and spires appear like a mirage over the city's clustered rooftops. I see Galata Tower, the Hagia Sofia and Topkapi Palace. Sights so familiar to my eyes. From here, I can see the three bodies of water that surround Istanbul: the Golden Horn, the silver ribbon of the Bosphorus, and the gleaming blue of the Sea of Marmara.

I lean against the window and try to reconcile the sights before me with the images etched in my memory. There are differences, of course—bridges where there had been none, modern buildings stretching upwards—but the heart of the city remains unchanged. Timeless.

The air greets me like an old friend when I step outside the airport. I inhale deeply. Sea salt, exhaust fumes, grilled meat, cigarette smoke, and something older—a scent that doesn't belong to any one thing. Memory. Age. Legacy.

I take a taxi from the airport, watching as the city passes by. The driver is young and plays Turkish pop music. He chats with someone over Bluetooth about *Galatasaray*'s recent match, oblivious to the turbulence in my heart. As we drive, we pass neighborhoods that spark recognition, even though they have changed—*Fatih, Balat, Eyüp*. Places I knew in another life.

We arrive near the *Süleymaniye* Mosque just before dusk. The driver drops me at a corner. I walk the last few blocks to my hotel, wheeling my small suitcase across uneven cobblestones. The shadows lengthen across the mosque's outer walls, and the golden light clings to the stones as if reluctant to let go. I stand at the gate for a long time, not moving. I have other sites to visit first, before this mosque. My heart will have to wait a while longer.

The Haseki Hürrem Sultan Complex is first. It has changed with time, but I can still feel my fingerprints in the stones of every wall. I stand in front of the soup kitchen and close my eyes, listening for the sounds of bubbling pots, the clatter of bowls, the laughter of hungry children being fed. I press my palm against the old stone wall and whisper, "I remember."

In the days that follow, I return to each place that matter. I sit at the edge of the Bosphorus watching the ferries dart across the strait like dragonflies. The air is sharp with salt. I dip my fingers into the water and bring them to my lips. It tastes the same.

I wander through the streets of *Üsküdar*, through the market where women once bought spices and silk. Some shops still sell rose oil and Turkish delights. The scent of roasting chestnuts drifts from a cart, and I buy a handful, burning my fingers as I peel them open.

I visit *Kandilli* and walk along the shore of the Bosphorus, looking for the old hunting lodge where the family sought refuge from the smallpox outbreak and where my little Abdullah died, but the sands of time have erased the pavilion from the modern landscape.

317

I find a little garden, as close to the location as my memory can surmise and say a prayer for my young son.

I visit their tombs one by one. Mihrimah's first. The marble is cool beneath my hand. I whisper her name and sit in silence, feeling the absence of her voice. I share with her now stories that I could never tell her at the time, about Boston, about university, about modern life. I tell her I miss her. She doesn't answer, but the wind picks up, swirling the hem of my coat.

I visit the tomb of Selim next and sit a long while, telling him how fiercely proud I am of him and how deeply satisfied his father would have been with his achievements. He ensured the legacy of our house. Through him, the House of Osman continued to reign until 1922.

Next, the tombs of Bayezid, Cihangir, and Abdullah. My poor sons. One so headstrong, so loving. The other, tender and sweet. And my little Abdullah, taken so young, so cruelly.

I visit Mehmed's tomb next. I weep harder here. His face comes back to me clearly—how he had laughed, how earnestly he had tried to be wise beyond his years. He had been so full of promise. His death has left a hollow in my heart I have never been able to fill.

Last of all, I go to Süleyman. I stand at the gates of *Süleymaniye* Mosque a long time before my feet eventually carry me forward. The courtyard is quiet. Tourists have mostly left, and only a few worshippers remain. I walk slowly, taking in every inch. His tomb stands beneath the vast dome of the mosque he had commissioned, and which Sinan had built in tribute to both Allah and Empire.

The marble gleams in the filtered light. I stand in front of the tomb of my beloved and sink to my knees, pressing my forehead against the cold stone. I close my eyes and feel it all over again—his hands in my hair, his voice reading poetry to me in the early hours of the morning, his laughter, his anger, his endless love. I cry, silent sobs that leave my chest aching. Here lies my Süleyman. The lawgiver. The poet. The Sultan.

"I found you again," I say to him. "Across time. Across death. I remember it all."

I do not know how long I have been kneeling here. The guards let me stay. Perhaps they sense something. Finally, I stand. My legs are stiff. I look once more upon the tomb and whisper to Süleyman in the heavens, "Wait for me. I will find you again."

Then I walk to my own tomb. It is smaller than his. More delicate. The tiles are blue and white, and the dome above is soft in its curves.
I stare at the marble sarcophagus, wondering: Can one be dead and alive at once? Am I truly Katherine, standing here in jeans and a coat, or am I lying beneath that marble, wrapped in silk, dust returning to dust?

I leave the tombs and walk through the gardens where I had once held Süleyman's hand. Flowers are still in bloom. I pick a single petal and tuck it into my notebook.

Later that evening, I sit in a small café near the Galata Bridge, drinking strong Turkish tea. The city buzzes around me with calls to prayer, children shouting, ferry horns on the water. Istanbul is alive. And so am I. I do not know what this means. Whether I have dreamed my past life or lived it. Whether I have been given a second chance or am caught in some divine loop. But I am here. And I remember.

As the sun dips below the horizon, painting the Bosphorus in fire and gold, I declare to the sun, to the wind and the trees, to the water and the fish in the sea, "*Teşekkür ederim*, Süleyman. Thank you. For everything."

The wind answers with a hush of warmth. And for the first time in a long while, I feel at peace.

Chapter 45
The Proof

I have one thing left to do before returning home to Boston. One last thread to follow, to pull loose from the fabric of my past and drag through the streets of a city that is no longer foreign.

It is strange—how quickly Istanbul has shifted from dream to memory, from mystery to home. I have touched stone and marble that knew my name. I have wept at tombs that had once housed the breath and laughter of my children. Now, all that remains is a door I have not yet opened. Topkapi Palace.

I approach at dawn. The city is quiet, the Bosphorus only just beginning to glitter under the rising sun. I come alone. No tour guide, no audio headset, no distractions. Just me and the weight of what was.

The palace grounds are already waking with light. The trees swish gently with whispers, and I swear I can hear the rustle of silk and slippers from ages past. The stones beneath my feet know my tread, remember it, welcome it. I walk slowly, not like a visitor, but like someone coming home after a long exile.

As I step through the Gate of Salutation, the silence shifts. My heart pounds. I know this gate. I have walked through it not as Katherine, the American university student, but as Hürrem, the chosen one, the Sultan's beloved. Each arch I pass under is a doorway to memory. Each courtyard is still and alive all at once.

I hear their laughter. My children. Not ghosts. Not illusions. Just laughter, bouncing off marble. Mihrimah teasing Selim. Mehmed calling for Bayezid to race him. Abdullah clapping his hands. Cihangir's quiet chuckle. The wind carries it all. I do not cry. I smile.

I pass through the Gate of Felicity and stand still. The harem waits, just beyond.

There is music. Faint, as if from another time. The note of a flute, low and aching, curls through the air. My feet move on their own. I follow the corridors that once held so many of my joys and fears. I turn left, then right, then descend the slight steps toward the private quarters. It has changed so little.

And then I see it. The door. The first private room I had been given. A space meant for solitude, for transformation. Where a frightened girl became a woman, and then a queen. I push it open. No one stops me.

The room is bathed in golden light. Dust motes dance like tiny spirits. I step inside, every breath tighter than the last. The bed is gone. The silk dresses are no more. But the air is the same. I drop to my knees.

And there it is. At the base of the central column. Half-hidden in shadow. Etched faintly into the stone.

K. E. D.

My initials. Not Hürrem's. Not a concubine or a consort. Mine.

Katherine Elizabeth Dubois.

I reach out with shaking fingers and trace them. I remember the night I carved them. The tiny knife I stole from the kitchen. The fear I would be caught. The strange need to leave a mark—not as property, but as self.

It was real. All of it. No matter how incredible it may seem. It all happened. My etched initials are proof. I did not imagine Süleyman's voice, or Mihrimah's curls, nor fabricate my sorrow, my joy, my rise. I hadn't conjured the scent of jasmine on Mehmed's blanket or the salty air from the Sea of Marmara.

I lived it. I loved and was loved.

I am Hürrem.

Still and always.

A strange calm washes over me. I am not angry that I have been returned to another time, to another name. I am not mourning the loss of that world anymore. Because I haven't lost it. It is with me, embedded in my skin, carved into my soul.

The room feels like it breathes with me.

And then, one question burns into my mind. A whisper. A prayer. A possibility.

Yesterday, I was Hürrem.

Who will I become tomorrow?

Made in the USA
Coppell, TX
06 February 2026

71285132R00198